ANNA SAYBURN LANE

# Folly Ditch

*A Helen Oddfellow literary mystery*

*For all my friends at Refugee Tales*

# Chapter 1

Paxton raised his binoculars and peered into the darkness of the English Channel. His boots dug into the scrappy turf, close to the edge of the cliff. The wind flung handfuls of sleet at his face. Far below, huge waves churned the shingle of the beach.

It was a rough night for a crossing.

He could pick out a few vessels at sea. Two small fishing boats bumped along close to the shore. A massive container ship, festooned with lights like a left-over Christmas tree, anchored up inside the Goodwin Sands to ride out the storm. A buoy, flashing red, warned of the hidden sandbanks beneath. A haze of sickly orange hung over the horizon: the lights of Calais reflected off the lowering clouds.

The bastard weather. He couldn't afford for it to be late.

At the bottom of the cliff blazed the port of Dover, gantries and docks floodlit. Lorries lined up in the big car park, snaking around the site. Men in high-vis jackets with clipboards stood stoic in the filthy sleet. It was all fixed, he'd been told. So long as they arrived before the shift change at nine.

And then he could see it, emerging from the darkness. The first ferry of the day steamed towards the port. Paxton checked his watch. It docked in fifteen minutes. Then maybe another half hour for the lorries to disembark. Hardly any private cars; early January wasn't the time for a jaunt to France and the hassle of travelling these days put most people off. Except for the illegals in their ragged inflatables, and there wouldn't be any of those today. Anyone stupid enough to try would be dead before they got out of French waters. There was something to be said for a storm.

Paxton stashed the binoculars away and stuck his hands deep in his pockets. He'd spent hours up here over the winter, monitoring the hordes of migrants with a few like-minded men. Patriots. People didn't want to hear about it, but you ask the fishermen. Or look at the piles of inflatables stacked up at Dover and Folkestone. The Kent coast had repelled invaders since Roman times, but some invasions took place by stealth.

He watched the ferry power through the waves until it reached the calm waters inside the harbour wall. Time to go. He trudged back through the freezing rain to the minibus and checked his phone. A message, from a number he didn't recognise: 'Docking now.' And a registration, Dutch by the look of it.

He drove along the winding roads past the mighty fortification of Dover Castle, stone walls standing like iron. The lay-by was a good one, by the Whitfield business park but away from CCTV cameras, screened by scrubby trees and bushes. Lorries used to wait up here for the ferry, but since Brexit most of the freight was routed along the M20. There were still signs, though. Bottles of urine littered the hedges, fast-food wrappers tangled in the branches of the trees. People had no pride. Kent: toilet of England. What was wrong with them all?

He waited. Paxton was good at waiting. He turned off the engine. Couldn't afford to waste petrol, even if the cab was freezing. An hour later, with the sky lightening as far as it was going to, a truck turned off the roundabout. A big artic refrigerated unit. He checked the registration number. That was the one.

The driver jumped out, baseball cap low over his eyes, and checked for cameras. He ran to the back of the truck and cut through the customs seal, shifted the bolts, and flung the doors open.

Paxton heard shouting in some language he didn't know, German or Dutch or whatever. A rabble of people climbed down. They looked in a bad way. Three men first, heaving tatty nylon sports bags and rucksacks stuffed with God knows what. Paxton frowned. They'd been told to bring the bare minimum. Their faces were weathered, heavily lined, and they wore cheap-looking leather jackets and jeans. One took out a tin of tobacco and started rolling a cigarette.

'No,' shouted the driver, shooing them towards Paxton. 'You go now.'

Paxton stepped out and opened the back of the minibus.

'Come on, then. This way, ladies and gents. I'm Gary. I'm taking you to the quarantine centre, all right?'

More were climbing down from the lorry, scrambling past rows of polystyrene boxes. A couple of middle-aged women, heads covered with scarves, bundled up in anoraks. Two more white men, younger, with ratty little moustaches. A tall black guy, skinny, his jeans almost falling off him. He wore only a sweatshirt and was shivering hard.

A girl with long dyed-blonde hair, helping down a woman with a massive wheeled suitcase. For Christ's sake. He took

3

another look at the girl, her face pale as sour milk. Young. Very young. Who the hell decided to bring her?

'This way, everyone. Got your documents?' He held out his hand.

'You don't need our documents.' The man with the cigarette. 'We need them.' His accent was strong, eastern European. Albanian, if Paxton had to guess.

Paxton sighed. 'It's just for the checks. Until you've tested negative for Covid. Then you get them back, OK?'

The man looked mutinous. Paxton held his gaze.

The lorry driver slammed the back doors shut and drove off, taking the roundabout at speed. They were on their own.

The man dropped his gaze, spat on the ground, and handed over an Albanian passport. Urtash Prenga. Paxton nodded and put it into a folder. He'd remember that one. This was the tricky bit. Get their documents and deliver them to the farm. Whatever happened after that wasn't his business.

'Can you help me?' asked the girl. She was trying, without success, to heave the big suitcase into the back.

'Shouldn't have brought so much shit with you,' he muttered. But he grabbed the handle and heaved it up. It was heavier than he'd expected. He needed to get back to the gym.

'Thank you, Gary,' she said with a wide smile.

'You speak English?' he said.

'I need to get better. I will go to school,' she said.

He sighed. That wasn't going to happen. She really was young. He scowled at the older woman with her, who scowled back. Silly cow, what had she brought a kid for?

'I am Aisha. This is Elira, my old sister.'

'Right. Come on, passports or ID cards, then get in.' He handed the girl a carrier bag containing a couple of bottles of water and a packet of biscuits. God knows when the poor sods had last eaten. 'Here you go. Make yourselves comfortable. Won't be long.'

Urtash Prenga was still looking suspicious, but his companions were lighting up evil-smelling cigarettes, showing terrible brown teeth as they laughed, happy that they had finally arrived in Britain. They wouldn't give him any bother.

Paxton climbed in and wound down the window, ignoring the sleet. He'd quit smoking when he got out two months back. Now the smell of it made him think of confinement, of men lying around on bunks with nothing to do and nowhere to go, simmering resentments building to ignition point.

He gunned the engine, heading northwest on to the single-lane tracks that led into the depths of the Kent countryside. The sooner they were there, the sooner this lot would be someone else's problem. It was like back-country Afghan out here. No-one kept anywhere near the speed limit. So long as he avoided the motorways, there was no chance of being flagged down by an over-zealous copper.

He felt excitement course through him, grinned as the van careered round tight corners hugged by high hedges. He took the Roman Road that led to Canterbury, then swerved around the city on drovers' roads, pilgrim paths. Up into the flatlands of north Kent, past Faversham, Sittingbourne. He ignored the shouts of protest coming from the back.

Delivery driver. That's what he'd told his parole officer. They hadn't bothered to check it out; everyone was a delivery driver these days.

Under the Medway River through the tunnel at Chatham, his old stamping ground. A mile or two later, he swung the wheel, took them off the road and on to the track that led to the farm. He stopped to remove the padlock from the steel gate across the path. Then on past the polytunnels, past the scruffy bungalow, guard dogs unleashing a volley of furious barking.

The second barn door was open. He drove straight in. The dark, cavernous space loomed around them. His passengers had fallen silent, but now the noise began again.

He got out with the folder of documents in his hand, listened. A shuffle of feet, coming closer.

'All right?' asked a voice behind him. Guren, his regular contact.

'Yeah. No problems.' He handed over the passports, unlocked the doors. The passengers piled out and the lights snapped on, illuminating the vast barn.

Six men stood around them. Huge bastards, dressed in black, hoods pulled low over their faces. Six baseball bats swinging loose in their hands. The passengers bunched together.

'Right, I'll leave you to it.' Paxton opened the door, avoiding Aisha's accusatory gaze.

The men closed in on him, yelling. But they knew, now. They'd been tricked. He needed to be out of here. He touched his hand to the leather handle in his pocket.

Someone grabbed his shoulder. He turned. Urtash Prenga, his face twisted, knowing he'd been taken for a mug.

'Fuck you!' A gob of brown sputum landed on Paxton's jacket.

He slowed everything down to a long waiting second. The angry men looming. The women standing scared behind them. The guys with baseball bats behind that, ready to back him up. Prenga's face, eyes darkening with fear.

Paxton flicked the knife open.

A streak of crimson appeared across the wrinkled brown cheek, bloomed, and overflowed. The man doubled over, clutching what was left of his eye. He screamed as his pain caught up with the facts.

'No, Gary!' The girl pushed forward, but her sister grabbed her arm, shushed her. Apart from a few gasps and the keening of the injured man, the rest of them were silent.

Paxton took a paper towel from the minibus and wiped the knife. He looked at the frightened faces of the men bunched around him. They shuffled back. He folded the blade down, got in and reversed out of the big double doors.

Minutes later, he was back on the lane, heading south. He glanced at the empty seat next to him. He should get a dog. He'd missed his dog when he was inside, more than anything. The smell of it, the warmth. In the confusion before his arrest, he'd left it tied up outside the cathedral. He never found out what had happened to it. He hoped someone had taken it in. It was a good dog, that one.

He'd get another.

# Chapter 2

Helen Oddfellow checked her watch and held up her finger. The little crowd hushed.

'Listen. We're just in time.'

A peal of five bells rang out from the tower behind them. Then seven slow tolls announced the hour. Helen shivered, hunching her shoulders inside her red wool coat.

'The Church of Saint Sepulchre, marking seven o'clock. For us, it means the end of the tour. But for the inhabitants of Newgate prison, which once stood directly opposite, those chimes were a darker signal.

'At seven in the morning, the condemned prisoners would hear the bells and know their time had come. And this road would be crowded with people – Londoners, sightseers, street-musicians and pickpockets – to watch the hanging. The scaffold was set up across from here, so you are standing in the most coveted position to see the action.'

Her charges shifted uncomfortably. One of the older men chuckled, nudged his serious-faced wife.

'Front row,' he said. She ignored him.

'Charles Dickens attended a hanging and wrote to *The Times* afterwards, calling for public executions to be banned.' Helen opened her folder and read aloud a little of the famous author's excoriation of the 'dreadful experience' he had witnessed.

Too much? she wondered. They were solemn, a little shocked.

'And at the end of *Oliver Twist*, Fagin spends his last night in the condemned cell at Newgate, refusing to repent his crimes.'

She decided against reading Dickens' grim words about Fagin's death. She wanted to give them something more cheerful to take home with them. Maybe she shouldn't have ended her Dickens at Night tour in the shadow of the gallows. Perhaps she should reconsider the route, finish at a jolly tavern or coffee-house.

'Thank you all for coming. If you're planning to go for a drink at one of the Dickensian pubs we passed this evening, I recommend the George and Vulture, down Saint Michael's Alley off Cornhill.'

The pub had been frequented by a young Dickens and was used to literary tourists. The group dispersed into the chilly London night. Helen watched them go, smiling until the last had turned their back.

Her shoulders slumped and the smile shut up shop. She sat on the low wall that circled the churchyard of Saint Sepulchre, hunched against the biting wind. At least the freezing rain had eased. The stone face of Old Bailey gazed down, impassive as the blindfold statue of justice that topped the building.

Eight people. Not bad for a cold Tuesday night in January. But eighty quid was not going to pay the tax bill at the end of the month. Without regular tourist crowds, guiding in London was a precarious living. And the curtailment of her teaching hours, as Russell University cut costs to make up for the loss of foreign students, meant she was more than usually dependent on walking tour income. She thought with fellow-feeling of Charles Dickens, always hustling and busy with some new venture, the spectre of the debtor's prison at his back. And he had a large family to support, not just himself.

Helen thrust her hands deep into her coat pockets and stared at the pavement. She should go home. She was tempted to go to the George and Vulture herself. The open fire and the buzz of conversation would be a lot cosier than her silent, cold flat.

But London pub prices were not going to help her financial situation. She'd pick up a ready meal, then do some writing. At least the enforced isolation of the last two years had given her time for that. Even if – unlike Dickens – she had no way to make a living from her pen.

Helen's long legs took her fast down a deserted Cheapside, past boarded-up sandwich shops, a gym and dry-cleaners. The familiar dome of Saint Paul's loomed off to her right, the London stock exchange to her left. God and Mammon, the twin pistons that pumped London's engine, had both fallen silent.

The city had endured for two millennia, since the Romans established their citadel on the banks of the Thames. It had survived fires, plagues, bombings, and Boudicca. Surely it would survive this?

How had previous generations of Londoners felt as the city underwent one of its periodic disasters? The medieval merchants of Cheapside, their customers and neighbours dropping dead around them as the Black Death cavorted through the streets. The Restoration insurance clerks, watching as their houses and coffee-shops were consumed in the Great Fire. East End market traders listening to the wail of the air-raid siren as they huddled underground, wondering what would be left of their homes when they emerged from the shelters.

The future of London must have seemed even more in doubt then. The people would return. But how would she keep going until they did?

At Bank tube station, she paused and checked her phone before heading underground. There was an email from her new head of department, Professor Brown. Helen tensed for bad news. He asked if she could call into his office for a chat. That sounded ominous. Not more belt-tightening, she hoped.

'Also, do you happen to be free on Saturday night? Apologies for late notice – there's an event I'd like you to attend in Rochester.'

Helen wished she needed to check her diary. As usual, she planned to spend Saturday night alone, eating pizza in front of the television and drinking cheap red wine. Rochester, though. Would he expect her to pay for her own travel? It was an hour or two by train from London, further than she'd been since the pandemic began. She pocketed her phone and headed down to the deserted platform.

It rang as she disembarked at Deptford Bridge. Her heart squeezed tight as she saw the name and she scrambled to answer, pressing herself into the corner of a building to get out of the wind.

'Hi!' She tried to keep her voice light.

'Helen? Can you hear me? You're very faint.'

You bet I am, thought Helen. 'Loud and clear. Is this better? Are you OK?' She pressed the phone to her ear.

'I'm good. Where are you?'

'Deptford. On my way home from a tour. How about you?'

11

'On set, but we've wrapped early for the day. I'm going hiking in the hills with some of the cast.'

'That sounds nice.'

Gregory Hall had been in Los Angeles to film a Hollywood blockbuster when the pandemic erupted. He'd stayed there while the filming stopped and restarted through ever-more-onerous travel restrictions. Her tentative relationship with the actor, barely begun at the time he left for America, was on ice. Helen wondered whether it could possibly be defrosted. They'd stayed in regular contact at first, but his calls had become less frequent. She wished she could think of something interesting to say, but their lives had diverged. She tried to imagine hiking in the Hollywood hills, or swimming off Malibu beach.

'I also thought you should know… there might be something about me in the papers this week. It's just stupid gossip, but you know what the press are like.'

'Uh-huh?' Helen's stomach tightened. 'What sort of thing?'

'Oh, just some photos from a cast night out.' His voice had struck a false note, jarringly light-hearted. 'Apparently there's one of me and Saskia which could be misinterpreted. I didn't want you to think…' He trailed off.

Helen couldn't breathe properly. Saskia Minski, his co-star, one of the most beautiful young women on the planet. She tried to laugh, but it came out as a gasp.

'Think what? Greg, it's been two years. I don't expect you to live like a monk. I'm glad you're enjoying yourself.' She wished that was true.

'Well… that's nice of you. I didn't want you to be upset. Anyway. What are you doing this weekend?'

Helen wanted to get off the call, scared her voice would

betray her urge to cry.

'Off to Rochester for a work thing. Got to go now. Have fun!' She hung up and wiped away a treacherous tear.

Fun. Helen stomped along the busy road as lorries thundered past, trying to remember when she'd last had any fun.

She turned the corner at the big old Victorian house, its windows dark. Damn. She'd been too distracted to buy dinner. What remnants were lurking in the bottom of her fridge?

She checked for post in the silent hallway, then climbed the stairs to her flat, hauling herself up the four storeys. In the freezing kitchen, she made cheese on toast and devoured it with her coat on, standing at the window. She took great slugs of an iceless, lemon-less gin and tonic.

'I know,' she whispered, raising her glass to the distant lights of the city. 'Sacrilege. Sorry, Crispin.'

She imagined his outraged response. 'If you're going to drink alone, darling, at least do it properly.'

Of all the losses that the pandemic had brought, Helen felt none so keenly as the death of Crispin Kent, her eighty-two-year-old neighbour and closest friend. The house was desolate without knowing he was there, five storeys below in the basement flat.

The law of three. You can have a great flat, she reminded herself. Or a great relationship, or a great job. You can't have all three at once.

She had a great job. She only hoped she'd still have it after her chat with Professor Brown.

# Chapter 3

Helen arrived early on Wednesday morning, taking advantage of the empty buses and quiet roads. She had not been to her Bloomsbury office for weeks. Russell University encouraged all staff to work from home when possible and teaching sessions were often delivered online.

Helen missed her students, their enthusiasm and fresh responses, the way you could see understanding suddenly dawn on a face during a tutorial. You didn't get the same interaction over a computer screen.

She picked up a handful of post from her pigeonhole and decided to brave the office kitchen.

'Hello! Haven't seen you for ages. How are you?' Jessica, the gossipy secretary, was filling the kettle. Helen felt unusually pleased to see her.

'Yeah, I'm fine. How about you, Jess? Did you have a good Christmas?'

'Lovely. Just me and the boyfriend. Very cosy.' She looked smug, and Helen hoped she wouldn't ask about her own dismal festivities.

Helen spooned instant coffee into a chipped mug while

Jessica chattered on about her new man. Then the woman stopped, clapped her hand over her mouth and stared at Helen.

'What?'

'I'm so sorry. Listen to me going on about Darren. I should be more sensitive. I suppose you've seen the photos on Instagram?'

Helen tried to keep her hand steady as she poured boiling water. 'I don't really do social media.'

Jessica dug out her mobile phone from her jeans pocket. 'Look. Gregory Hall, with that Saskia Minski. He was your boyfriend, wasn't he? You must be really upset.'

Helen flushed with humiliation. 'Not really. We got to know each other when the Marlowe play was on, but I haven't seen him for years.' She glanced at the tiny image, despite herself. Greg wrapped around a long-haired platinum-blonde woman about half Helen's height. It hurt more than it should.

'Oh.' Jessica was clearly disappointed.

Helen grabbed her coffee, slopping half of it over the floor, and made for her office. She closed the door, blinking away tears. Bloody hell. Why did the end of her relationship have to be anyone else's business?

Her phone buzzed. She noticed a handful of missed calls from numbers she didn't recognise. But this one she knew.

'Hullo, Nick. If you're phoning for a comment, please sod off.'

'Come on, girl. I don't do celeb stuff. You know that. I saw the stories, though. I wondered if you needed any media help. I suppose the vultures have started calling.'

She sighed. 'That's nice of you. There were a few calls, but I haven't taken any of them. I had my phone on silent and didn't notice till just now.'

'Right. Leave it like that, don't reply to any of them and if anyone gets through, tell them no comment. They'll get bored and move on soon enough.' He paused. 'Are you all right, though? I don't know if you were still seeing him…'

'Not for ages. I'm fine,' she said, firmly. 'Look, it's good to hear from you, but I've got a meeting with my boss in five minutes.'

'OK, I'll let you get on. But you take care. Let's meet up soon for a drink, yeah?'

Helen hung up, feeling a little cheered. She hadn't seen Nick for ages. The journalist was an old friend, and they'd been through some stuff together. She needed to get out more. She'd been lonelier than she'd like to admit in recent months.

She went through the post. Flyers mainly, for upcoming conferences and exhibitions, new journals she might want to subscribe to, university newsletters that she'd already received by email. One heavier cardboard envelope. She saw the publisher's stamp on the front and her heart jumped.

Carefully, she unwrapped it. A slip of paper from the editor – 'Congratulations!' – and the book itself. Pale grey cover, a delicate line drawing of a skull with a flower growing through its eye socket. Above the image, the title: *Outcast Dead*, by Helen Oddfellow.

She handled it gently, a soft smile on her face, flipped through the pages to be sure that this was true – her poems, the work of the past five years, collected together and printed in one volume.

The poems had been inspired by the Cross Bones burial ground near London Bridge, where the outcast dead – those not deemed worthy of a proper burial in consecrated ground – lay. Prostitutes, paupers, the destitute and uncared-for. The place had been adopted by Londoners in recent decades as a kind of shrine, a memorial garden. Helen found it incredibly moving.

She'd worked on the poems in secret for so long, not daring to show them to anyone. When she'd finally shared one or two with a friend, they had pressed her to submit them to poetry magazines. She'd been surprised when they were quickly accepted and an editor got in touch to ask if there were more.

Helen had worked on them all through the long lockdown days, tuning in to the ghostly voices she had somehow conjured from London's streets. They had pressed in as she hunched over her desk, warming themselves around her glowing laptop screen as she searched patiently for the right word, the perfect phrase to give them life. Disregarded lives, the countless nameless Londoners whose bones lay in churchyards and plague pits, burial grounds both ancient and modern, heaping up beneath the pavements of the modern city.

And here they were: bound in paper and card, out in the world for anyone to read. A quiet solace among all that had been lost.

There was a rap on the door and Jessica inserted her head. 'Emmanuel wants to know if you're ready?' she asked.

Helen had forgotten her appointment. She got to her feet, beaming.

'On my way,' she said. 'Thanks, Jess.'

Helen tapped on the door of Professor Emmanuel Brown, the head of department who had arrived at Russell University from Harvard the previous September. The professor had made his reputation in his surveys of African American literature and also had a special interest in the novels of

Charles Dickens. He had been enthusiastic about the chance to widen the curriculum of the English department while continuing his Dickens studies in the author's home city. Helen had taken to him immediately, and he'd helped her to develop her Dickens walking tours, delighting in melding his knowledge of the author's work with her familiarity with the streets and alleys of London.

'Come!' He sat at a wide desk, cleared of everything but a sleek laptop computer and a silver-framed photograph of his wife and two children. He wore a well-cut dark wool suit with a crisp white shirt and striped tie, his salt-and-pepper hair clipped short and neat as his goatee beard. He always made Helen feel fearfully scruffy.

He broke into a broad smile, tipped back his chair and waved Helen to a seat.

'Good morning, Helen. Will you have coffee?'

The professor had taken one look at the kitchen facilities on his arrival and installed a shiny coffee machine in the corner of his office.

'Thanks. I'd love one.' Helen had let her mug of nasty instant get cold.

'Help yourself.'

She sat with a scaldingly hot, fragrant espresso. He leaned across the table.

'I'll be straight with you, Helen. The department is in a hole. We were so dependent on overseas students and numbers have fallen off a cliff in the past two years.'

Hell. He was going to cut her hours again. Or – even worse – make her redundant. How would she survive? She twisted her fingers together in her lap.

'I've been looking over the figures. The university wants

me to cut costs. We may need to lose some dead wood.'

She flinched at his phrase. 'I suppose so.'

He looked startled at her strangled tone. 'Not you, Helen! Goodness me, you're one of our shining stars! I was thinking of… actually, strike that. With luck, we'll have some early retirements, before I need to start putting posts at risk. But this is the point: I didn't come here to make cuts. I came here to bring in new money, new investment. And I need your help.'

He picked up a flyer from his desk and passed it over. Helen recognised it as one that had been stuffed in her pigeonhole.

'I've been advising the curator of this exhibition in Rochester – A River Runs Through It: Charles Dickens and the Thames. It opens at the weekend, and there's a reception on Saturday evening. Drinks and canapés, speeches and so on. I'd like you to come along. Are you free?'

'Sure.' Helen was surprised. 'It sounds interesting.' She wasn't keen on official functions, but the exhibition sounded intriguing.

'There are some people going that I want to cultivate. Potential donors, people who might want to set up a bursary or have a library named after them or something. I think they could be very useful for us. One in particular, an English guy who runs a big property company. His great-grandpa was a duke or something. I'd like him to have a good time, get to know some of the younger members of faculty. Especially people like you, Helen, with an interest in Dickens.'

'Right.' Helen bristled at the thought of being laid on as entertainment for some rich toffs.

'It starts at six o'clock.' He looked awkward for a moment. 'And – I know you academics are very casual here, but maybe

19

you could wear something more formal?'

Helen looked down at her jeans and black polo-neck. 'Yeah. I'll see what I can do.' She hesitated, and then decided to ask anyway. 'Is it all right if I claim back the train fare? Only it's quite expensive unless you book up ages in advance.'

He looked surprised again. 'Of course. And stay over. I don't want you travelling back alone late at night. Tell Jessica and she'll arrange the hotel and train tickets.'

She rose to go.

'One other thing,' he called.

She turned back. He had in his hand a copy of her little volume of poetry. She'd not mentioned it to anyone in the department, feeling simultaneously too shy and too anxious about what proper academics might think of it.

'This is fantastic. Why didn't you tell me about it before it was published? We could have held some kind of launch event for you. I didn't even know you wrote poetry until I saw a notice about it in the *Poetry Review*.'

'Oh. Well, I suppose… I didn't want to blow my own trumpet.' Helen was blushing like a kid. She couldn't resist asking, 'Did you read it?'

'I did. I loved it. And I despair of you. If you won't blow your trumpet, how does anyone get to hear about your work? At least tell me when you do something like this. Then I can blow the trumpet for you.' He laughed a low, warm chuckle. 'And believe me, Helen, I blow loud!'

# Chapter 4

The pup was young. Too young, probably, to be away from his mother. He whined all night. Paxton had to let him sleep on his bed, just to get some sleep himself.

But he'd been cheap. Paxton had been gobsmacked by the price of dogs. Four hundred quid for a crossbreed? This one had no sort of pedigree, although he looked like he had a bit of Staffie in him somewhere. He was strong already, his little jaws clamping Paxton's wrist whenever he tried to stroke him.

He needed to get the dog house-trained, fast. His room was starting to smell of piss and he wasn't having that. Besides, someone was bound to complain. There were a few bare square metres of concrete outside the hostel by the steps that led up to the street.

'Cooper! Outside.' He dragged the dog by his collar out of the utility room door. Cooper looked up at him, confused. 'Go on. If you're going to crap, do it over there, by the drainpipe.'

The dog scampered around the area, tail wagging madly, stuffing his nose into corners where wet leaves piled up. Paxton sat on the iron steps that led up to the road. This was a shitty place. But it was only for a few more weeks, then he'd have enough cash and the liberty to find himself a bedsit somewhere.

He had plans for the future. A boxing gym, somewhere young lads could come and get themselves fit. The sort of kids who had no direction. He could harness that, bring them into the fold, make patriots of them. They'd be needed, and they'd need to be in shape. But it would cost and Paxton was broke. No way would he have taken up with the traffickers if he hadn't needed the money.

On cue, his phone buzzed. 'Yeah?'

'Got your stuff, and another job for you. Usual place.' It was Guren.

Paxton watched the dog crouch by the drainpipe, a look of concentration on his face. Good boy. You're learning.

'All right. Give us an hour.' The pup bounced over to him, tail wagging frantically. Paxton pulled his silky ears, rubbed his head.

He put the phone down on the step, let the dog take hold of his wrist with his needle teeth. Guren ran a horrible business, Paxton knew that. And he wasn't immune to the irony: his own political commitment to keeping the immigrants out versus the necessity of bringing the illegals in, feeding the machine.

He'd preferred his old business, security. You knew where you were with that. Protecting property, keeping order. The sort of job that fitted a man with his skills. But you couldn't get a licence to be a security guard – not even a doorman – with a criminal record. So, he'd made the connections inside; worked out how things operated. They needed men like him, brains as well as brawn. Organised crime, he'd realised, was full of crackheads who couldn't organise a kid's birthday party.

People like him, who kept sober and didn't sample the goods, could make money fast.

He thought again of the girl, Aisha. Her wide smile, crooked teeth, decent English. She'd been the only one of them with the guts to stand up to him when he knifed that guy. She must be about the same age as his son, he guessed. Fourteen. Just a kid.

He hadn't seen the boy in two years. Jackie brought him to visit twice when Paxton was still inside, but her contempt drained all pleasure from their encounters. Luke had seemed so uncomfortable, scared and hunched into himself in the visitor room, answering his dad's questions about school in monosyllables. Hating it.

Paxton had told her not to bring the boy again. He'd not seen either of them since, but he sent money for Luke's birthday and Christmas. Maybe he'd get in touch again, see if Luke wanted to meet Cooper. Kids liked dogs. They could go to the beach when it got warmer.

The pup pissed on his trainers. 'Oi!' He pushed Cooper away, harder than he'd meant to, and the dog yelped. Paxton needed a new pair of trainers anyway, but didn't have the cash.

He got up, stretched. He'd run up to the rendezvous instead of taking the van. Down the Old Folkestone Road to Samphire Hoe, up the back-breaking path to the top of the cliff, pushing himself till he wanted to throw up. Then drop and pump out a score of press-ups on the short turf at the top, face to the watery sun hovering over the horizon. He remembered struggling to lift the suitcase, the strain on his muscles. He couldn't let himself get soft.

'Come on, Cooper,' he told the dog. 'We're going for a run.'

Up at the top, breathing hard, he took shelter beside a huge concrete block. The wind was blowing up from the east again, bruised-looking clouds chasing across the wind-whipped sea. A few spots of rain had fallen. Cooper was shivering, pressed up against Paxton's legs. He was getting cold too, the sweat from his run cooling rapidly. He took off his backpack and pulled on a hoodie.

Paxton liked it up here. He liked the brutal concrete, like modern art or something, a big concave depression scooped out of the front of it, facing the sea. But it wasn't some stupid sculpture; it was a clever piece of defence. Back before radar, before modern air defences, the sound mirrors along the south coast had been listening posts, able to pick up the drone of incoming aircraft as they crossed the 20-mile stretch of sea that divided England from enemy territory. He'd read up on it, how trained operators could pick up the exact angle from which the sound was coming, meaning they could send signals back to headquarters with the calculated position of the aircraft. Then the gunners would be ready, the RAF could be scrambled, and the invaders repelled. A good system, ingenious.

In better weather, the coastal path attracted its share of hikers, most of whom stared in dumb incomprehension at the structure. There were nerds, too; enthusiasts who drove around the country visiting decommissioned military bunkers, sound mirrors and old gun emplacements. The Kent coast was littered with them, the frontline against invasion since the time of the Romans.

But today, the weather had kept the hikers at bay. Paxton narrowed his eyes. A dark figure was coming along the path. The man was average-height, thick-set with broad shoulders and the rolling gait of a heavyweight boxer who'd taken one punch too many. He had a cigarette cupped in his hand, from which he took deep drags. Paxton looked further along the path. Guren usually had a couple of heavies in tow, but he couldn't see anyone today.

'Shit weather.' The man flicked his burnt-out cigarette into a puddle at the base of the concrete.

'Yeah. Sorry about that, boss. Next time I'll order sunshine.' The sarcasm was lost on Guren.

'Job for you, this weekend.'

Shit. Paxton wanted to go to the protest on Saturday. It was going to be big. He couldn't get involved, but he wanted to see what was going on.

'What day?'

Guren shrugged. 'Your call. There's a shopkeeper up in Rochester. He takes care of some stuff for us. He's got a load of stuff that the boss wants. It should be boxed up; you just need to collect. Take the van. And he owes us money. He's behind with his payments, so you might need to lean on him a bit. He's a civilian; shouldn't be too difficult. We won't need him for much longer.'

Paxton nodded. 'Address?'

'On the High Street, number 26.'

Guren reached into his waterproof jacket. It was a Barbour, one of the posh ones, not knocked-off. He pulled out a big manila envelope and handed it over.

'What's this crap?' Paxton pulled out a handful of plastic gift cards. 'I said cash.'

Guren shrugged. 'New system. Easier this way. Less noticeable. No-one uses cash anymore. You can't even spend it.'

Paxton used cash. So did the local corner shops he went to,

25

the bloke in the pub he bought Cooper from. Also, you could count it.

'I want notes.'

Guren smiled, an unpleasant sight at the best of times. 'So, you sell them. Easy. Or order stuff and send it back. Get refunds. Untraceable, yeah? Safer than running everything through a stupid little bookshop. Or do you want Bitcoin next time?'

Bitcoin. Paxton knew blokes who reckoned they could make a fortune with cryptocurrencies. There was a guy in prison who claimed to be a crypto millionaire; spent all his phone credit putting through orders to his broker. But Paxton was old school, analogue. He didn't like money you couldn't see. The cards would have to do.

'There'd better be enough.'

'There is. £110 on each card. Sell them for £100; you're still covered.'

'OK. Where do you want the boxes?' asked Paxton.

'Bring them to the farm. We'll take care of it from there.'

Paxton waited a beat. 'Everything OK up there? Those migrants giving you any trouble?'

Guren grinned again, exposing tobacco-brown teeth. 'Not since you sliced that guy. They're all shit-scared of you. All we have to say to get them in line: "I'll call Gary." Maybe you should do that every time. One each cargo, keep them quiet.'

Paxton clamped down on his urge to ask about the girl. None of his business, and the less he knew, the better.

Guren pulled up his collar, hunched his shoulders and walked towards the Folkestone Road. The rain blurred his outline until he was a dark, squat column moving against the hedgerows.

Paxton walked around the sound mirror and stood in its curved depression, listening to the amplified sound of the waves as the wind lashed in from the sea.

# Chapter 5

Something was going to kick off. Nick Wilson had been at enough of these demos to know when trouble was brewing. The last couple had been damp squibs; a few dozen ugly-looking guys in yellow vests who made a lot of noise and sat in the road, filming each other getting arrested. This time, it felt different.

There were more of them, for a start. Far more. And they were still coming, streaming down from the town centre and pouring off coaches parked all along the sea front, England flags draped over their shoulders.

The coaches were the first sign. Most of the far-right groups Nick had investigated could barely get together the bus fare to their local town, but someone had paid for dozens of coaches from all over England. The British Patriot Party had cash to burn.

Where was the money coming from?

There were more police, too, a lot of them surrounding a small group of scared-looking people clutching 'Refugees Welcome' placards. Nick wanted to tell them to get the hell out of there, head home while there was still time.

He listened to the crowd. It was too quiet. There was an

intensity, a purpose. A feeling of readiness. They should have been shouting idiotic slogans, laughing, taunting the counter-protestors. Instead, they walked past in near-silence, grinning or spitting at the ground. They went quickly and quietly, taking their places behind the BPP banner stretched across the road into the town centre.

The official route would take them from the seafront into the town, past the council offices and the big pedestrianised square, ending up at a park for a rally. The police were worried they'd stage sit-downs on the main road and block the lorries heading for the ferry port. There were vans of riot police all along the port road. But it felt too big, too important, for a sit-in.

'This is weird,' said Angus, Nick's cameraman. 'Which rock have all this lot crawled out from?' Simon, the sound guy, giggled. He was new, inexperienced. He looked like he'd rather be somewhere else.

Nick didn't answer. Angus was one of the good guys, reliable and tough. They'd worked together on several documentaries. But he didn't experience it the way Nick had all his life. There was racism everywhere. Mostly it manifested as muttered comments, ugly looks. The occasional bit of trouble from a group of thugs. But here the thugs were all gathered in one place, carrying banners.

The team had a reporter undercover who had been tagging along with one of the south London groups for a couple of months. Ollie had tipped them off that this anti-migration demonstration was being whispered about as something different. Not one they'd want to miss.

Nick was monitoring Ollie's social media posts, watching out for any messages. It was risky, and Nick wished he could have done the undercover work himself. But his face was too well-known. There weren't enough black guys on the far-right for him to pass unnoticed. Some marchers had already spotted him, pointed him out to each other. One had drawn his finger across his throat, hissing with fury. Nick had found whole pages dedicated to him on the far-right websites, especially since his last documentary aired on Channel Four.

'#PatriotArmy Armed and Ready. Just waiting for the Off,' he read, next to a photo of Ollie, his face half-obscured by a Q-Anon T-shirt pulled up over his mouth and nose. Nick scanned the crowd, trying to work out where he was. But that was stupid; he couldn't risk catching Ollie's eye.

Nick and his two-man crew were near the middle of the march. A bunch of men next to a van milled around, handing out official British Patriot Party placards from the back: 'No More Migrants'; 'Send Them Back'. And, most frequently, 'Keep Your Promises'.

This, Ollie had reported, was the trigger for the protest. The government had recently rowed back on crowd-pleasing pledges to ship new arrivals from Calais straight to Rwanda for 'processing'. Their plans had run into immediate legal difficulties and been suspended, to derision from the far right. Some saw the recent opening of a new immigration processing centre at Dover's Western Docks to cope with the increased numbers making the 20-mile journey by sea as evidence of the government's betrayal of that promise.

Nick scanned the crowd again, looking out for faces from previous encounters. He stiffened, stopped. The crowd had shifted for a moment, giving him a glimpse through to the grass verge on the other side of the road. Then the gap closed. But it had been him, he was sure of it.

He grabbed Angus's arm. The man's height gave him an advantage.

'Over the other side. Big guy, in his forties, wearing a zip-up jacket, hands in his pockets. Short brown hair, shaved at the sides.'

Angus craned his neck. 'Lots of them about, Nick. Someone you recognise?'

'I should do. He broke my wrist and tried to strangle me. Three bloody operations to fix it.' Nick touched his fingers to his forearm, traced the scar over the metal pins. 'Gary Paxton. Last I heard, he was safely banged up.' If there was one man who deserved to be in prison for the rest of his life, it was Paxton. What the hell was he doing here – day release to re-train as a Nazi?

Nick pushed through the crowd.

'Don't be an idiot.' Angus restrained him. 'Wait here. Look, something's happening.'

The protesters were shuffling over to one side, allowing passage for three sleek black limousines, sinister with tinted windows. The motorcade swept slowly down the seafront, heading for the rear of the march.

'Trouble.' Nick set off at a trot, heading in the direction the cars were going.

'We'll be right at the back,' grumbled Simon.

'Trust me.' Nick darted away, leaving the crew to follow on, lugging their heavy equipment.

The crowd stretched all the way along the smartened-up seafront, past the lines of guest houses and hotels, seafood restaurants and the yacht marina. He'd almost caught up with the cars when they came to a halt, horns blaring. The tail of the march was at the end of the esplanade, towards the

Western Docks entrance. Nick picked up his pace.

There were fewer police around. The guys at this end of the march weren't holding placards or banners. They looked hefty; some wore balaclavas or scarves tied around their faces. They wore lumpy-looking backpacks, heavy belts. He saw the glint of a knuckleduster on a fist.

Men in combat gear leapt out of the front passenger seats of the limos and opened the rear doors, saluting. A man got out of each car, each one dressed in a long greatcoat, wearing a military-style beret. Twats in hats, thought Nick. He waited for his crew, catching his breath. He didn't want to be on his own in this crowd.

'What's happening?' asked Angus, puffing up with his camera over his shoulder.

'Not sure. But they like playing soldiers.'

The three men were addressing the crowd, their faces serious. Nick wasn't close enough to hear their words.

Nick's phone buzzed with another message from Ollie's account.

'#PatriotArmy About Turn!!!' read Ollie's post. It wasn't the only one; the whole social channel lit up with the same message.

The mass of men turned smartly, almost as one. With a roar, they ran towards the entrance to the Western Docks.

# Chapter 6

Nick and the crew ran with them.

'Shouldn't we wait for the police?' asked Simon. Nick didn't waste his breath answering. The police were focused on the town end of the march, where it would cross the main road to the port. Fighting the last war, like always.

'The processing centre,' he shouted to Angus. Of course. He should have realised that would be the target. He hoped to God someone at the centre had realised the threat, ensured the place was impenetrable.

The crowd surged across the narrow bridge over the water and up to the tall gates at the entrance to the Tug Harbour. A lone security guard ran out of his sentry box and looked in horror at the hordes pushing at the gates. Sensibly, he retreated to his box, shouting into his radio. A couple of men with backpacks and balaclavas were ushered through to the front of the crowd, where they extracted bolt-cutters and made short work of the padlock. The vanguard broke through and flung the gates wide.

Nick followed, Angus close behind him. There was a roaring in the air, hundreds of men with their fists raised, a terrifying wall of sound. It coalesced into a chant: 'Send them back.' After a moment, it changed. 'Throw them back,' Nick heard. He looked behind him for any signs of police activity. Far off in the distance, he heard a faint siren wail. Too late.

The centre was a five-storey modern building, sitting by itself at the end of dock surrounded by empty tarmac. Nick had joined the press on a tour when it opened. The brisk woman who managed the centre showed them the immigration documentation offices for staff on the ground floor, doctors' surgery for those in immediate need of medical attention, kitchen for serving up gallons of soup. Upstairs, the emergency accommodation and bathrooms. Eight to a room in single-sex dorms, plus a few rooms for the family groups that arrived together. It was spartan, but not inhumane, and infinitely better than the inadequate temporary facilities in place when the trickle of small boats became a daily armada of the desperate back in 2020.

The new building could accommodate two hundred and fifty people at a time, the press had been told, until they could be dispersed to suitable facilities around the country. Enough for a winter night, Nick remembered suggesting, but what about when the weather improved?

Two hundred and fifty. How many men, women, and children, exhausted from a perilous sea crossing in an open dinghy, were in that building now?

The building had wide glass doors, the sort that slid open automatically. He saw a woman in a blue skirt run from behind the reception desk. She reached up, stretching towards the lock that would close the doors. One man from the cars, a big guy in a floor-length greatcoat and epaulettes, blocked them with his foot. She stood her ground for a moment, then one of the other men picked her up and carried her out of the way. The crowd swarmed through.

'Christ, Nick. What do you want to do?' Angus was at his shoulder, filming as the men rushed through the doors. Simon, looking green, was behind him.

Nick hesitated. They should probably wait. This was a dangerous situation, and he had to think of his team's safety.

'Let's do a quick piece to camera and wait for the police,' he said, reluctantly.

They crouched in front of the building as Nick explained to viewers what they had seen. The men kept rushing past, through the open doors, whooping. Nick stood, saw the expression on Angus's face. The cameraman was battle-hardened and had been with him in plenty of tight spots before.

'Come on, Angus. Let's go in.' He glanced at Simon. 'Not you. Keep back here. When the police arrive, tell them we're inside.'

Hoods up, Nick and Angus joined the throng flooding into the centre and struggled through the crowded foyer. He heard a woman screaming from the office, another shouting into a phone, pleading for help. Where the hell were the security guards? Nick would bet they were happy to charge in if there was any trouble from the refugees. Angus, brawny from shouldering his camera, pushed his way up the stairs, Nick close behind.

A scuffle had broken out in the corridor; half a dozen defiant young African men attempting to hold back the thugs. There was a lot of posturing and shouting. The young lads weren't backing down. Nick supposed they'd already been through hell; this was just one more ordeal. But the numbers were against them. One of the serious-looking thugs from the back of the march swung a punch, followed it up with a hook that brought a spray of blood from an African boy's mouth. His mates roared, faces distorted with rage.

Nick saw a silver blade flash, heard a man scream as blood sprayed across the wall. This was going to be a massacre. And he would be part of it, if he wasn't careful.

He backed into a side room, saw a woman in a headscarf clutching a small child to her breast, her eyes wide and terrified. Nick clocked the wardrobe behind her.

'Get in there,' he told her. Shaking, she did as he said, and he closed the door.

He glanced out the small, barred window. Police vans were pulling up, officers piling out.

'What's in here?' yelled one protester, pushing Angus back into the room. 'What are you filming for?'

'Keep your hair on. This room's empty. I'm documenting it for the patriots,' said the cameraman, keeping Nick well behind him. 'Can't leave it all to the mainstream media.'

Mercifully, the man moved on.

Nick heard running feet, laughter. 'There's a bunch of women on the top floor. You coming?' yelled a voice. 'Or do you want to watch?'

He heard shouts from below, the police finally arriving. Then a pair of terrified eyes behind a balaclava appeared at the door.

'What the hell are you doing? Get out. There's a fire exit. Follow me.'

It was Ollie.

'Wait.' Nick pulled the wardrobe open. 'Come with us,'

he told the woman. Nick took the child, who started to scream. They pushed past people in the corridor, the woman sandwiched between him and Angus.

'Here.' Ollie pushed through a fire door and on to a metal walkway. 'I'm going back in. Can't be seen with you. I'll follow when I can.'

Nick nodded. 'Good luck. The police are on their way in.'

He pushed the woman ahead of him and they clattered down the stairs. Nick was relieved to see others – young men in tracksuits and older guys in thin jackets, a handful of women – were also on their way down.

He handed the baby back to her mother. 'Go, now. Get right away from here.'

He and Angus turned the corner from the steps and walked right into the arms of a brace of police.

'Get in there' shouted Nick as they flung him to the ground. His face hit the gravel. 'We're TV. They need you inside.' The man with his knee on Nick's back didn't seem impressed.

'They're going to set it on fire,' yelled a voice from the top of the steps. Ollie.

The pressure on Nick's back eased.

'What did you say?'

Nick turned his head, just far enough to see a plume of smoke coming from one of the upper windows.

Ollie clattered down the stairs to the police. 'Quick. I know you want to arrest me, but I don't want any part of this. There are men with petrol bombs on the top floor. You've got to get everyone out of there.'

The police got to their feet and ran, shouting into their radios. Nick and Angus scrambled up.

'Get filming,' Nick told Angus. Unnecessarily; the big man

was already training his camera on the smoke coming from the window. They both knew how serious this could be.

'Ollie...'

'Shut up. I'm going to leg it. Don't blow my cover,' he said. He swung a punch at Nick's head, slowly enough that he could dodge it, but clearly enough for anyone watching. Then Ollie took off, running as fast as his legs would take him away from the centre, out of the docks.

Nick stood at Angus's shoulder and watched, helpless, as the flames spread.

# Chapter 7

Helen walked along Rochester High Street, dazzled by the bright sunshine that had broken through after a night of rain. She'd taken the train down from London in the morning, eaten lunchtime sandwiches en route, and was ready to explore. A weekend somewhere new and unfamiliar might shake her out of her low mood.

The town was lively with shoppers; well-dressed prosperous-looking types who all seemed delighted to be out on a sunny Saturday, browsing the antique shops and buying Kentish produce in the expensive delicatessens. A fully costumed town crier outside the cathedral was posing for photographs with tourists.

Rochester certainly made the most of its Charles Dickens connections. The author had lived in a country house at Gads Hill, a few miles out of town. Helen spotted a Miss Havisham Tea Parlour, a wine bar called Pickwick's, and a vintage store inevitably called Ye Olde Curiosity Shoppe. She paused by the quaint red-brick Eastgate House with its twisting chimneys and turrets, apparently the original model for Miss Twinkleton's seminary in *The Mystery of Edwin Drood*, and admired Dickens' rather grand writing hut, a two-storey

Swiss chalet which had once stood in his garden in Gads Hill. It was bigger than Helen's entire flat. She tried to imagine having the use of such a place solely for writing poetry.

She couldn't relax. Even with Emmanuel's reassurance about the safety of her post at Russell University, she was barely making enough to pay the bills for her studio flat. The prospect of ever being able to afford a bigger place, one with a separate room for study and writing, was remote. She thought for a moment of Greg, living it up in Los Angeles. His East London flat was great; high ceilings and a balcony overlooking Victoria Park. She supposed it was still empty. She shook her head, tried to distract herself; she wouldn't be seeing the inside of that flat again.

She came to a halt beside a table of paperbacks, tatty and dog-eared, outside a rather run-down looking second-hand bookshop. Books were catnip to Helen, her biggest temptation.

She browsed the table without finding anything interesting, then peered in the small, rather grubby window of the shop. Leather-bound volumes with woodcut prints were artfully arranged, beckoning her in.

She hesitated. The books inside were older, probably more expensive. But it wouldn't hurt to have a look. An old-fashioned black-and-gold painted sign above the door announced the name: Thomas Chapman and Daughter, Booksellers.

She raised her hand to push the door open, then paused. A sign on the door announced the place was closed, even though there were lights on inside.

While she hesitated, a teenage girl wearing baggy black clothes and holding a skateboard marched up to the door. A boy about the same age tagged behind her.

'I think it's closed,' said Helen.

'No, it's not.' The girl pushed the door open. 'Dad!' she yelled. 'You left the sign on closed again. No wonder we don't sell anything.'

A man up a ladder turned, flustered. He was small with round-framed spectacles and curly dark hair, a rumpled white shirt untucked at the back.

'Oh dear. Silly of me, very silly.' He turned to Helen. 'So sorry. Come in, have a look around. Ask me if you need anything.' He had an old-fashioned air about him, as if he was playing at being a Dickensian character.

Helen smiled at him. 'Thank you. I will.'

She inhaled the familiar smell of leather greased by years of handling, the malty scent of crumbling paper. Dark shelves criss-crossed the shop, laden with old books with gilt lettering on their heavy spines. Poetry; military history from the nineteenth century. Twentieth-century novels that no-one read anymore.

She almost tripped over a cardboard box on the floor, steadied herself and knelt to investigate. Piles of maps, Ordnance Survey from the 1920s. She unfolded a map of Kent and traced a road north over the Medway to Cooling Church, another place that had inspired Dickens. She thought of the row of little gravestones beside the flint church. Pip's graves, out on the marshes, huddled together for company. Maybe she could make a pilgrimage out there before she headed home tomorrow. She was planning a Dickens tour of Kent, for tourists who wanted to go further afield.

There was another box next to the maps, stuffed with books. Helen picked one off the top, flicked through. It was an early

Victorian topographical survey of Kent, with notes on the towns, villages and key features of the county, complete with drypoint engravings. Underneath was a green cloth-bound volume, paper furred at the edges. The gilt lettering was dulled.

'*London and Londoners: or a second judgement of Babylon the Great,*' she read. That sounded more up her street. She turned to the title page, checked the author's name. Robert Mudie, second edition, 1836.

Interest piqued, she read the first page, adjusting her attention to the ornate phrases. The author promised to take the reader on a perambulation through the unfrequented streets of the capital, not shrinking from the less gentle thoroughfares. The reader would learn of the wickedness of the law courts, the commerce of the docks and the criminal dens of iniquity that marred the face of London.

It sounded fantastic and could be a great help in constructing future walking tours. Helen checked for a price, but found nothing.

She weaved her way through the shelves back to the desk, almost hidden beneath piles of papers and stacks of books.

'Hello?'

The man looked up, startled, and knocked a teetering pile of books. He seemed to have a nervous disposition.

'Sorry, I made you jump.'

'Not at all, not at all.' He steadied the books with a practised hand. 'Now, what have you got there?'

Helen handed over *London and Londoners*. 'It doesn't have a price. I found it in a box behind that bookshelf.'

He took off his glasses, which hung on a chain around his neck. 'Ah. Yes, indeed. I haven't got around to cataloguing those yet. They came from a big house sale quite recently.'

He paused, a troubled look passing over his brow.

'In fact… I'm not sure I should sell those, really. There's a collector…'

'Fuck's sake, Dad!' The girl and her friend were sitting on a baggy leather sofa beside the desk, reading comic books. 'Just sell it already! We need the cash.' She scrambled out of the sofa and took it from his hand. 'Come on, I've never even heard of this one, and the binding's nothing special. Sell it for a fiver. Don't be such an idiot.'

Helen tried to repress her laughter. 'Five pounds would be fine,' she said. She could manage that, surely. Especially as her trip was paid for by the university.

'Now, Wiz. Language,' remonstrated the girl's father. He turned to Helen. 'But my daughter is right, of course. Five pounds it is.'

Helen smiled at the girl, whose fierce pale face was sharp beneath a curtain of jet-black hair.

'Thank you. That's perfect.' Helen found some cash in her purse and handed it over. 'What are you reading?' she asked the girl. 'Looks interesting.'

She shrugged. 'Manga. I'm a collector. We're going to start a section for illustrated books and comics,' she said.

'Well, we've talked about it,' said her father.

'There's nowhere you can buy stuff like that in Rochester or Chatham,' the girl said. 'We'd get all the local kids coming in buying things. Wouldn't we, Lev?'

The boy looked up at her from under a greasy blond fringe, adoration in his pale-blue eyes. 'Yeah. No problem,' he said.

The bookseller slipped the volume inside a brown paper bag and handed it over to Helen.

'I hope you enjoy it. Are you visiting Rochester?' he asked.

'Yes, for a work thing. The new Dickens exhibition at the Guildhall? There's an opening event tonight, so I'm staying at the hotel opposite. Making a weekend of it.'

'Ah, yes. That exhibition sounds fascinating. We sell a lot of Dickens-related books, of course. I must get along to it. Well, we're open on Sundays, if you fancy another rummage.'

Helen wandered back into the street, the bright sun making her squint. She was getting hungry. She eyed Miss Havisham's Tea Parlour warily. What were the chances of getting a decent cup of coffee amid the chintz?

# Chapter 8

Helen spent a couple of hours touring the ancient cathedral, its heavy Romanesque architecture reminding her that it had been established long before the Norman conquest. Back outside, she strolled past the elegant Georgian houses of Minor Canon Row, another street immortalised by Dickens, then walked up to the remains of the castle, its square Norman keep looking like a toy fort, commanding the high ground above the bend of the river. She scrambled around the ruins and up into the keep, looking out across the wide river with its moored yachts and bridges. The sun lowered behind the cathedral and the day cooled.

Tired, Helen checked into the hotel, which was modest, but clean and friendly. Her feet ached. She sat on the bed with its frilly pink bedspread, took off her boots and glanced at her watch. There were still a couple of hours before she had to be across the street at the Guildhall for the exhibition opening.

She took her evening outfit from her travelling case: a midnight blue velvet trouser suit she'd bought five years ago, when she'd been invited to speak at lots of conferences and talks about a newly discovered Christopher Marlowe play. It had always felt a bit too glamorous even then, so she'd not worn it much. With luck, it would meet Emmanuel's expectations of smart evening wear.

After a quick shower, she flopped on the bed and checked her phone. She'd missed a message from Nick, asking her to call him. She tried his number, but it went straight to voicemail.

She switched on the TV news. There appeared to be a riot going on, with sirens wailing, people running about and smoke pouring from the top floors of a building. Helen turned up the sound.

'...At least two people have been confirmed dead, but it is unclear how many were in the immigration processing centre at the time,' the newsreader said, her voice sombre. 'The centre was opened late last year to deal with the increased numbers of people crossing the English Channel in small boats.'

Helen felt sick. The hostility directed at people seeking asylum in Britain in recent times horrified her.

'The Home Secretary has called for an investigation into how the anti-immigration march, which was due to take place in Dover town centre, was able to get out of control. The British Patriot Party, which organised the march, is likely to be declared a proscribed organisation, she said.'

The scene switched to the docks, where men were streaming through gates in front of a big building. With a shock, Helen saw the camera pan to Nick crouching by the side of the road.

'We've followed the protestors from where they rallied along the seafront to the Western Docks, where the new immigration processing centre opened just a month ago,' Nick said into the camera, his voice raised above the noise of men shouting. 'This looks very much like a pre-planned attack. Questions are bound to be asked about why the police were unprepared for such a possibility,' he continued.

The news programme switched to a bland police spokesman who used a lot of words to say nothing, before moving to the results of the day's football matches. Helen switched off the TV, grabbed her phone and tried Nick's number again.

'Hi.'

'Are you OK? I've just seen you on the news.'

'Yeah.' He sounded tired, lacking his normal bounce. 'It was pretty bad.'

'They're saying some people died…'

'I know. Bastards.' His voice cracked. 'We were right inside. They were going after anyone, Helen. There were women with babies inside. The women's dormitory was on the top floor. I don't know how many of them got out.'

'God. How awful.'

'Yeah.' He paused. 'I can't talk long. I've got to work. But there's something else. Back at the start, when they were all lining up on the seafront, I saw someone. But maybe I got it wrong. It's hard to be sure now.' He stopped again.

'Go on. Who?'

'Gary Paxton. But I thought he was still in prison. I mean, surely they can't have let him out already?'

Helen almost dropped the phone. 'No. It can't be.'

'At the time, I was pretty sure it was him. But so much happened after and I didn't get a photo or anything. I thought maybe you could ring your policewoman mate, find out if he's still inside.'

Helen's heart was thumping. Gary Paxton had almost broken her. She hadn't seen him since the day in the courtroom six years ago, when the judge had sentenced him to twelve years for manslaughter, GBH and false imprisonment.

She'd hoped never to see him again.

'Yeah.' Her voice didn't sound real, as if someone else was carrying on this conversation for her. 'Yeah, I'll phone Sarah.'

'Thanks,' said Nick. 'Let me know, will you? I can't believe that bastard is back on the streets.'

Helen hung up. She stared at the phone. Maybe Nick had got it wrong, like he said. It would be difficult to identify one person in a big, shifting crowd. Helen herself had thought she'd seen Paxton several times. A glimpse of a hefty shoulder, seen from behind. A man with short, neat dark hair. A high-pitched male laugh. But after a few crashing seconds of terror, whoever it was would turn around and she'd realise she'd been wrong.

After fumbling with nervous fingers, she managed to find the number she needed to call DCI Sarah Greenley.

'Helen! How're you?' The policewoman's voice was wary. 'Where are you? I only hear from you when something's wrong.'

'Gary Paxton,' said Helen. There was a pause. 'Is he out?'

Sarah sighed. 'I'm sorry. I only just found out myself. A former colleague at the Met told me. I should have called you. He got parole a couple of months ago. Which in my view should not have happened. They appealed it, of course.'

'Where is he?'

'He's at a hostel here in Kent somewhere. Dover, I think.'

Helen felt sick. Nick had been right, then. 'I see.'

'Helen, I am sorry. Are you OK? How did you know he was out?' The policewoman sounded uncomfortable.

'Nick Wilson called me. He was in Dover, at that protest. He saw him in the crowd.'

'Not the migrant protest?'

'The anti-refugee riot. The one that burned down an immigration centre and killed who knows how many desperate
people.' Helen felt her own anger mounting and tried to
swallow it. There was no point taking it out on Sarah.

'Right. Well, Paxton shouldn't have been there. Leave it
with me – I'll let my colleagues in Dover know. If he was
involved in storming the centre, we'll have him back inside
so fast his boots won't touch the ground.'

'Yeah. OK. Thanks, Sarah.'

'You take care. And don't worry. He's not allowed anywhere
near Deptford. He has to keep away from you, and from his
former associates. If he breaks parole terms, he's straight back
inside.'

Helen ended the call and stretched out on the bed. Don't
worry. Like that was even possible. She opened her phone's
map application, slightly reassured to see that Dover was 50
miles away from Rochester, at the southern tip of the county.
She sent Nick a quick text message to update him, then got
up and paced around the room. There was still more than an
hour before she needed to get ready for the reception.

Helen remembered *London and Londoners*, the book she'd
bought earlier, and took it from her backpack, hoping for
distraction. She sat back down, flicked through. The opening
targets – the convoluted courts of Chancery – reminded her
of Dickens' *Bleak House*. A later chapter outlined an orphan's
progress, made into a criminal by the cruelty of the Poor Law
and London society. *Oliver Twist* sprang irresistibly to mind.

Before long, Helen was immersed in a description of a
London 'flash house', where gangs of thieves congregated
to sell their acquisitions to a fence. It sounded very much
like Fagin's gang of pickpockets, from the youthfulness of the

thieves to the squalor of the back alleys and the abandoned warehouse in which they roosted.

Helen paused and looked again at the date of publication: 1836. Robert Mudie's whole book seemed to be filled with subject matter later explored by Charles Dickens. Had he read it? It was the year before Queen Victoria's reign began; around the time that Dickens was writing his first proper novel, *Oliver Twist*; conjuring up Fagin, the Artful Dodger and Bill Sikes. She wondered if Mudie's book had been identified as a source of inspiration for Dickens. His novels were generally supposed to have sprung from his own life and wanderings in the streets of London, but surely, he would have read up on his subjects too? She could ask Emmanuel Brown at the exhibition launch, if she got a moment.

She turned a page. Stopped. Between the pages, flattened as if it had not been moved since the day it was put there, was a yellowed piece of newspaper, covered in small print, about eight inches by four, folded in quarters.

She moved it carefully, feeling its brittleness. Was it a contemporary newspaper cutting? Perhaps something that the reader had inserted to mark a place. She turned it over, looking for a date, but found none.

The paper was in danger of disintegrating. It was divided into long, narrow columns, the print slightly smudged. Helen read first the sections that were visible on the outside of the fold. A report about trouble on the Gold Coast, where a General McCarthy had declared war on the Ashanti people. The newspaper described the general's attempts to 'rid this important trading coastline' of the warriors who had disrupted British interests with their 'tribal skirmishes'. Then army notices, naval appointments, shipping intelligence.

Interesting, she supposed, but she couldn't see the relevance to the section of the book she'd been reading. Just a handy book marker perhaps – but then why had it been preserved?

The familiar tug of mystery to be unravelled. There was something here. Helen cautiously parted the folded pages, her anxiety over Paxton forgotten.

News from the police courts and magistrates. A merchant was fined for a fire that had destroyed several warehouses full of gunpowder, and a dozen surrounding houses, down by the docks. Two boys from Saffron Hill were to be transported for being 'most incorrigible and persistent thieves.'

Then, halfway down the third column, in capital letters, the cross-heading: Murders. Helen smiled. The newspaper obviously knew its readers would go straight to such a headline, with all the gory detail in one place.

She read on, smile fading. A woman had been burned to death in a lime kiln in Birmingham by jealous fellow prosti-tutes. A man's body, his head bludgeoned, was discovered in a ditch in Taplow. Real lives, brutally ended.

And another, in London. 'On Sunday morning, an unfortu-nate young woman was found most barbarously murdered on the Surrey foreshore at the foot of the steps from London Bridge, by person or persons unknown.

'Her neck had been broken and her skull was dreadfully fractured by blows of some blunt object. The perpetrator of the foul outrage has yet to be apprehended. Friends of the young woman reported to the magistrate that a man by the name of Buller has been "on the run" since her death.'

Only in the final line of the report was the victim named: Miss Nancy Love, of Lant Street in The Borough.

Nancy. Murdered on the steps of London Bridge. And the

clipping, folded inside a book that detailed what could have been the backdrop to *Oliver Twist*.

Helen felt the hairs rise on the back of her neck. She turned again to the front of the book, looking for signs of ownership. Whose book had this been? There was no Ex Libris bookplate, no scribbled name or address. Only a few faint marks at the end of the book, dots and curved lines that meant nothing to Helen.

She photographed them; and the cutting, folded up where she'd found it, and then opened to show the report of the murder. The newspaper name was visible at the bottom of the page: *The British Press*. She could look up the clipping later, find out the date.

She sat back, read over the clipping again. Miss Nancy Love, of Lant Street. Who were you, Nancy? And what happened to the man who killed you? And – most intriguing of all – who had cut out the newspaper clipping of your death and placed it here in Robert Mudie's book about London?

Her phone buzzed. A message from Nick, thanking her for the information.

'Catch you later,' he added. 'Time we caught up.'

Time. Helen jumped to her feet. The reception started in ten minutes, and she wasn't even dressed.

# Chapter 9

Paxton sat in the van and listened to the six o'clock headlines. At least two dead, more missing. Stupid bastards. The police would be all over the BPP now, and they'd squandered public sympathy.

You had to keep the public onside. Paxton talked to people, read the local papers. They hated the boat people, the African men turning up in dinghies from Calais. Hated how stupid it made the immigration system look, hated to see people jumping the queue. There was plenty of support for the march in and around the town – you only had to see how many had turned up on the day. But now they'd all be running like hell, pretending they weren't there and knew nothing.

Much like him. Paxton had stayed on the seafront when the crowd charged towards the docks. For one thing, he couldn't risk getting arrested. He knew he'd been jammy to get parole when he did; he had no intention of finding himself back in the slammer for the sake of marching with a bunch of meat-heads.

Once he'd realised what was going down, he'd slipped back into town, picked up Cooper and gone for a nice long drive around the coast. They'd stopped for lunch at Ramsgate, fish and chips down by the harbour, the dog barking his head off at the bloody seagulls that kept nicking his chips. Paxton kept the receipt in case he needed an alibi. Then they'd walked up on to the promenade above the town and taken the cliff path as far as Broadstairs.

Back at the van, he'd decided he might as well keep going; west by the A299 that rode the spine of Thanet, heading into the Thames estuary via Herne Bay, Whitstable, Faversham. He'd reached Rochester just as the shops were closing. He'd been for a quick stroll with the dog. The van was parked around the back of the shops and he could see light from the downstairs back window, a shadow moving to and fro. There wasn't much time. He had to be back in Dover before eight.

A small figure opened the back door and slipped out. Baggy clothes, hood up, skateboard in hand. The bloke's daughter, according to Guren, although you could hardly tell it was a girl. Paxton watched while she stepped on the board and glided off down the backstreet, past the van. At the corner, another figure raised a hand and they headed towards the town centre.

'Stay,' he told Cooper, opening the van door. The dog whined and started barking. 'All right. But behave yourself.' He fixed the lead, rolled his shoulders. 'Come on, then.'

The girl had left the door unlocked. He pushed his way into the back room and almost tripped over a box. He flicked the light on. The place was a tip. Boxes everywhere; a kitchen table littered with the remains of a pizza, crusts still in the cardboard container; a couple of mugs with cold tea in them; various sections of *The Guardian* newspaper scattered around.

'Back already?' The voice came from the stairs which led up from the corner of the room. Paxton said nothing; waited.

The dog yapped.

'Sorry, who's that? We don't allow dogs…'

The man descended the stairs and stopped at the bottom, staring. He was small, slight like his daughter, with the unhealthy look of a man who spent all his time indoors. He'd pose no difficulties. Paxton noticed his white shirt was crumpled and the collar showed a line of grime. His lip curled.

'I'm sorry. Who are you?'

Paxton pointed to a chair piled with magazines.

'Sorry.' The man licked his dry lips, shifted the magazines to the floor, and offered him the chair.

'Sit,' said Paxton. The man sat; shoulders hunched.

Paxton walked closer until he could smell the sour sweat of fear that had broken out in the man's armpits.

'I'm here to collect,' he said.

The man nodded. 'Of course.' He pointed to a pile of boxes in the corner. 'They're over there. Shall I help you with them?'

Paxton counted.

'There should be six. Where's the other one?'

The man swivelled in the chair, licking his lips again. 'Let me… maybe it's under the table.' He got down on his knees, checked, counted the pile of five boxes again.

Cooper started to growl. Paxton slipped off his lead and let him go to the man.

'Sorry, could you… I'm not very good with dogs.' His shirt stuck to his back.

'Better find that box, then.'

The man stood, eyes desperate. 'I suppose it might have… Oh!' He stopped. 'I think it was in the shop. Someone… there was a lady who was looking through it this afternoon.'

Paxton walked closer to him again. 'So go and get it.'

The man hurried to the door into the shop and turned on the lights. It was even more chaotic than the back room, if that was possible. Boxes all over the floor, shelves lined with books and dust.

'She said it came from behind this shelf…' The man was muttering away to himself as he blundered around the shop. Paxton sighed. What a waste of time. Why did Guren even need him to do this one? Anyone could have picked up a few boxes of books or whatever it was.

Cooper nosed into one of the corners, then raised a leg against a shelf. The man came back, carrying a cardboard box in his arms.

'Here we are.' He saw the dog pissing and opened his mouth to protest. Paxton said nothing and the man changed his mind.

Paxton looked at the box. The brown tape had been torn off and the box opened. He moved his face close to the man.

'If there's anything missing, I'll find out,' he said. 'You hear?'

The man looked away, too quickly. 'Yes,' he said.

Paxton grabbed his chin. 'What have you got to tell me?'

The man's eyes, frightened. 'I – I'm sorry. We might have sold one. Before my daughter knew they weren't for sale.'

'Get it back.'

'But I don't know where it is.'

'That's your problem. You've got a week. I'll be back for it. Now. Money.' Paxton pushed a pile of debris from the desk on to the floor and sat down. 'Five hundred notes, as of this morning.'

'The thing is…' The man licked his lips again. 'Since the system changed, there's not that much going through the till, you see. It's difficult.'

'That's your problem. You signed up for this.'

The man opened the till. 'This is all I've got. Honestly. Business is terrible now.'

Paxton held out his hand and counted it up. Three hundred and twenty, plus odd change.

'I'll be back. Same time next week. I want the book you sold and five hundred quid, plus the two hundred you owe from today.'

There were tears in the man's eyes. 'Please. I can't do this anymore. I only borrowed five thousand. I must have paid it off by now, even with the interest.'

Paxton almost laughed. 'You stupid bastard,' he said softly. 'You don't think you can pick and choose if you take money from us? We're not Barclays bleeding Bank. You've been running our cash through your books for months.' He brought his face close again. 'We own you, Chapman. Get used to it.'

The man straightened, took a step back. Paxton saw him gather what shreds of pride he could muster. He recognised that look. The man was about to do something incredibly stupid.

'You don't. I could go to the police. Tell them about the boxes you had me store here. What was it, drugs? I could call them tonight.'

The knife was at the corner of Chapman's eye before he saw it coming.

'You really don't want to do that,' Paxton told him. He eased the tip of the knife under the eyelid, just enough to scratch. 'Do you?'

He flicked it away and a thin line of blood spattered the man's glasses. Chapman screamed, clutching his hand to his face.

'Next week,' said Paxton. 'And when you've finished making that noise, you can help me load the boxes in the van.'

# Chapter 10

Helen arrived at the Guildhall out of breath. Her velvet suit still fitted, thank goodness. She'd swiped on red lipstick, slicked back her hair, and changed into a pair of patent leather pumps. She drew the line at high heels. With luck, she'd live up to Emmanuel's American standards of grooming; she really needed a proper haircut.

The grand Victorian building was full of people clutching glasses of white wine and chattering. It was strange to be at a party again, crowded in with lots of others, all breathing over each other and laughing. She took a glass of wine from a circulating masked-up waitress and eased her way through the crush. She spotted two of her colleagues huddled in a doorway.

Her heart sank. One was Helen's former PhD supervisor, Jeremy Fraser, the archetypal image of a fusty academic. Armoured in tweed and disapproval, he crunched messily on a canapé while boring on about something or other.

Beside him, the department's Bloomsbury Group expert, a woman with a severe iron-grey bob and pink floral frock, waved at Helen as if she was hailing a taxi. She had coral lipstick on her teeth. Helen joined them and wondered whether to tell her about the lipstick. No wonder, she thought disloyally, Emmanuel had wanted some of the younger staff along.

'Helen. I'm surprised to see you here,' said Jeremy. 'I thought it was senior faculty only.' He looked quite put out.

'Emmanuel asked me,' she said. 'Have you seen him?'

'He's cosying up to the sponsors. Trust the Americans for that,' said the Bloomsbury Group woman waspishly.

Helen decided not to mention the lipstick. 'Thanks. I'll go and say hello.'

Helen slipped into the room beyond the doorway and quickly spotted Emmanuel at the far side, surrounded by people. There was a short woman with curly dark hair and round glasses in a gold-sequinned dress wearing matching sequinned Doc Marten boots. Helen liked the look of her. A jolly-looking Asian man with a chain displayed resplendently around his neck was obviously the town mayor. Emmanuel was laughing at something he'd just said. Beside them stood a tall, broad-shouldered man with his back to Helen.

Emmanuel caught Helen's eye, beamed, and beckoned her over.

'May I introduce Dr Helen Oddfellow, one of our rising stars at Russell? Helen recently published her first poetry collection, *Outcast Dead*, which I heartily recommend. Helen, this is Miss Hester Sussman, who curated this exhibition; Rochester's Mayor Mr Hardeep Singh; and Sir Augustus Cumberland, whose company Vermillion has kindly sponsored the exhibition.'

Helen shook hands with everyone. The tall man was quite handsome, in a very English sort of way, with bright blue eyes and a floppy blond fringe. He was younger than his rather pompous name suggested, maybe in his thirties or early forties, and was presumably the one that Emmanuel wanted to impress.

But Helen was rubbish at small talk, and now she had an ulterior motive for talking to a Dickens expert. 'I'd love to hear more about the exhibition, Hester. What was the inspiration for it?'

The curator was enthusiastic and keen to talk. Helen liked her immediately. The exhibition was sparked by Hester's research about the importance of the River Thames in Dickens' fiction, especially in his late great novel *Our Mutual Friend*, she explained.

'It's my favourite of his novels,' said Helen. 'I love the way the river appears and reappears through the narrative.'

Hester nodded. 'Me too. And then I realised how often the river and its bridges appear in the novels – from *Oliver Twist* to *Little Dorrit*, and of course the estuary and the marshes just north of here in *Great Expectations*. And I knew they were looking for a new exhibition for the Guildhall, so…'

They were soon deep in conversation. Helen thought again of the stairs down to the Thames at London Bridge, and Nancy.

'I found a book today,' she said. 'In a local bookshop, on the High Street. I wondered if Dickens might have read it. It has lots of references to themes from *Oliver Twist*, in particular.' She pulled out her phone and showed Hester the cover.

'Ooh, that sounds interesting. *London and Londoners*. I'd love a look at that.' Hester screwed up her face, as if trying to squeeze out a thought. 'Wait a minute. There was something… What's the author's name again?'

'Robert Mudie.'

'Yeah. Check *The Dickensian* journal, last year sometime. Mudie was a journalist and worked with Dickens, or something. I can't remember the details. But there was a paper published about how the book could be a source for Oliver. Give me your email and I'll see if I can find the reference.'

'That's so kind of you.' Helen handed over her card and was about to tell Hester about the clipping she'd found in the book when Emmanuel swooped.

'Sorry to interrupt, ladies. Hester, you and I have to give our speeches. Helen, maybe you could…'

She saw an urgent appeal in his eyes and looked around. Sir Augustus Cumberland was leaning against the mantelpiece, his eyes glazed. Jeremy Fraser was holding forth, spraying vol-au-vent crumbs as he talked.

'Of course.' She grinned. 'It'd be a pleasure.'

She promised to be in touch with the curator again and launched herself at the two men.

'What's your interest in Dickens, Sir Augustus?' asked Helen, cutting in as Jeremy paused for breath.

Cumberland turned his gaze on her, his bright blue eyes crinkling at the edges.

'Call me Gus, please.' His accent was upper-class, a lazy drawl that suggested he was used to people listening to him. 'I suppose I read Dickens at school,' he continued. '*Oliver Twist*, *Christmas Carol*, that sort of thing. But I pretty much stopped reading fiction once I got into business. Only just picked it up again recently. Interesting chap, isn't he?'

'I've always found Dickens rather jejune,' interjected Jeremy. 'I'm not sure anyone should read him as an adult.' He snickered at his own joke.

Helen ignored him. 'And what is your business, Gus? I'm

sorry, I don't think I've heard of Vermillion before.'

He laughed, showing even white teeth. 'Don't worry. That's the way we like it.' He drained his glass of whisky and waved at a waiter. 'Would you like one, Helen? Better than that nasty white wine.'

Once they'd both been supplied, he continued. 'Vermillion is a property company. We own a few shopping centres, commercial sites and so on. We buy up sites with development potential.

'But I'm more interested in the family estate, to be honest. We've been farmers for generations. Since I took over from my father, I've been trying to establish the farm on organic principles, with a bit of re-wilding, nature conservation and so on. Yurts for campers and rare-breed cattle for organic meat. You know the sort of thing.'

She smiled. With his immaculate dark suit and shiny shoes, he was hard to imagine striding across muddy fields in his wellies.

'I've heard about it. I'm pretty much a townie. This is as far as I get from London before I start to panic.'

'Nothing wrong with London,' he said. 'I've got a place there myself. Where do you live?'

'Helen's a devoted south Londoner, Sir Gus,' said Jeremy, who had a much-envied house in Hampstead. 'She enjoys slumming it down in Deptford.' He hadn't been offered whisky and was waving his empty wine glass about in an ostentatious fashion. Helen wished he'd go away.

She sighed. 'I love it. There's so much history along the south bank of the river. I do guided tours, mainly with literary themes. Shakespeare, Marlowe, and the Elizabethan theatre. I do a Dickens tour, too, in the City and around the Borough, where the Marshalsea prison stood.'

'Wow.' Gus looked genuinely interested, not just polite. 'That sounds great. You'll have to give me a private tour of the south bank. And I'd love to show you Vylands. It's really very beautiful.'

There was a general shushing around them. People were being encouraged towards a clutch of microphones on a stage at the end of the room.

'Come on,' said Jeremy, bossily. 'We need to show our support.'

He pushed through the crowd towards the front. Gus looked at Helen and grinned.

'Let's go upstairs and look around the exhibition before he comes back. I've heard enough speeches to last me a lifetime.'

Feeling a bit like a naughty schoolgirl, Helen followed as he headed up the stairs to the exhibition rooms. They passed the Bloomsbury woman, standing on her own in a corner. She gave Helen an enormous wink.

Well, Emmanuel had wanted Gus to have a nice time, after all. Somewhat to her surprise, Helen realised that she, too, was having rather a nice time. She drained her whisky. She was even, perhaps, having fun.

# Chapter 11

'Honestly, I'm fine.' Helen hiccupped again and giggled.

She really shouldn't drink whisky. She hoped she hadn't made too much of a fool of herself. She dug around in her suit pockets until she discovered the key and flourished it with relief.

'See?'

'Let me at least see you to your room,' said Gus. 'Unless you'd like a quick nightcap in the hotel bar?'

Helen shook her head. 'I think I've probably had enough.' More than enough. She remembered Jeremy's outraged stare as Gus had steered her through the Guildhall to the exit, the party still in full swing. She really hoped Emmanuel hadn't seen her, although she supposed Jeremy would spread the word soon enough. Oh, let him. She'd had two years of being careful, behaving herself, sitting alone in an empty flat and staring out of the window at the deserted street.

She swayed and wished the hotel carpet was less swirly and disorientating. Gus put a steadying arm around her shoulders. He smelled nice, a citrussy sort of smell like a gin and tonic.

'Come on, Dr Oddfellow.' He called the lift and she leaned

against the mirrored wall. He was about as tall as she was. Thank God she hadn't worn heels.

She watched their reflection in the mirror opposite, as if observing someone else. He moved towards her, put his hands on her shoulders, bent his fair head. She closed her eyes, tasted whisky, felt a prickle of stubble around his mouth as he kissed her. A slow, deliberate kiss. God. It had been a long, long time.

The lift pinged and the door opened. He took the key from her hand, and they walked along the corridor. She tripped and he steadied her again.

'Careful, now.' He looked amused. Presumably he was used to drinking half a bottle of whisky without falling over.

Helen thought, fleetingly, of Greg. Remembered the photograph of him with Saskia. Having fun. That's what she was doing.

'This way,' she said.

As he inserted the key, she heard a scuffle and the sound of something being dropped on the floor.

'What the hell?' Gus flung open the door. It wasn't locked.

The room was almost dark, lit only by streetlamps from outside. Helen was pretty sure she'd closed the curtains before she left, not to mention locking the door.

'Wait.' Was this even her room? She had a sudden panic. Maybe she'd got the wrong number. Maybe the keys opened all the rooms. But no, that would be silly.

Gus walked in. 'Where's the damn light switch?'

As he fumbled along the wall, a shadow detached itself from a corner and launched itself towards the door. Helen gasped as the figure collided with her.

'Sorry,' muttered a man's voice, his hands pushing her out

of the way.

The light went on and Gus spun around as the figure disappeared into the corridor.

'Stay here!' he shouted. He ran after the man.

'No,' called Helen. 'Gus, come back.' Whatever had happened, it wasn't worth anyone getting hurt.

She gazed around the room. It was the right one. It had been turned over, drawers and wardrobe doors all standing open and empty, bedside table knocked askew. With so little luggage, Helen hadn't bothered to unpack.

Gus reappeared. 'I'm sorry, I shouldn't leave you. Are you hurt?' he asked. He surveyed the room. 'Damn. Looks like we interrupted a burglary. Have you lost anything?'

Helen checked her pockets. She had her wallet and phone on her. Her backpack was on the floor by the window, up-ended. Her change of underwear and nightdress were scattered on the floor next to the bag, and she shoved them back in, embarrassed. What else?

The book. Embarrassment forgotten, she emptied the bag out again. Nothing. Had she put it back in after reading it? She checked the bedside table, looked down the side of the bed and under the desk.

She sat on the bed and sighed. 'I think he took a book. Something I bought today.'

'A book?' Gus sat next to her. 'Are you sure? Why would anyone do that?'

Helen frowned. 'I don't know.' She wished her head wasn't so fuzzy. 'It was… it might have been important. I found it in a local bookshop. It was quite old and I thought it could have been something that Dickens had read. There was all this stuff about gangs of thieves and parish boys…' She tailed

67

off.

'Go on.' He gripped her wrist, his face serious. 'Tell me more.'

Helen stared at the floor. His face was too close. She could smell whisky fumes on his breath. Feeling a little nauseous, she shuddered. She was cold and suddenly felt quite sober.

She pulled her hand away and got to her feet.

'I think I should call the police,' she said. 'Let's go down to reception. And then you'd better be getting on your way.'

'I think I should stay with you. What if whoever it was comes back?'

Helen thought of the moment the man had collided with her. The shock, the whispered apology.

'I don't think he will. I think he was as scared as I was,' she said.

'Damn it, Helen. Don't let it spoil things.' Gus moved closer, as if to kiss her again. She twisted her face away.

'Please.' She tried to smile. 'I just want to get this sorted out, then go to sleep. I'm really tired.'

Just for a second, she thought she saw annoyance flash across his face, the expression of someone used to getting what he wanted. Then it was gone, replaced by smooth concern.

'Of course. I quite understand.'

The hotel receptionist was polite, but at first sceptical. Was Miss Oddfellow quite sure? And had anything of value gone missing? Not until Gus weighed in with his title and air of authority did she agree to call the police. The manager of the hotel was summoned, looking distressed.

'I'm so sorry,' she said. 'There was a man, earlier. He said he was a colleague of yours from the university and needed to borrow a book. I told him the room number, but I don't know how he got in if it was locked.'

Helen persuaded Gus to leave. 'You didn't see anything more than I did. I'll give the police your number, in case they need it,' she said.

She went back to her room, double-locked the door and put a chair under the handle. She wrapped her coat around herself and sat on the bed, shivering. A colleague, a man. Emmanuel and Jeremy were both staying at the hotel, but she'd told neither of them about the book, and what possible reason would they have to break in? Jeremy certainly disliked her – but no, he'd been at the Guildhall when she was leaving.

Checking her phone, she saw the message from Nick, thanking her for letting him know Gary Paxton's whereabouts. It hadn't been Paxton; that was for sure. The man who'd been in her room had been much shorter and slighter. But she couldn't shake the fear that this was something to do with him. Years ago, on the night that Richard was killed, Paxton had arranged for a team to break into her flat, looking for Richard's notebook. And now someone had stolen another book, with clues to another mystery.

She opened the photos on her phone and looked at the pictures she'd taken. The strange squiggles inked on the fly leaf. The newspaper cutting, with its grim tally of murders. What secrets did the book hold, and why did someone care enough to break into her room to steal it?

# Chapter 12

The weather was grim again after the sunny weekend. Helen's umbrella blew inside out and she gave up on it, sprinted across Gordon Square with the rain lashing down through the London plane trees, their patchwork trunks darkening. Eight o'clock on Monday morning and it was barely light.

Breathless, she pushed open the blue-painted door of the townhouse that held the English department of Russell University and climbed the stairs to her office. She hoped she'd be the first person – maybe the only person – in. The last thing she wanted was to be quizzed about her behaviour at the Dickens exhibition party. She had a tutorial to give later that morning, but a couple of free hours to do some research first.

She shrugged off her raincoat, raked her wet hair back from her face and logged on to the university's account with the British Newspaper Archive. Firstly, she looked up the title of the newspaper the clipping had come from: *The British Press*. To her surprise, she found it was published only for a couple of decades: from 1803 to 1826. Strange… how then could the cutting have been kept inside the Mudie book, which wasn't published until 1836?

Helen checked the photograph of the cutting. The right newspaper; and the right address, too: The Strand, just along from Fleet Street. She scanned the archive's article about the newspaper, its foundation, and its political interests.

One line leapt out at her. According to the memoirs of one of the regular journalists, the newspaper had for a time employed a very young Charles Dickens as a 'penny-a-line' stringer. This would have been the young man's first employment as a writer, she read.

Another link in the chain. She looked back at the photograph. Was Dickens working at the paper when Nancy Love had died? Might he even have written this article about the brutal murder? If so, what a find! Dickens' own apprentice journalism providing a plot twist for his first novel.

She frowned. She was letting her imagination run away with her.

She entered search terms from the clipping into the archive's holdings of *The British Press*: Nancy Love, London Bridge, murder. Three facsimile newspaper pages were returned, the search terms highlighted in yellow.

The first was the page which contained the cutting she'd found. The date: Wednesday April 14, 1824. Halfway down page three, below the promise of Murders: "An unfortunate young woman was found most barbarously murdered on the Surrey foreshore at the foot of the steps from London Bridge…"

Helen sat back and made a note. Nancy had died in 1824. More than ten years before Mudie's *London and Londoners* was published. Someone, then, had kept the newspaper cutting for more than a decade after her death. And when the book was published, that someone had taken the precious cutting and placed it between the pages. The pages which detailed the London flash house, which could conceivably have been an inspiration for *Oliver Twist*.

It was more than suggestive. Was the book Helen had found Charles Dickens' own copy of *London and Londoners*?

She checked the dates. Dickens was born in 1812 – so he'd have been just twelve years old in 1824. Could the twelve-year-old Dickens have cut out the newspaper report and kept it safe all that time? It seemed a bit far-fetched.

And the further link between the newspaper and Dickens… but no, surely the boy could not have been working at the newspaper at the age of twelve? She needed to check a decent biography, but wouldn't he have been at school?

Helen pushed back her chair and swung on it, gazing into space, her mind a whirl. If only she still had the originals to pore over. Where were the book and the precious cutting now?

She cursed herself again for drinking too much at the exhibition opening. She'd not been able to give much of a description to the police, other than that the man had been smaller than her, which didn't rule out that many people. And the hotel manager hadn't been much more help, even though she'd talked to the man who claimed to be Helen's colleague. Small, she'd said. Ordinary looking, as far as she could tell. He'd worn a medical face mask, which didn't help.

His voice – that whispered 'sorry' – nagged away at Helen. Why would a burglar apologise for knocking into the person he was robbing?

There was a rap on the door. Helen groaned silently, recognising the peremptory knock.

'Helen. Working away, I see? Not too many ill-effects from Saturday night?' asked Jeremy Fraser. He came in without being invited and sat on the edge of her desk. She pushed down her annoyance and decided not to rise to his jibes.

'I'm fine, Jeremy. Just following up on an idea,' she said, keeping her voice neutral. 'I'll be sure to let you know if it comes to anything.'

'I do hope so. I know how your enthusiasm can run away with you. I'm always happy to offer guidance. It's about time we saw you publish something new in the academic press. If you can find time away from your – ah – verses.'

So that was the source of his annoyance. He was jealous of her poetry book. Jeremy's last academic publication of any note had been the papers they co-authored about Helen's discovery of a lost play by Christopher Marlowe, several years ago. And she'd written most of the papers herself. He'd been terribly envious of her success, and doubtless the publication of her poems had wound him up even more.

He leaned over her desk to see what she was working on. She resisted the impulse to slam her laptop closed.

'Newspaper reports? Surely that's not relevant to renaissance theatre? You seem to be out of your comfort zone.'

Helen sighed. 'I'm looking up a reference to something in *Oliver Twist*. I've been doing a bit of work on Dickens for my London walks.' And I don't need to stay in my comfort zone, unlike you, she didn't add.

He shook his head, walked to the tiny window that gave a glimpse of the trees in the square. The rain was still lashing down.

'I think you're spreading yourself a bit thinly, Helen. Your wide-ranging interests are, of course, admirable, but if you want my advice, you will focus on your specialism. That is, after all, what you were employed here to pursue.'

'I'll bear that in mind.'

He turned, his thin lips pressed together in something she knew was supposed to be a smile. 'And, if I may offer another word of advice? Do try to behave professionally at evening receptions where important people are present, even if there is free alcohol. The department cares about its reputation, even if you seem rather careless of your own.'

That was going too far. Helen flushed with anger. She leaned across the desk.

'I do not need your permission to have a drink at a party,' she said, furious. 'And Emmanuel asked me to talk to Gus, to stop you from boring him to death. Now, if you will please leave me alone, I have work to do.'

His eyebrows shot to his receding hairline and he shook his head again, slowly. 'There's no helping some people,' he said. 'Well, I'll be off. Before I bore anyone else to death.'

He shut the door behind him with exaggerated care. Helen sat back, heart hammering, and sighed. She shouldn't have said that. No doubt he would be straight on to Emmanuel to complain.

Helen hadn't seen or heard from the boss since Saturday night. Despite her outburst to Jeremy, she felt terrible about getting drunk at a work event, and really hoped she hadn't made too much of a fool of herself.

She'd had a text from Gus on Sunday asking how she was and suggesting they got together in London: 'I want to know more about Dickens,' he'd said. 'And you'. She wasn't sure how to respond. She'd liked him, but it had been so long since she dated anyone. She felt nervous at the thought of seeing him again.

Time was running out and she needed to prepare for the tutorial. Helen took one final look at the newspaper archive and downloaded copies of the pages from *The British Press*. At least she had the date, April 1824. She'd need to find out how that fitted with Dickens as a twelve-year-old boy reporter. Maybe she should get back in touch with Hester from the museum. If she hadn't annoyed Hester as well by disappearing with the exhibition's sponsor.

Her eyes lingered on the final lines of the report. Nancy Love, of Lant Street in the Borough. Who had she been? Where was she buried? Helen thought of the gates of the Cross Bones burial ground, decorated with tattered ribbons. It too was in the Borough, a few minutes' walk from Lant Street, across the Marshalsea Road. Did Nancy rest there, among the other outcast dead?

Whoever Nancy Love had been, Helen would find out.

# Chapter 13

Nick pulled off the motorway and rode up to the motorbike parking near the service station entrance. He removed his helmet and walked inside, past the burger bar and newsagent and on to the bridge that crossed the motorway. Traffic droned away beneath him, the constant flow of lorries and cars mesmerising if you looked down for too long.

Halfway across, he stopped at a chain cafe where a bored-looking kid with acne was wiping down the counter. Nick ordered a flat white and glanced around the seating area. It was quiet at mid-morning, after the rush hour had faded. Ollie was there before him, in a booth at the back. He walked over, slipped on to the shiny vinyl bench.

'All right?'

Ollie looked up from his phone, his eyes flicking quickly beyond Nick and around the deserted cafe.

'All right,' he confirmed. His thin face creased into a grin. 'Man, it's good to see you.' He reached over and shook Nick's hand.

'How's it going? Are you OK? Any fall-out from Saturday?'

Ollie shrugged. 'Not that I know about. Obviously,

76

everyone's really antsy since they banned the BPP. There have been quite a few arrests, people chased down from the social media coverage. And Angus's news footage too, of course. Everyone saw that. There's nothing a fascist likes better than seeing himself on the telly.'

'I'll bet. But no suspicions about you?'

Ollie blew out his cheeks. 'A couple of the lads noticed me talking to Angus inside. I told them I'd asked what he was doing and he'd said to me that he was filming it for the patriots.'

'OK. Did they believe you?' That was what Angus had told others inside the centre, Nick remembered.

'I think so. No-one saw me talking to you, I don't think. Or the police. Everyone's keeping their heads down. The BPP leadership – you know those guys who got out of the cars? They were arrested, but they've been bailed. They're apparently looking forward to making a big splash about it at the court case. Got the lawyers all lined up.'

Nick digested this. 'Plenty of dosh, then.'

'They're loaded.'

They grinned at each other. 'Follow the money,' they said in unison.

Nick got out his phone and made notes. 'You know any of their names? The blokes in the silly hats, I mean. I've got a list of names of those who've been charged from the police, but I don't know who's who.'

Ollie called something up on his phone, then showed Nick a profile in a chat room. 'That's the one who always gives the speeches. Weird bloke; always going on about the second world war; talking about his time in the army, like he was an officer or something. But according to one of the lads, he's never been a regular; got chucked out of the Territorial Army for being too keen on guns. Which you wouldn't think was a problem for them, really.'

Nick looked at the weaselly face, pointed chin and sharp nose beneath a military-style beret, like the ones the men from the limousines had worn at the demo.

'Jonnie Johnson. I'll look him up.'

'Not his real name. There's a rumour he's called Sebastian.' Ollie chuckled, his pale blue eyes narrowing. 'But that's what we need you to find out about, Nick. The guys I hang out with – they haven't got a clue about the money. Useful idiots, a bit of muscle when required. They're bottom feeders. But someone is funding this movement like it's never been funded before.'

Nick nodded. 'Yeah, I noticed. Any idea where it's coming from? There were a few Russian guys on the march...'

'There were loads. That confuses the hell out of the anti-immigrant crowd. But the far-right semi-fascist scene is pretty big in that part of the world. I think you could be right. Russian money – maybe even State money – spreading confusion and division. Either that or it's organised crime.'

That reminded Nick. 'Talking of criminals, I spotted my old mate Gary Paxton, right at the start before it all kicked off. Fresh out of Belmarsh, making a new life for himself in Dover. You heard anyone talking about him?' He found a mugshot of the man on his phone and pushed it across the table.

Ollie scrutinised the picture. 'I've heard the name. People still talk about him, about what he did to you and that woman. He's a bit of a hero to some of the more moronic south London element. Some of them used to hang around with him, back in the day. I've never seen him, though. I don't remember anyone saying that he was out of prison. I can ask around a bit, if you like? Maybe tell people I saw him on the march?'

Nick drained his coffee and checked his watch. He didn't want to push their luck by keeping this meeting going too long. It was a good place for a meeting: halfway between London and Dover, and they could arrive from different directions. But you never knew who else might be passing through.

'That'd be handy. Text me if you hear anything. And send me the names of the rest of those guys from the cars, if you have them.'

Ollie nodded. 'How much longer, do you think?' His voice was business-like, but Nick sensed the anxiety beneath it. Working undercover was exciting, but a strain. You got lonely; you missed being able to kick back and just be yourself. Having to watch yourself the whole time, having to think before you spoke. It was tiring.

'Give it a couple more weeks, if you can? If it gets too much, text me and we'll work out your exit strategy. I feel like we're just getting somewhere interesting.'

Ollie nodded and pulled on a hooded anorak. 'No problem.' He walked out of the coffee shop, head down and eyes on his phone.

Nick gave him ten minutes while he looked up 'Jonnie Johnson'. The guy was all over the far-right internet; mad videos, mainly, where he called himself 'The Captain' and spouted hate-filled nonsense about Jews and Blacks and a conspiracy to undermine European civilisation.

As Ollie had predicted, there was no-one with that name on the list of people charged after Saturday. But there was a Sebastian Johansson, with an address in Folkestone. That was a start. Maybe a trip out that direction would be in order –

once Nick had tracked down Gary Paxton in Dover.

# Chapter 14

Helen strode across Russell Square, where handfuls of snowdrops were pushing their way up through the bare earth. It was a shivery, damp morning. Dodging red London buses, she crossed in front of the big hotel and turned into Guilford Street, its terraced brick houses darkened by centuries of soot.

The London Metropolitan Archives were an easy half-hour walk from the Russell University, and even with the chilly weather Helen was glad to get out into the fresh air. The last two days had been uncomfortable, to say the least. Jessica had made sure Helen saw the newspaper photographs – which she hadn't remembered being taken – of her and Gus laughing together at the party, his arm around her shoulders. Her colleagues, apart from Jeremy, had treated her with a mixture of embarrassment and concern. She still hadn't seen Emmanuel, who had been closeted in his office with the faculty accountant, working on the budget for the year ahead. Everyone was jumpy, knowing that cuts were coming.

Gus had called, proposing lunch at his London flat at the weekend. She'd panicked, pleaded work pressure and wondered how long she'd be able to put him off politely. Or even whether she wanted to. It made a nice change to be pursued.

In the few minutes she'd been able to take away from her teaching work, Helen had established that her best chance of finding out more about Nancy Love would be parish records. Before the mid-nineteenth century census, the baptism, marriage, and burial registers for the parish churches had been the most comprehensive records of people's lives.

Helen had done a preliminary search online, which had returned records for the Love family around the late eighteenth and early nineteenth century from both St George the Martyr church, close to Lant Street, and St Saviour's, now Southwark Cathedral, at the other end of Borough High Street. She couldn't tell from the online results whether it was the same family, or perhaps relatives.

She'd done a few calculations. Nancy had died in April 1824 and been described in the newspaper as a young woman. That could have been anything from fifteen to thirty years old, Helen supposed. She could have been born any time from around 1794 to 1809. A fifteen year period to search, with two parishes, looking at separate baptism, marriage, and burial records. She'd better get a move on.

Helen quickened her pace, past Great Ormond Street Hospital, past the turning with Doughty Street, where the Dickens Museum occupied the home that he and his wife lived in soon after their marriage. Maybe a visit there would be useful, too. It was, after all, where he had written *Oliver Twist*. Helen remembered that Hester, the curator of the Rochester exhibition, said she worked there part-time. Perhaps Helen could meet her for a coffee.

The Metropolitan Archives were held in an ordinary-looking building opposite a park in Clerkenwell; not easy to find in the maze of backstreets unless you knew where you were going. Helen produced her card, stowed her belongings, and went up to the bright open-plan archive study area. She'd already ordered the parish registers for the years 1794 to 1824.

She opened the St Saviours baptism register and carefully turned the pages, scanning for the Love family name. Familiar as she was with the records, she always got a thrill from seeing the handwriting of long-dead clerks and clergymen, the last traces of the countless Londoners who had made the city their home.

She struck lucky in 1797 with a baptism in June. But not a baby, and not what she was expecting.

'George Frederick Love, a Black of St Christopher's Island in the West Indies,' she read, 'Aged twenty-five Years.'

What was a West Indian doing in Southwark in 1797? The slave trade in Britain was not abolished until 1807, and slavery itself persisted until 1833. If George Love had been born in the West Indies, he had probably been born a slave. He might even have been brought to London while enslaved. What happened then – had he been given his freedom, or simply run away, disappeared into the teeming streets of the capital? Perhaps his baptism had been a way of asserting his status as a Christian and a free man.

She turned the pages. In April 1800, she found the record of a baptism of a girl, Frances Love, daughter to George and Patience Love of the Mermaid Tavern. So, George had married and had a child. But was this the right family? No sign of a Nancy, yet.

She scanned more pages, and more. Eventually, she found

it. Baptised May 1802, Nancy Love, daughter to George and Patience Love. Helen took a quick photograph of the page. There you are, Nancy. The unknown murder victim had a family, a home. A baby girl, sister to Frances. Helen did a quick calculation. Nancy had been twenty-one years old when she died at London Bridge.

Two more Love children followed: Sally in 1804 and Tom in 1805. Almost one a year, thought Helen; poor Patience.

Helen came to the end of the book, which finished in 1809. She switched to marriages.

The first mention of the Love family baptisms had been George in 1797, followed by Frances in 1800. Helen quickly found the missing event: in September 1799, George Love of the Mermaid Tavern, Borough High Street, had married Patience Wheeler, also of the Mermaid Tavern. George Love was described as a labourer. Patience's father was Thomas Wheeler, landlord; her mother Frances Wheeler. George had lived and worked at the Mermaid, then – and married the boss's daughter? What had been the attitude of Patience's family to this black man, their employee, marrying their daughter?

Helen did a quick count on her fingers. Patience had been pregnant with their first child, Frances, when they were married. Perhaps the marriage had been a matter of urgency.

Helen kept on turning the pages, noting the variations in the occupations of the fathers – labourer, tavern-keeper, hatter, mariner, ostler – reflecting the lively mixture of society in this part of south London. But there were no more Love marriages in St Saviour's records.

Helen swapped to burials, noting with sadness the frequent deaths of young children during the early years of the nineteenth century. In 1806, she spotted a relevant record – Thomas Wheeler, Patience's father, still proprietor of the Mermaid at age fifty-eight. The family had stayed together in the tavern; Patience and her growing family living with her parents, Thomas and Frances, at least until Thomas's death.

Towards the end of the book, she stopped, gave a little cry. Two burials on the same page. George Love, aged forty-six. And his son Tom Love, aged eleven. Both dead in 1816, a crowded year for local burials by the look of it. What had happened? wondered Helen. Cholera? Typhus? The Love family must have been hard-hit.

Helen came to the end of the book and returned the St Saviour's registers.

'Next volumes?' asked the assistant. Helen hesitated. She'd already found Nancy Love in Borough High Street. Maybe it would be better to switch to St George's closer to Lant Street to be sure the records were of the same family.

'No, thanks. Can I see the records for St George the Martyr from about 1815?'

Helen skimmed through the marriage register first. Nothing, for page after page. Finally, just as she was about to give up, she found one.

'June 1818. William Carter, of Sanctuary Street, married Frances Love, daughter of George (deceased) and Patience, relict of the same, of Lant Street.' Nancy's elder sister, married at age eighteen. Perhaps the family had moved to Lant Street because of George's death.

Helen switched to burials, knowing that there was one more to find. A brief notice, Wednesday April 20, 1824. Burial of Nancy Love, spinster, of Lant Street, daughter of Patience Love. Almost a week after the newspaper report of her death.

There was no information about the manner of Nancy's death. But it was a sound start. Helen had the woman's date of birth, the names of her parents and siblings, the two addresses she'd lived in during her brief life. There was more – much more – she wanted to know.

It was almost half past twelve. Helen ought to go back to the department. She returned the registers to the desk.

'Thanks. I'll be back as soon as I can manage it.'

Back outside, she checked her phone. There was an email from Hester, the curator from the exhibition, forwarding the article she'd promised to send about Robert Mudie's book. And one from Emmanuel. Could Helen call by his office whenever was convenient?

Damn. Helen wasn't sure she wanted to know what that was about. She hesitated, then called Hester's number.

'Hello?' The woman sounded harassed.

'Hi, sorry to bother you. It's Helen Oddfellow. Thanks so much for sending me that article. I'm near Doughty Street now and I wondered if by any chance you were at the Dickens Museum? I thought I could get you a coffee and tell you more about the book.'

'Hang on.' There was a muffled sound of movement. 'Sure, that'd be great. I'm trying to sort out the curtains on Dickens' bed. We've just had them cleaned. The glamour of museum life.' She laughed. 'I'd love an excuse to take a break.'

'Fantastic. I'll see you in fifteen minutes.'

# Chapter 15

They sat outside in the weak sun that had broken through the clouds and was warming the small courtyard garden. A fountain trickled quietly from a mossy sculpture of a lion's head.

'Your book was stolen that same night? God, that's a bit weird,' said Hester, her face creased with concern. She wore a green crushed-velvet smock with leggings and red DM boots, big gold hoops sparkling from her ears. Helen couldn't help thinking that she looked a bit like a Christmas tree.

'I know. I reported it to the police, but I don't suppose anything will come of it. It was pretty creepy, knowing someone had been in my hotel room.'

'I'd have been terrified,' said Hester. 'Especially on my own.'

Helen blushed. 'Luckily I had someone with me,' she said, trying to keep her voice neutral. 'So, it wasn't too bad.'

Hester looked confused for a moment, then light dawned. 'Oh…' She bit her lip. 'Well, that's OK then.' She looked away.

Helen sighed. 'Look, Gus just saw me to my room. And saw off the burglar, then helped me call the police.'

Hester shrugged and took a sip of her coffee. 'None of my business, Helen. Don't worry.' Her voice had cooled noticeably.

This wasn't how Helen had wanted their discussion to go. She cursed herself again for drinking too much and flirting with Gus. I might as well have let him stay over, she thought. Everyone thinks we slept together, anyway. And she'd got on so well with Hester at the opening.

'How's the exhibition going? Plenty of visitors, I hope.'

Hester thawed a bit. 'Yeah, not bad. We had some nice write-ups in the local paper, and in a couple of the nationals, too. Emmanuel made sure they came along. He's brilliant, isn't he? Seems to know everyone. I bet he's a great boss.'

Helen nodded, remembering his email summons. 'He's very effective. I don't think the department quite knows what's hit it. But money is tight – well, I'm sure you know what that's like. We're all a bit nervous right now.'

Hester rolled her eyes. 'Tell me about it. Most museums are in all sorts of trouble. We've been closed, or only able to let in half a dozen people at a time. Now we can open properly, but the overseas tourists haven't come back. They're our life-blood. We're almost completely reliant on ticket sales and merchandise.'

Which means sponsorship from someone like Gus Cumber-land is vital, thought Helen. Having sponsors distracted by floozies from academia, when they're supposed to be admiring the exhibition they've funded, must be annoying. She wished she knew how to make amends. She decided to share her discoveries about Nancy Love.

'I wanted to tell you about something else that I found in the Robert Mudie book. But I didn't get time at the opening.' She pulled out her phone and found the photograph she'd taken of the cutting. 'I've been trying to find out more about this woman in the Met Archives this morning.'

Hester took the phone and enlarged the photo. Helen watched her read, her eyes widening.

'Wow. This cutting was in the copy of the book you bought?'

'Yeah. It's from *The British Press*, April 1824. Ten years plus before the book was published. And I know it's a bit fanciful – but a woman called Nancy, bludgeoned to death on the steps at London Bridge? And the cutting kept in a book that could have been a source for *Oliver Twist*? I thought it was worth investigating, at the very least. What do you think?'

'It's amazing.' Hester frowned. 'Lant Street. Wasn't that… Hang on. Let me check the dates.' She jumped up and grabbed a leaflet from the cafe. It gave a timeline of Dickens' life. 'Yes!' She thrust the leaflet at Helen, her face shining with excitement. 'Look at that! Lant Street, 1824. Dickens was living there, while his father was in the Marshalsea Prison for debt.'

'Oh my God.' Helen took the leaflet. 'Of course. He was working at Warren's Blacking when he was twelve. How did I forget that?'

The novelist had kept secret his stint as a child labourer in a boot-polish factory, confiding only in one close friend, John Forster. There had been a sensation when Forster included the episode in a biography written after Dickens' death.

Helen realised the implications. 'Wait… Charles Dickens was living in the same street as Nancy Love at the time she was murdered? He'd have known about the murder…'

'He might even have known Nancy,' said Hester. The two women grinned at each other. 'Bloody hell. What a find!'

Helen sighed. 'Except all I've got are the photographs. And the burglar has got the book and the cutting.'

'Yeah.' Hester thought for a moment. 'We can find the original of the article in the British Newspaper Archive, of course. And there are other copies of Mudie's book around – the British Library should have one. But it makes you wonder why someone nicked your copy, doesn't it?'

It did. An ordinary burglar would have taken money, her laptop… not a second-hand book. She thought again of the figure who'd brushed against her in the corridor. His apology. He wasn't a hardened burglar, that was for sure. She remembered the nervous bookseller in Rochester, his initial reluctance to sell. What had he said? There was a collector interested in the box of books she found it in. And then his bolshie daughter had insisted he sell it because they needed the money.

'I think I should talk to the man who sold Mudie's book to me,' she said. 'Or maybe his daughter.'

'What have you found out about the murdered woman?' asked Hester. 'You said you'd been up at the Met.'

Helen explained how she'd traced Nancy Love's family. 'Her father was black, from the West Indies. George Love worked in the Mermaid Tavern on Borough High Street and married the boss's daughter. They lived there until at least 1816, when George died. The family moved to Lant Street sometime before 1818, when Nancy's sister was married from St George's. Then nothing until Nancy's burial in 1824.'

Hester collected a couple of flapjacks from the cafe. 'We should celebrate. It sounds like you might have found Dickens' Nancy.' She chewed meditatively. 'You know, there's something odd about the fictional Nancy. Don't you think? Dickens told Forster that she was based on a real person. But she doesn't seem real to me at all. She's so melodramatic –

all that tearing her hair and flinging herself to the ground; impassioned speeches in highfalutin language. If she was based on a real woman who grew up in a pub, you'd think she would be a bit more down to earth.'

Helen took a swig of coffee. 'Confession time,' she said. 'I haven't actually read *Oliver Twist*. I thought I had, then I realised I've seen the film and a TV adaptation, and of course the musical, and I suppose I thought I must have read it because I know the story. But then I used a copy for reference when I was designing my Dickens walk and I realised I hadn't read the original. I only started it this week.'

Hester laughed. 'Shows how strongly he gets into the culture, doesn't it? I bet loads of people who talk about Scrooge or Miss Havisham haven't read *A Christmas Carol* or *Great Expectations*. Like your Sir Augustus, for example.'

'Oh?' Helen raised her eyebrows.

'I probably shouldn't say. But when we were putting the exhibition together, Gus was around a lot, pumping me for information. He seemed really interested in Dickens' history in Rochester and Chatham. So naturally I talked a bit about the books set locally, and I realised he hadn't read them. Maybe he has now.'

Helen frowned. 'That's odd. If he's so keen on Dickens, you'd think he'd have read the novels. I suppose there are a lot of them.'

Her phone buzzed. Jessica's sing-song voice: 'Hello, Helen? Professor Brown wondered if you'd seen his message about calling into his office today. Or should I tell him you're too busy?'

'I'm on my way,' said Helen.

# Chapter 16

Professor Brown was looking serious as Helen came through the door.

'Why didn't you tell me someone had broken into your hotel room? Helen, I don't allow my staff to be menaced or put in danger. You should have called me right away. I'd have come over and talked to the police with you.'

Helen sat down. 'Sorry. I didn't want to bother anyone. And anyway...' She paused, tried to find the right words.

'I know. Sir Augustus was there. We spoke on the phone this morning. He told me about the burglary.'

Helen blushed hard while trying to look nonchalant. She felt like she'd been hauled up before the headmaster for snogging behind the bike sheds. Which had never happened at school, because the headmaster had been her father and she'd been too tall and unpopular for any of the boys to snog.

Emmanuel leaned back in his chair.

'So, are you going to tell me about it? Because I get the impression that my potential departmental donor is forming something of a special interest in my star researcher. And I'd rather know from you what the situation is, before I put my big feet in it.' He cracked a smile.

Helen took a deep breath. 'OK. Sorry, I should have told you – although there's not much to tell. He walked me back to the hotel after the exhibition opening. He saw me to my room and we discovered the burglary in process. The burglar ran off. Then we went down to reception and reported it, and Gus went home. I haven't seen him since.'

Emmanuel watched Helen's face for a moment longer, then nodded. 'Fine. Thank you, and I apologise for prying into your personal life. It's your business, of course.'

'Except it's your business too, if it affects a potential sponsor,' said Helen.

The man spread his hands across the desk. 'And that's why I wanted to hear your thoughts. Sir Augustus wants to talk further about some opportunities with the university – possibly funding a research fellowship about Dickens. We're having lunch next week with the vice-chancellor. He asked if you would be there and said he had you in mind for the fellowship.

'I told him – which is nothing but the truth – that you would not normally be involved in such a meeting. And that if we did develop a fellowship, it would be for the university to make the appointment, not the sponsor. He seemed disappointed. I wanted to know if you would feel uncomfortable attending a lunch in those circumstances.'

Helen squirmed. She couldn't remember a more awkward conversation. 'I suppose… I mean, I have no objections to having lunch with you all. But it's not the sort of thing I would expect to be much use at.'

The thought of sitting over lunch as some sort of eye candy, while the important men got on with business, was excruciating. Helen felt hot with embarrassment just thinking about it. She'd never even met the vice-chancellor, and he'd know she was there just because Gus liked her. Anyway, did she even want a Dickens fellowship? She liked the freedom to pursue her own academic interests. She wondered what she could suggest instead.

'I have a better idea,' she said. 'I said I'd give Gus a tour around Bankside, show him the Dickens connections in the area. I'd be far more comfortable with that than just sitting around at lunch. Why don't I call him?'

Emmanuel's brow cleared. 'Great idea. That sounds much more appropriate. If you're sure you're OK with that?'

That would be better than lunch, or dinner for two. They'd be outside and Helen would be on firm ground with her knowledge of the local area. She could even investigate Lant Street while she was at it. And she had to admit, she wanted to see Gus again.

'That would be fine,' she said. 'It's what I do. I could do it this week. Friday.'

Emmanuel seemed very relieved not to be organising an awkward lunch party. 'Jessica tells me you were off doing some research this morning. Anything interesting to report?'

Helen smiled. 'Funny you should ask that. I think I might have tracked down the inspiration for Nancy in *Oliver Twist*. But best not to tell anyone until I can prove it.'

# Chapter 17

Helen stood on London Bridge, looking north towards the glittering city. She still felt uncomfortable with what Emmanuel had told her about Gus Cumberland. It suggested he felt entitled to her company. But then he'd been charming when she'd called him to suggest the walk and accepted with enthusiasm. She waited to see which version would turn up for the tour.

Low January sun flashed off glass tower blocks across the river. Downstream, wide passenger boats ferried commuters along the Thames, past the moored grey bulk of the warship HMS *Belfast*. Tower Bridge, festive with its Gothic towers and gilding, was silhouetted against the bright sky. London was putting on one of its clear winter days, bracingly cold but full of light. A good day for a walk.

'Hello.'

Helen jumped. Gus had arrived silently from the south side of the river, padding up behind her on spotless trainers. He was muffled against the cold in a soft navy blue scarf, tucked inside the collar of a fawn leather jacket. His fair hair gleamed in the sun. She'd forgotten how good-looking he was.

'Hi.'

'You're admiring my view.' He leaned on the parapet next to her.

'Your view?' She smiled at his proprietorial air.

'I have a flat in that building.' He pointed beyond the converted warehouses that lined the south bank of the river. 'You can see this view from my terrace. I'm a south Londoner, too.'

Helen followed his gesture, saw a huge brand-new block of glass and timber, swags of greenery cascading like a waterfall down its terraced frontage.

'Wow. That looks great,' she said, surprised. It wasn't the sort of place she'd expected.

He beamed. 'Thanks. It is rather good. I only bought it last year; sold off the crumbling old flat in Belgravia after lockdown. None of us were using it. I'll show you later.

'It's lovely to see you again, Helen. And I'm eager to learn about Charles Dickens' London. Where do we start?' He was excited as the keenest tourist.

'London Bridge is a good enough place,' said Helen. 'This isn't the original, of course. The bridge that Dickens knew as a child was about thirty metres upstream and was demolished in 1831. And the view has transformed. No Tower Bridge in Dickens' day; no tower blocks or smart apartments. Imagine sailing ships unloading in the Pool of London, docks with warehouses full of goods. And muddy stairs down to the foreshore, the river washing up to the end of the street.

'The river was a bigger part of London life in Dickens' day. Fewer bridges, so people used boats to get across. More people made their living from the river, especially around the docks. Dickens often wrote about the riverside dwellers, as we saw in the Rochester exhibition.'

She led them down the steps to the riverside path and under the sleek concrete structure of London Bridge itself. They passed kids queuing for the plastic thrills of the London Bridge Experience, buskers plodding through another rendition of *The Streets of London*, homeless people huddled into arches. As always, Helen dropped a coin into the plastic cup of one rough sleeper. Gus raised an eyebrow, quizzical.

'What difference does that make?' he asked.

She shrugged. 'Not much.' She had no illusions about that. It was just something she did; like paying a toll to cross the bridge.

'You won't get rich like that,' he said with a smile. 'Giving it away.'

She gave him a sideways glance. 'Who says I want to be rich?'

She indicated a blue plaque by the side of the bridge. 'That's our next Dickens connection,' she said.

'Nancy's steps,' he read. 'Nancy who?'

'Nancy from *Oliver Twist* – the woman from Fagin's gang who befriends Oliver.' She wondered whether to tell him what she'd discovered about Nancy's real-life namesake.

'Of course. The prostitute who gets strangled by Bill Sikes.'

'That's one way of putting it. Dickens never says she's a prostitute,' said Helen. 'And Sikes didn't strangle her.'

'But she was murdered here?' He read the plaque again.

'No, actually. In the book, Sikes beats her to death in his lodgings. But she was overheard on London Bridge steps, talking to Oliver's protector.' That settled it, Helen thought. As Hester had suggested, Gus hadn't read it. Helen was now immersed in the novel, revelling in the rich characterisation and evocation of London life.

She looked down to the brown water lapping at the shore, imagining a bedraggled body, hair and clothes coated in silt. Nancy Love, the real Nancy, at the foot of the steps. Her skull dreadfully fractured by some blunt object.

'You're looking very pensive.' He smiled. 'What other lies do the tourist guides tell gullible visitors?'

Helen laughed. 'I'd be drummed out of the Guild of London Tour Guides if I admitted to those. Come this way.'

She led him through the tangle of streets around Southwark Cathedral and through the bustling Borough Market. Borough High Street was busy as usual, and Helen was glad to step through a set of big wooden gates into the shelter of The George, one of the last galleried coaching inns in London. It was a preserved corner of London's past, a little time capsule from the eighteenth century.

'Have you read Dicken's first serialisation, *The Pickwick Papers*?' she asked, mischievously.

'Of course.'

She wasn't going to test him on it. 'Great. Then you'll remember the scene set in a coaching inn, very like this one, where Sam Weller is cleaning the boots outside the inn's rooms.'

She pointed to the row of doors beyond the wooden gallery on the first floor. 'That's the sort of accommodation where Mr Pickwick and his friends would have stayed on their travels,' she said. 'Coaching inns were everywhere before the railways. Dickens travelled all over the country by stagecoach as a young journalist, reporting on elections and political meetings. He wrote about racing other journalists back to London, bribing the turnpike and the coach driver to get back first with his copy.' She smiled. Those stories seemed to her to show the best of Dickens, his enthusiasm and energy and irrepressible love for life.

Gus spotted the sign on the wall. 'And William Shakespeare. He came here too?'

Helen laughed. 'It's certainly possible. The theatres he wrote for were just down the road, and there has been an inn on this spot for a very long time.'

She had a sudden, piercing memory of Richard. This was where they'd first met, when he came on her guided tour. He'd teased her about embroidering for the tourists, conjuring up pictures of Shakespeare and Christopher Marlowe sinking pots of ale together at The George.

Some days she felt his loss everywhere. He'd have loved her quest for the real Nancy, she thought. He'd have understood, in a way that she didn't think Gus would. Helen wondered if she would ever again find someone who would understand her passion for history, who felt it too and had made it his life's work.

'You're looking sad,' said Gus. 'What's the matter?'

She slapped a smile on her face. 'Not at all. I was just remembering something.' It's a job, she reminded herself. Stop daydreaming.

She led the way along Borough High Street to the church of St George the Martyr, a Georgian classical-style building in red brick and white stone. The parish church where Nancy's sister, Frances, had been married, and where Nancy's funeral was held.

'Are we going in?' asked Gus. He peered into the dark interior.

'Not today.'

Helen circled the building and entered the small park, once

the churchyard, behind it. The park was deserted, gloomy. Pigeons scrabbled in the dust below a big pollarded plane tree, bare branches raised like clenched fists threatening the sky. As in so many former graveyards, most of the gravestones had been cleared away. Helen checked the names on the remaining stones. Somewhere in this little park lay the body of Nancy Love. But she knew the chances of finding the exact spot – or of there being a surviving tombstone – were low. She'd come back on her own, have a proper look.

Set in the high brick wall to one side of the churchyard was a pair of iron gates. Helen put her hand on the cold metal.

'This is what remains of one of the most notorious prisons in London,' she said. 'The Marshalsea, where London's poor were imprisoned until they could pay off their debts. Including John Dickens, Charles Dickens' father. The whole family – except for Charles – moved into the prison.'

'Really?' Gus took hold of the metal gates and shook them. 'How did they pay? How can you earn money in prison?'

'Good question. In the case of John Dickens, he was lucky enough to inherit money within a few months. Others were here for years.'

Helen looked up at the high brick walls.

'The prison was demolished in 1834, but it had a profound effect on Dickens. He set much of his novel *Little Dorrit* in and around the prison, among people on the periphery of society, always close to the edge financially.

'He told very few people about that time in his life. He was twelve and he worked for his living, pasting labels on to bottles in a boot-polish factory at Hungerford Stairs. After a long day's work, he'd visit his family in the prison before going home to his lodgings.'

Gus stepped back and looked up at the gates. 'So, he learned to earn his living early. Like me. And not to rely on his father, his family.' Helen heard something damaged in his voice, a vulnerability beneath his privileged veneer.

'You started work young?' she asked.

He nodded. 'I wasn't twelve,' he said, with a short laugh. 'But I was still at Oxford when my father became ill. He couldn't run the business after that. I ditched university, packed my trunk, and moved back to the circus.' His smile was sad. 'I've been working ever since. Now it's time to fill in some of the education I missed. This is great, Helen. Where next?'

Lant Street, quiet and unassuming, still had some early nineteenth-century terraced housing, as well as warehouses repurposed into smart, expensive flats. Helen walked down the short stretch of road, wondering. Where had Nancy Love lived with her family?

The street ended abruptly, cut across by the playground of the Charles Dickens Primary School.

Gus laughed. 'Everything's named after Dickens around here.'

Helen looked back along the street. 'Poor Charles. He was desperately unhappy about being taken out of school to work. It's ironic – this street is where he lodged, while he was working at the factory and his family was in the Marshalsea. He lived with one of the constables from the prison.'

'No blue plaque?' Gus examined the houses. 'I suppose there's no way to tell which of these it would have been. Or even whether these are the original houses.'

He stopped, looked again at Helen. 'Come on. What is it? You've got that look on your face again. Like something from the past has just come back to haunt you.'

Helen shivered, despite herself. His blue eyes were resting on her with curiosity and, she thought, kindness. Maybe he would understand.

'I found a newspaper cutting,' she said. 'In the book. The one that was stolen in Rochester.' She hoped he wouldn't comment on the circumstances of the burglary. 'The cutting was about a woman who lived here while Dickens was lodging in Lant Street. She'd been murdered. I was trying to find out more about her. And I was wondering about her life.'

He raised his eyebrows. 'Wow. A historical murder mystery. That sounds so interesting. What have you found out so far?'

'Her name was Nancy. Nancy Love. She was twenty-one years old.'

'Nancy?' Gus's eyes lit up. 'Like the girl in *Oliver Twist*?'

Helen nodded. 'Exactly.'

'And was she killed by a man called Bill Sikes?'

Helen tried to smile. Nancy's death wasn't a joke.

'No. But her body was found on the steps of London Bridge. The cutting said that a man called Buller was a suspect.' She needed to follow that up, she remembered. There had been other references to Nancy Love's murder in *The British Press* which she'd not read yet.

Gus rocked back on his heels, hands in his pockets. 'You're a dark one, Helen. This is fascinating.' He checked his watch. 'I want to hear more. But can we get something to eat first? I didn't manage breakfast this morning and I'm starved. We're only about ten minutes' walk from my flat. The housekeeper was going to leave me some lunch and I said there would be two of us.'

Helen's stomach rumbled and she acquiesced. She was curious to see the inside of the apartment, she had to admit.

# Chapter 18

Nick was buying drinks in the Duke of Wellington, which he reckoned had a fair claim to be the roughest pub in Dover, despite stiff competition. His companions were a gap-toothed old boy with an appetite for extra-strong lager and whisky chasers at lunchtime, and his nephew, a shifty-looking bloke in a tracksuit who had already tried to sell Nick a bag of skunk. They happily looked at Nick's photo of Gary Paxton and claimed to have seen him around, but seemed to need more lubrication to unlock their memories. Nick had the feeling he was being taken for a ride.

He looked around the dingy bar. It was down a scruffy side street, between the boarded-up chain stores on the High Street and the dual carriageway that sliced through Dover, cutting the town centre off from the seafront. He could hear the lorries thundering down to the ferry terminal over the jangle of the fruit machines that were in constant demand.

There were plenty of customers for a Friday lunchtime, presumably lured by the low prices rather than the sticky tables or swirling patterns of the carpet, which must have been quite colourful before twenty years of dirt was trodden into them. Maybe he should give up on the duo he'd befriended and ask around further.

'Oi, Sancho!' The old guy beckoned over a thick-set shaven-haired man who'd just walked up to the bar in grubby jeans and work boots. He didn't look much like a Sancho.

He joined them, eyeing Nick with suspicion.

'Nick here will get you a pint, won't you?' said the old man. 'Sancho knows everyone.'

'What can I get you?' asked Nick.

The man stared at him for a minute, narrowed his eyes. 'You're not police, are you? Home Office?' His accent was eastern European. Definitely not a Sancho.

Nick shook his head. 'No way. I'm a journalist, like I've been telling your friends here.'

'I'll have Carlsberg. What do you want to know?'

Sancho downed half his pint before he felt able to look at the photo on Nick's phone. He looked for several seconds, then switched his gaze to Nick's face.

'How do you know this man?' he asked. 'Is he your friend?'

Nick tried to read the man's impassive face. With no clues, he decided honesty might be the best policy.

'No. Last time I saw him, he tried to kill me,' he said. 'Well, the time before last. But I saw him in Dover last weekend, at that big march. And I'm trying to track him down, find out what he's up to.'

Sancho switched off the phone and put it back in Nick's hand. 'Don't go asking everyone about him. You need to be careful. He works with some people I know. They would try to kill you too, if they knew you were looking into their business.'

'Friends of yours?' asked Nick.

He shook his head vehemently. 'Not anymore. I keep away

from them. You should, too.'

Nick slipped the phone back in his pocket. 'OK. I get that. But you don't know where he hangs out, do you? Where he lives or anything? His name's Paxton, Gary Paxton. But he might not be calling himself that now.'

The man shrugged his heavy shoulders. 'I just work on the building sites. I don't get involved with no-one, don't want no trouble. But you tell me. He has been in prison?'

Nick nodded. 'Just got out a month or two ago.'

'OK. That's normal, for them. They have people who make friends with you in prison, then they follow you when you get out. Give you some money, tell you to do some jobs for them. If you have a good head on your shoulders, you say no.' Nick got the feeling the man was speaking from personal experience.

'If he's just out of prison, he is maybe in the bail hostel by the cliffs. That's where they usually put people. It's not a nice place. They are not nice people. You should be careful.'

He drained his pint, raised a hand to Nick's two companions.

'That's all I can tell you. Back to work.' He strode out of the bar.

'Told you he knew everyone,' crowed the old geezer, exposing his missing front teeth in a grin. He flourished his empty glass. 'How about another?'

A bail hostel. Of course. Why hadn't Nick thought of that before? He signalled to the barman and opened the map application on his phone. By the cliffs, the man had said. He zoomed in, tried a search.

There it was. White Cliffs Hostel, East Cliff, Dover. Tucked between the main approach to the ferry terminal and the cliffs.

Nick paid up and walked out into the drizzle. Time to see if anyone was at home.

# Chapter 19

The flat didn't disappoint. The lift from the shiny marble atrium took them directly to the penthouse. Helen stepped in and gasped. A wall of glass framed an astonishing view of the river, sunlight sparkling off the waters and softened by trailing greenery from above.

Gus opened the sliding doors to the terrace and they stepped out on to the wide wooden deck.

'You're practically on top of Tower Bridge,' said Helen. 'What an incredible view.' The square white block of the Tower of London was across the river, a clutch of City skyscrapers rising incongruously next to it.

'You should see it at night, with all the lights on,' said Gus. He put a hand on her shoulder. 'I hope you will, soon.'

She leaned over the parapet and looked downstream. 'And you're quite close to another notorious Dickens landmark. See down there, the other side of Tower Bridge, where there's an inlet and a green surrounded by housing? That was Jacob's Island, the notorious slum Dickens wrote about in *Oliver Twist*.' Where Bill Sikes was cornered by the mob and died, she remembered, thinking again of Nancy Love.

The housekeeper had left a warming pea and ham soup, a

couple of quiches and crusty sourdough bread. Gus opened a bottle of white wine. They ate perched on stools at the breakfast bar, Helen admiring the gleaming chrome open-plan kitchen.

The food was delicious, and Helen realised how hungry she'd been. What bliss, to have someone prepare the food for you, keep the place clean and get the shopping in.

'You obviously needed that,' said Gus with a grin as she laid down her soup spoon.

'Sorry, I eat too fast. It comes of living alone,' she said. She usually shovelled down food while reading. Sometimes she didn't even sit down, but ate straight from the fridge. She wasn't going to tell him that.

'Do you like living on your own?'

She liked the fact that he'd asked; hadn't assumed she was a tragic, lonely spinster. Even if she had felt like one in recent years.

'It suits me, mostly,' she said. 'Lockdown was tough, though. How about you?'

He smiled, a little rueful. 'My mother lives in Vylands with me. And there are plenty of people around to keep the place running. I was down there for lockdown. It was a bit much, to be honest. I like having a London flat as a bolt-hole. It keeps me sane.'

Helen thought for a moment. 'You said your father was ill? Is he still around?'

Gus finished eating. 'Yeah.' He put down his knife and fork and pushed the plate away. 'My father is… not sane. He's in a mental-health unit. What they used to call an asylum. Mad as a box of frogs, unfortunately.' He forced out an unconvincing laugh.

'I'm so sorry. That must be difficult for you. And your mother.'

He shrugged. 'Thanks. It's been a long time. We're used to it.' He sighed. 'You'll see stuff about it online if you look me up. Surprised you haven't, to be honest. Most people do, these days.'

Helen wanted to reassure him she had more interesting things to look up online, then wondered if that would sound rude. She said nothing.

'Poor old Pa went off the rails back in the late nineties. He took a hunting rifle up to Buckingham Palace and started waving it around, saying he should be King. Not surprisingly, they locked him up. He was lucky they didn't shoot him.'

'Wow. And he's been in hospital ever since?'

'Not quite. He's been in and out. He's back in now. To be honest, it's easier when he's in. Ma and I can just get on with our lives, without worrying what havoc he's going to cause next.'

He smiled at her. 'So that's me. Now, tell me more about Nancy Love. Your mysterious murder victim. I want to hear everything.'

He made coffee using the same sort of machine that Emmanuel had in his office, while Helen filled him in on Nancy Love and her family. He seemed properly interested, asked intelligent questions, and didn't make everything into a joke, as she'd feared. Maybe his tendency to joke about things came from his experiences with his father. She could only imagine how a bunch of upper-class Oxbridge boys would tease one of their number whose father was sectioned.

He carried the coffee over to a low glass table beside a sleek leather sofa.

'And this newspaper cutting was in the book that someone nicked that night in Rochester? That's weird,' said Gus. 'It's like they were after the same thing.'

Helen sat next to him and pulled up the photographs she'd taken of the book and the cutting.

'Yeah. I have an idea about that. I wish I could show you the originals.' She handed him her phone.

He scrolled through the images, enlarging them to see them better.

'What are all those squiggles? Is it shorthand or something?'

Helen grabbed the phone back and looked. Shorthand. Of course. Dickens had been a parliamentary reporter and had prided himself on mastering shorthand. She gazed at the faded blue ink markings, a series of dots and curved lines.

'I hadn't thought of that,' she admitted. 'But it could be.' She thought for a moment. There had been articles in the news recently about a project to decipher various documents in shorthand belonging to the author. She looked up 'Dickens shorthand' and found the website for the project.

'Listen.' She read aloud the introduction. Dickens had adopted a complicated system, Gurney's Brachygraphy, which he'd taught himself from a manual, and then personalised, making it incredibly hard to read. But not impossible – teams of researchers across the country were working on it.

'That's brilliant, Gus. I'll get in touch with them and see what we can find out,' she said. She felt the thrill of a puzzle to solve. 'Thanks so much.'

'No problem. Don't forget to tell me what you find. It was my idea, remember?' His smile was teasing. 'Maybe you should work from here, where I can keep an eye on you. Help you out when you get stuck.'

Something about his words made Helen want to return to her own territory. She had a sudden longing for her laptop, her own desk. Perhaps she was too used to her own space for a relationship.

'I should be getting back,' she said. 'I won't forget to keep you updated.' She rose from the sofa, walked over to the windows. 'I can't get over this view.'

'Come to Vylands next time,' he said, helping her into her coat. 'And don't leave it too long.' He leaned over and kissed her forehead, an intimate gesture that took her by surprise. 'Thanks, Helen. It's been a really good day.'

It had, she thought, walking back along the riverside to London Bridge to hop on the train home. Better than she'd expected. On impulse, she looked up Gus's country estate near Canterbury. It looked gorgeous: a lovely house surrounded by countryside with a river running through the grounds. Perhaps she could combine a visit with another trip to Rochester to see the Dickens exhibition properly.

Which reminded her. She leaned against the river wall, reached for her mobile phone, and fished a card out of her wallet. The phone rang five times.

'Hello, Chapman and Daughter Booksellers.' The man sounded out of breath.

'Mr Chapman? It's Helen Oddfellow. I bought a book from you last weekend. Robert Mudie, *London and Londoners*. Remember?'

There was a pause. 'Sorry, we see so many people. I'm not sure I do. Can I help?'

His voice had moved up a pitch. He was lying, Helen was sure of it. The shop had hardly been overrun with customers.

'The book was stolen from my hotel room, Mr Chapman.

111

Just a few hours after I bought it. I thought you might have been offered the stolen book for resale.'

'Oh dear. How dreadful. I'm so sorry.' He sounded flustered. Helen remembered the figure who had bumped into her, the way he'd muttered 'Sorry'. Was it the same man? She felt almost sure it was.

'Well? Has anyone been in with it? Or asking about it?'

'No. No, definitely not. I'd have remembered. But I'll make a note of it, Miss…'

'Oddfellow. Dr Helen Oddfellow.' Helen rarely used her academic title, unless she wanted to make a point.

'Of course. Sorry. Now. Remind me of the title again?'

Helen spelled it out, annoyed at his pretence. How could he be so certain no-one had been asking about it if he couldn't remember the title?

'I'll be down in Rochester again soon, I expect,' she said. 'Perhaps I'll call in to see you. I'd like to know more about the book. Where it came from, for a start. I think you said it was part of a house clearance?'

'Um. Yes, that might have been it. So hard to remember, really. Sorry I can't be of more help.'

Helen hung up. She should go to see him. If it had been him burgling her hotel bedroom that night, she felt sure she'd be able to tell.

# Chapter 20

White Cliffs Hostel was, if nothing else, a remarkably accurate description. The building, part of a tottering row of Victorian terraced houses, leaned against the foot of the chalk cliffs. It was in a canyon of permanent shadow, the sea view blocked off by a much taller row of hotels which had themselves seen better days.

Nick booked a single room at the back of one of the cheapest-looking hotels. The landlady offered him a double with a sea view for the same price, but he pretended to be worried about noise from the port and said he'd prefer to be on the back. The small window, shaded by greying net curtains, had a lovely view down on to the bail hostel.

Nick and a glum-looking French family were the only guests at dinner, served at an uncompromising six o'clock. Amy, the landlady, had brought them a surprisingly decent meal of chicken and chips, before hitching her sizeable hip on to the table next to Nick for a gossip.

'Where your family from, then?' was her opening gambit.

He grinned. 'Belfast,' he said, to tease her.

'Nah!'

'Well, my mum is. Dad's from Trinidad. I grew up in Liverpool. You?'

'Jamaica. And it was my grandparents, not my parents, I'll have you know. My grandaddy got off the boat, looked over the road, saw this place and decided he'd done enough travelling for one lifetime.' She pointed across the road to the ferry terminal.

'Really?' asked Nick, laughing. 'He only got this far?'

'Pretty much. He'd been in France after the war, but didn't like it. Said the people was too unfriendly. He crossed over and shacked up here. Met my grandmother, who was a chambermaid in this hotel. Started working here himself. Eventually they bought it. It was crumbling to pieces.'

She sighed, looked around. 'My parents always said they would do it up nice. And then I said I would, too. One day.'

He shook his head. 'It's a tough business. And this part of town… It looks like it needs some money spent on it.'

She bounced up from the table, nodding vigorously. 'Too right. We need smart hotels and decent restaurants. Instead, we get bed-and-breakfast places for homeless people, criminals, immigrants straight off the boat.'

Nick thought that was a bit rich, given her own family history, but didn't want to divert her flow. 'Criminals?'

She put her fingers on her lips. 'That place across the road? It's for people who should be in prison. They let them out early, put them in there. Opposite decent hotels like this one.'

Nick nodded. 'That's tough. Do they come over here, use the bar and restaurant, then?'

She shook her head. 'No chance. Anyway, they're under curfew. Have to be in at eight o'clock. Then they can't go out till six in the morning.'

114

Nick glanced at his watch. It was just past seven. Well, that was handy. He could keep an eye out, see if he could spot Paxton coming back. Then he just needed to wake up early and follow him when he left.

He faked a yawn. 'Long day tomorrow,' he said. 'I'm on an early ferry. I need to do some work, then get a decent night's sleep.'

He perched on his bedroom windowsill, the net curtain hooked back and the light off, flicking through social media on his phone. The footage Angus had taken of the attack on the processing centre would be included in a documentary on immigration that evening. Lots of people were expressing various degrees of outrage or concern about the attack. But he was more interested in how it had gone down on the far right. He used one of his aliases to log on to a chat room that attracted the madder end of the political spectrum.

The attack on the centre was being hailed as a victory. Sebastian Johansson, better known to his mates as Captain Jonnie, had posted a video of himself ranting about the attack, saying that it was 'inevitable that decent patriots would call the government to account'. He said the BPP would need to regroup and be ready for the next action, and warned about journalists.

'Careful who you talk to. We think someone was talking to the media before the action at Dover. The film crews arrived on the spot too fast,' he said. Nick sucked in his breath. 'Be suspicious. Remember, anyone in your cell could be a spy cop or an undercover reporter for the mainstream media. Think before you share information. Check out anyone suspicious. You'll know what to do if you find a rat.'

Shit. Was that a threat against Ollie? Nick and his crew

had been the only journalists present at the storming of the immigration centre, although that had been more about Nick's quick reactions than any inside information. His first instinct was to call his reporter, but an unexpected phone call at the wrong moment could put Ollie in more danger. He sent a message to an encrypted service that Ollie could log on to when he was alone.

It was a quarter to eight. Outside, streetlamps threw dim pools of light down on to muddy puddles in the pot-holed road. There was a scuffle that could have been rats or foxes behind a cluster of bins in the hotel's dark back yard.

Then he heard the dog. A low growl, followed by a frenzy of barking. A man's voice, shouting at it to shut up. The animal slunk down the street, straining at its lead. Behind it came the man, thick-set in jogging bottoms and a hoodie. Hair shaved at the sides, longer on top. Nick couldn't see his face, but he recognised the bulk of him. He remembered the terror of trying to fight him off, the way his breath had been knocked out of him by sheer force.

Paxton paused in front of the bail hostel, crouched, and gave something to the dog that made it quieten. Another figure emerged from the darkness and greeted him. A long, dark coat, the streetlamps glinting off gold braid on the shoulders. A beret with some kind of cap badge pulled military-style across his forehead. Bloody hell, thought Nick. Captain Jonnie and Gary Paxton. My two least-favourite people, teaming up.

The men appeared deep in conversation. Nick cracked open the window, but still couldn't hear what they were saying. No point in watching if he couldn't hear. He slipped out of his room, ran lightly down the back stairs and out of the door next to the kitchen.

The yard stank of rotting food and general rubbish. Nick crouched behind the big plastic bins, hearing a tell-tale squeak of rats. He tried to still his breathing, tune into the voices. Were the men still there?

'Trouble is, someone's looking for you, Gary. Asking questions, down in the Wellie,' said the first voice, pitched low. Nick recognised the mock cockney accent from Captain Jonnie's videos. He cursed himself for being too obvious in the pub. Word got around.

'Who?' Paxton, his voice guarded.

'The same black bastard who got into the migrant centre. The one off the telly. You know him? Rides a motorbike.'

Nick wished he could calm his heartbeat. It banged so loudly in his chest, he could hardly believe it wasn't audible to the men on the other side of the gate.

'Nick Wilson.' Paxton sounded resigned. 'Yeah. I'll deal with him.'

'That's good. But you've got to be careful, Gary. Now, you know we want to work with you. A lot of the lads look up to you. We could learn a lot from each other. But we don't want the wrong sort of media attention, you get me? Not now, with the police crawling all over us.'

Paxton called sharply to the dog. 'Oi. Stay here.' Nick heard it whimpering, growling. Perhaps it could smell the rats by the bins. Or maybe it could smell him.

'What makes you think I want to work with you?' Paxton asked. His voice was cautious. 'You've got yourselves banned. I just got out. I'm busy getting some dosh together. I don't like the way you work, all this social media bollocks. Dressing up like a soldier and making videos. You need to get your boys trained up, ready to fight. Then pick your targets, focus your efforts somewhere that's going to get public support. Half this town works down at the docks. All you've done is piss them off.'

Johansson was silent a moment, then forced a laugh. 'You see? We could learn from each other. And you say you need money? We've got it, mate. More than you could possibly imagine. Friends in high places. Come on. We know who you're working for. Everyone does. How long before that blows up in your face? Nasty lot, they are.'

'Mind your own business,' growled Paxton.

'Go on, how much do you want? A couple of grand? I can give you that, cash. How long is that going to take you to earn, driving a van for those bastards out on the farm?'

Nick tried to get closer to the gate, to see if Johansson had got the cash on him. He trod on something soft. It shrieked, clawed at him and pulled away. He gasped and jumped back, before realising it was a cat.

'What the fuck?'

The gate swung open and Nick saw the outline of a big man against the streetlamp. A dog leapt through the gate, teeth bared. Nick shrank back behind the bins and crouched to the ground, praying. The cat shot past him and out of the gate. The dog pivoted and followed, letting off a volley of barking.

'Just a bloody cat,' said Johansson, at Paxton's shoulder.

'Maybe.' Paxton walked into the yard. 'But something set it off.'

Nick held his breath. A beam of light shone out from Paxton's phone. It swept across the detritus of the yard: a split bin bag with banana peel and food packaging spilling out; a discarded mop handle; a rusting kid's bike. The beam came closer, catching the edge of the blue plastic bin. Nick closed his hand around a discarded glass bottle, swallowed hard.

The beam stopped. Nick looked. It had found his trainer.

'There you are, you little fucker.' Paxton's voice was soft. Nick saw the gleam of a blade in his hand.

# Chapter 21

Nick chucked the bottle at Paxton's face as hard as he could. The man yelled and took a step back. The bottle bounced off his head, smashed against the ground. Nick was on his feet, clambering on top of the bin, then on to the wall next to it.

Paxton's hand closed around Nick's ankle, pulling him off-balance. He swayed for a second, grabbed the wall in both hands, then kicked hard and twisted free. He ran along the top of the wall. Paxton was heaving himself up, coming after him already.

Nick knew he had no chance in a stand-up fight with Paxton on his own; much less against two of them. But he was quick, his reactions sharpened by the training in mixed martial arts he'd been doing since the last time they'd met. If he could keep out of Paxton's hands, he could out-run him.

He headed for the fire escape which met the wall at the corner of the building, grabbed the edge of the metal stairway and swung himself up on to the platform. He banged on the dark window of the adjacent room. No response.

He ran up the metal steps to the next floor. Paxton clattered up behind him, panting. Maybe Nick was imagining it, but

Paxton didn't seem as light on his feet as he used to be. Nick swung himself up to the next floor; tried the fire exit door. Locked on the outside, of course.

As he went, he yelled for help and banged on the windows. But Paxton was close behind him and there wasn't much further to go. What would he do when he got to the top?

As he reached the third floor, he turned and braced himself against the railing. A well-aimed kick might just send Paxton back down the stairs. The man thundered towards him. Nick took a deep breath. One chance to get it right.

The lights came on behind him and the fire escape door swung open.

'What the hell is going on?' yelled Amy. She stood in the doorway, arms folded.

'Please…' Nick begged. 'Let me in.'

She looked at him with disdain. 'What are you doing out there? Get in.'

He ducked through the door. 'Lock it,' he said. 'He's after me.'

She stepped out on to the fire escape and looked down at Paxton, who had paused halfway up the steps.

'You are trespassing on my property,' she said. 'I'm calling the police. And if you are from that den of criminals over the road, I will have that place shut down. You hear me?'

Paxton decided that retreat was the best option. Without further comment, he clattered down the steps and out of the yard. Nick checked the time – ten past eight. With luck, Paxton would get bollocked for being out after curfew.

Amy closed the door and secured it. She turned to Nick.

'Now, you going to tell me what all this is about, Mister Journalist who I've just been watching on my television?

121

Before I call the police and get them to throw you out of here.'

He followed her to her little sitting room. She sat on a small sofa covered in a crocheted blanket. The immigration documentary was playing on the big TV.

'They just showed a picture of you up at the docks,' she said. 'With all those nasty types setting fire to the migrant centre. What are you doing in my hotel and why was that man chasing you up my fire escape?'

Nick sighed. She'd quite possibly just saved his life. He owed her an explanation – and he hoped she wouldn't suffer as a result. Gary Paxton didn't make a good enemy.

'The man who was chasing me was with those guys who stormed the centre,' he said. 'I'm trying to find out more about them. About who's behind them, who is paying for all the coaches to bring people to the marches, that sort of thing. He was staying at that place opposite, so I booked in here. I saw him talking to someone, so I went down to listen. Then they found me.'

She stared at him, implacable. 'How did they find you?'

'Um, I trod on a cat.'

'You trod on my cat?' Her voice rose in outrage.

'Sorry. I didn't see it. But it was OK. Only it ran away, and they came to investigate.' Nick remembered the dog; hoped the cat had got away from that beast in one piece.

She nodded, then unlocked the door to a seventies-style sideboard. 'I don't drink,' she said. 'Except when I've had a shock.' She brandished a bottle of ginger wine. 'Want some?'

Nick returned her grin. 'Not my usual tipple, but go on then.'

She poured the sticky liquid into tiny shot glasses with the

122

Jamaican flag painted on the side. He took a sip, grateful for the sugar rush and the alcohol. His legs had started to tremble.

'Ooh. That's good. OK, then.' He explained his previous acquaintance with Gary Paxton, trying to keep the story simple. 'He kidnapped a friend of mine because she'd found out something his boss wanted to know. I was trying to find her and I got trapped with him. He broke my wrist, then tried to strangle me. My colleague rescued me just in time. And Paxton got sent down for twelve years, six years ago.'

'And they let that so-and-so out of prison?' Amy was outraged.

'Yeah. Listen, I'm really grateful for what you did tonight. I think he would have done me some serious damage if he'd caught me. But I'm worried it's put you in danger. You should at least report it. Tell the police someone from the bail hostel was climbing on the fire escape.'

She looked at him over her glass. 'And what about you? Are you going to tell the police that thug came after you with a knife in his hand?'

He looked down. 'Nah. It would complicate things.'

'Then why do you think I should call the police to my respectable hotel?'

He shrugged, palms up. 'In case they come back. In case they cause you trouble in the future.'

'Future can look after itself,' she said. 'Now, what are you going to do? How we going to make sure you don't get jumped the minute you leave this place?'

'Good question.' Nick thought. Paxton knew he had a motorbike. 'Do you do all the washing and stuff for the hotel here? Or do you use a laundry service? What time does it come in the morning?'

# Chapter 22

Helen yawned and got up from her desk to make tea. She'd been working all evening on deciphering the notes scribbled in the back of the Mudie book, but was no closer to an explanation.

She'd found the online *Dictionary of Dickens Shorthand* at the shorthand researchers' website. To her excitement, the symbols looked very similar to those in the book. A note on the website suggested researchers should cross-reference any symbols they found with the original Brachygraphy manual. Any symbols only found in Dickens and not in the Brachygraphy could indicate this was Dickens' work.

The work was laborious. As with many shorthand systems, it mostly omitted vowels, giving a string of consonants like a bad Scrabble hand. Only the context would provide the meaning – and she didn't know what the context was. Each symbol could have several meanings, and it was up to the reader to work out which was the correct one to fit with the other letters and any full-word symbols. Helen had ended up with a row of tentatively identified letters, separated by dashes that showed word breaks. She couldn't see any pattern in them.

Her eyes were tired. She took her tea to the window, looked out across the dark rooftops that stretched down towards Deptford Creek and the river. Maybe she needed a change of tack. Before she started on the shorthand, she'd been focusing on finding out about Nancy. And there were more references in the newspapers she had yet to chase up.

Back at her desk, Helen logged into the British Newspaper Archive. A week after the report of Nancy's death, *The British Press* had devoted a column to her funeral. Helen's eyes widened as she read.

'Much of London's theatrical world gathered at the church of St Geo. Martyr on Tuesday last, for the sad interment of Miss Nancy Love. Miss Love, an acclaimed actress who has delighted audiences with her many leading roles at the Surrey Theatre, was brutally murdered last week, and her killer remains at large.'

An actress. Helen wanted to cheer. Nancy was not a prostitute, forced to sell sex for a living. She had been a professional actor, a leading lady. There was a line drawing next to the article, showing a young woman with plentiful dark hair in a fairy costume with wings, captioned 'Miss Love as Titania'. Helen gazed at the image, fascinated. Nancy finally had a face. Her eyes were dark, her expression bold and challenging. She wore a smile, and something about the image looked as if she was having the most tremendous fun.

Helen downloaded a copy of the page. She remembered her conversation with Hester in the Dickens Museum – Hester's description of Nancy in *Oliver Twist* as melodramatic. Well, perhaps that was the reason. Perhaps the boy Dickens had seen Nancy Love onstage. And when he drew her character in his novel, perhaps it was her stage mannerisms, her passionate speeches that he remembered.

Helen read down the page. There were eulogies for Nancy from her colleagues and the owner of the Surrey Theatre, who described her as 'a perfect professional' with 'many ardent admirers'. The newspaper even described the flowers that were heaped on her coffin: 'Very fine, from her many admirers both known and shy of public identification'.

The third article featuring Nancy had news of the investigation into her death. Tom Buller, the man who was suspected of her murder, had recently frequented Miss Love's performances and waited for her after the curtain fell. They had walked away from the theatre toward the river on the last night on which Nancy was seen alive.

The man, who had served in the Royal Artillery during the wars against Napoleon, had not been seen since and had left unpaid debts of two shillings and sixpence at his lodgings. The manager of the theatre had put up a reward for anyone with information leading to his capture. He was, the report said, not known in the locality, and had rented his room in Mint Street for only five weeks.

An infatuated fan whose advances had been rebuffed? Perhaps. Helen opened an academic search engine and looked up the Surrey Theatre.

The name was one of many that graced the theatre, circus and music hall at St George's Circus near Blackfriars, she read. She glanced at the map of London that hung on the wall above her desk. It was a short walk from Nancy's home in Lant Street, maybe a quarter of an hour?

Helen found a paper in a theatrical studies journal outlining the theatre's history. The place seemed to have had appalling luck: burning down several times and eventually going out of business because of the popularity of the nearby Old Vic.

In 1824, the theatre was being run by the landlord of a nearby pub, who presumably did rather well out of the customers coming and going to the performances. Helen wondered if the publican ownership was a link back to Nancy Love's family – would they have known each other through Nancy's father at the Mermaid Tavern?

The article showed an image of a playbill from the period with a dizzying variety of acts performing in a single evening. A 'tragic-comic' play was followed by a display of gymnastics, with an interlude of comic songs followed by a romantic comedy.

The playbill was reproduced 'with kind permission of the University of Kent's special collections', she read. Right. Helen navigated the university's online library catalogue. It had a collection of theatre memorabilia, including Victorian playbills, scripts, and photographs. Several holdings related to the Surrey Theatre, or the Royal Surrey, as it was later called. They made the collection accessible to researchers on site at the university campus, just outside Canterbury.

Helen's phone rang. Gus's number.

'How's the research going? Any more progress?' He sounded genuinely interested.

Helen smiled. 'Lots, actually. I'll tell you when I see you next. It looks like I'll need a trip down to Canterbury to the university library there.'

'Fantastic!' His voice was full of enthusiasm. 'Why don't I take you? Save you getting the train. I'm driving down tomorrow morning.'

'Well…' It was tempting. Train fares were expensive, and it would be nice to have someone to go with.

'Oh, go on. And come for dinner at Vylands. My sister will be down, too. It'll be fun. We could work on that shorthand stuff. And I can run you to Canterbury station on Sunday, if you need to get back.'

A country house weekend, meeting Gus's family. Helen felt a prickle of alarm. Was she ready for that? Her weekends tended to involve solitary walks around London. But there had been a lot of that sort of weekend. She needed to push herself back into meeting new people, seeing fresh places. What the hell?

'Why not? That'd be great.'

If only Crispin had been there to ask for wardrobe advice. Helen remembered how cold it had been at Cobham Hall, her only other experience of country houses. Jumpers, she reminded herself. Wear a lot of jumpers.

She could take her hiking boots, she supposed; they'd see her through any amount of mud on the farm. But what about dinner in the evening?

Helen charged up her mobile phone, packed her notebook and pencils for the library at Canterbury. She looked again at the string of half-identified letters from the shorthand.

She wished more than anything that she could run downstairs with the scribbled symbols and get Crispin's brain on to it. He'd been amazing at cryptic crosswords and had helped her to solve many puzzles in the past. Even after his last stroke, he'd been able to fill out *The Times* crossword while waiting for the kettle to boil, his spidery script moving quickly across the paper.

Crispin and Helen had looked out for each other during the first lockdown. Helen fetched his shopping and anything else he needed, and they chatted several times a day on the phone.

He had carers who came twice a day, although he said they were in and out so fast, he barely got time to say hello.

Helen had been so happy when Crispin had gone for his first vaccination, thinking he would be safe. Then, just the next day, the cough had started. She'd called the emergency services, terrified by his blue lips and sunken eyes as he struggled for breath. The paramedics hadn't let her go with him in the ambulance. She'd promised to look after the flat, told him he'd be back in no time as they wheeled him up the steps from the basement. She never saw him again.

She wiped her eyes. Stop that, she told herself. He would hate you to cry over him. She looked down at the first line of letters through a blur of tears.

M/pr/nci/fr?v/y/ch?i/f/fls?/frtd/b

The phrase swam up to meet her. M/pr/nci. My poor Nancy. Of course! A smile broke through her tears. Thank you, Crispin.

She blotted her eyes. He'd have relished this puzzle and would probably have finished it by now. But he'd helped her to find the key, the first words. Now it was up to her. She wrote the words down in her notebook and turned to the next few letters.

By midnight, she had managed the first paragraph. She pushed the papers away, yawning. She needed to pack, then get some sleep, but she read over the words she'd deciphered:

'My poor Nancy. Forgive your Charlie for a foolish, frightened boy. Your [bully?] scared me so I did not deliver your letter. I have it still, a dozen years later. I will give it into the safekeeping of Mr Pickwick.'

So many questions. Was this a message from Dickens to the dead Nancy, twelve years after her death? That meant that –

as she and Hester had suspected – he knew the dead woman. Forgive your Charlie? It sounded like they had been close, intimate even. But as he said himself, he was just a boy, aged twelve at the time of Nancy's death.

A letter, undelivered. Had Nancy used him as a messenger, delivering letters for her? And what did he mean by giving the letter to Mr Pickwick for safekeeping? *The Pickwick Papers* had been published the same year as *London and Londoners*, to great acclaim. Was Mr Pickwick also based on a real person? Surely not.

The questions swam in Helen's head. She needed sleep. And to talk to someone who knew more about Dickens than she did. She'd give Hester a ring on Monday, after she'd investigated the theatre archives at Canterbury.

Helen closed her notebook and slipped it into her overnight case. It was almost one o'clock. She undressed and fell into bed. She'd do the rest of the packing in the morning.

# Chapter 23

Paxton couldn't sleep. That was unusual; not much kept him awake at night. He'd learned in the army to kip anywhere, anytime. And in prison too, no matter what madness was kicking off on the wing, he could usually get his head down.

He gave up around two o'clock; flicked on the bedside light and wished he had a cigarette. There was too much stuff coming together at once. He just wanted to earn his money, then start to rebuild. But the jobs he was being asked to do were getting dirtier, riskier. There was the bookseller to sort out. The immigrants up at the farm to be kept in line, and more coming in to be collected next month. Girls, he'd been told, from Romania this time. Groomed for service, ready for shipping to brothels around Kent. Filthy business.

He thought again of Aisha, the girl at the farm, tried not to think what might be happening to her. Just a kid. Smart with her languages, and fearless. Imagine having a kid like that and not taking care of her. She shouldn't have been there. She should have been back home, at school. It made him sick, the whole business.

So why not take Captain Jonnie up on his offer? They

believed in the same cause, wanted the same thing, knew the same people. He could use BPP money to set up his gym, train up the lads for them. Teach the Captain about strategy, get a plan in place. And despite what he'd said, Paxton knew they needed to use the internet. Social media was tedious, but it enabled you to get a network together. You could scale up quickly, mobilise far more people than just with word of mouth.

He didn't like the man. Jonnie Johnson was a loudmouth, ridiculous in his beret and military posturing. He'd not been near a battlefield in his life, Paxton could tell. He'd met his sort before, always happy to take the credit for someone else's hard work. The type that would double-cross you without a second's thought, cut you loose as soon as they no longer needed you. Take all the glory, none of the risk. And he didn't know what sort of strings might be attached to Jonnie's offer.

And yet, he said he had money. And Paxton needed dosh.

Cooper whimpered in his sleep, ears twitching. Dreaming of catching cats or rats. Paxton placed his hand on the dog's belly, felt the rise and fall of his breathing. It had taken him half an hour to find the pup, shivering in an alleyway near the castle, after he'd come down from the fire escape. By which time Jonnie was long gone, and he'd had to grovel to the hostel warden not to report his late return to the probation officer. Cooper's escape had given him a decent-enough excuse.

'You're a good dog,' he told him. He wouldn't have even known that the bastard journalist had been there if Cooper hadn't gone for the cat.

Nick Wilson. He should have killed the bastard while he had the chance. He might have guessed the journalist would come poking around after him. He'd heard about the kid's move into television documentaries, his obsession with right-wing activists and his determination to bring them down. Well, he knew who he was messing with. He'd have to be taken care of. And that bitch at the hotel, too.

Paxton could do it tonight. Buy a couple of jerry cans of petrol down at the service station, tip it through the letterbox and around the back door. A bottle with a burning petrol-soaked rag, straight through a window. The whole shitty place would go up and take the two of them with it.

Cooper sighed, got up and turned around three times, before settling back down on Paxton's leg.

He couldn't do it tonight. He couldn't even get out tonight. The warden had warned him he'd be keeping a close eye on him and that any further infringement of the curfew would have consequences for his parole report. Paxton shoved the dog off, sat up and looked out of the window. The hotel was almost within touching distance across the narrow street. Somewhere in there, Wilson was sleeping.

Paxton must have fallen asleep, because when the alarm sounded, he was lying on top of the bedclothes with Cooper across his chest like a heavy pillow. Shit. He'd intended to keep watch on the hotel.

He pushed the dog to one side, checked the dark street. Five-thirty. He was meeting Guren at seven. He wanted to be out of here at six, when the curfew lifted. He dropped to the floor and did a set of push-ups. Cooper got down on the floor with him, getting in the way and making him laugh. He washed, dressed and was out of the house as soon as the warden unlocked the door.

'Somewhere important to be?' asked the man, his voice sarcastic.

'Work, mate. Full day of deliveries,' said Paxton, jangling his keys. He checked the hotel, but there was no sign of life. Wilson rode a motorbike, he remembered. There was a line of them parked in a bay along the street, but no way of knowing which was his. Paxton checked around him. No-one in sight. He pulled the knife from his pocket, flicked it open and dug it into the front tyre of each of the bikes. That'd slow the bastard down.

He waited for Cooper to do his business, then got into the van and headed through the quiet streets. Guren was there before him this time, standing four-square on to the sea, cigarette cupped in his hand against the wind.

'You're late.'

Paxton checked the time. He wasn't.

'Seven o'clock,' he said.

'If I'm here first, you're late.' The man turned to look at him. 'And you look like shit.'

Paxton rubbed his face. God, he was tired. 'What's the problem, boss?' He hated calling Guren that, but the man seemed to find it reassuring.

'The boxes of stuff you gave us. There's a book missing. He hasn't made his full payment this month. He's getting to be a nuisance.'

Paxton nodded. 'Yeah, I know. I'm going back to sort it out. He's started making stupid threats, too.'

'Today. You are going today.'

Paxton considered. He'd rather deal with Nick Wilson first. But Guren didn't seem to be in a good mood. Best not to argue.

'All right.'

'Get the book. If you can, get the money. But we don't want

him around no more. Understand? Get rid of him.'

Paxton caught a whiff of tobacco smoke. He really wanted a cigarette. Get rid of him. He could, of course. But to do it well, carefully – these things took planning.

'Today?' he asked, cautiously.

'Today. Get rid. Understand? Or you want me to draw you a picture?'

Paxton clenched his fists. He'd had enough of this. 'How much? More risk, more money,' he said. 'You want it done quickly? You pay premium.'

Guren laughed, threw his cigarette butt into a puddle. 'Enough. Don't worry about the money.'

Easy for him to say. He wasn't the one living in a shitty bail hostel on a hundred quid a week. Paxton shrugged, turned away.

'Send me a message when it's done. And bring the stuff to the farm,' said Guren. Then he trudged back up the cliff path.

Paxton stood in the shelter of the sound mirror and looked out over the channel. He really needed to get out of this business. He'd call Jonnie, set up a meeting. See the colour of his money.

But first, the man at the bookshop in Rochester. Go early, before it opened? Or wait until the evening, when the shops shut? There were pubs and restaurants all along the High Street, people coming and going into the night. Early might be best. He checked his phone. With clear roads, he could be there in less than an hour.

Then afterwards. He had no time to arrange a complete disappearance. He'd need to cover his tracks.

He thought about the nervous man, his anxiety and his money problems and his empty threats to talk to the police.

He reminded him of a recruit when Paxton first joined the army. The same sweaty defiance, a runt refusing to act like one. Trying to assert himself, stand up to them. Threatening to report them.

Paxton and his mates had made his life a misery, every single day. If he'd just been weak, if he'd fallen into line, laughed at their jokes, turned a blind eye when they played pranks on others, he'd have been all right. They'd have looked after him. But he didn't fit, never would. It had taken five months before he cracked.

Paxton remembered his sergeant at the time, the look of disgust on his face when he'd been called to see the naked body hanging limp in the shower block. At the inquest, the sergeant had sworn blind there had been no bullying, no pranks.

'Sadly, some people are simply not cut out for army life,' he'd told the coroner. 'Help was on offer, but he declined to take it.'

Yeah. Paxton watched a flock of gulls take off from the turf towards the cliff edge, white against the lowering sky. That was the way.

He trudged back to the van, deep in thought. He barely noticed the laundry van parked up at the other end of the layby, the driver with his cap pulled low over his face, absorbed in his phone.

# Chapter 24

The High Street was quiet, the shops not open yet. The town looked mildly hungover from Friday night: spilt beer and a few broken bottles in the gutters. A whiff of urine as he passed an alleyway outside a pub. It was a good time to do his sort of business, early morning, while people nursed thick heads and turned over for another half hour of sleep. All the shops had deliveries coming and going. No-one was likely to remember one more anonymous-looking van parked up on a kerb.

Paxton crossed the yard behind the bookshop and pushed at the door. Locked. He hammered on it with his fist. A few seconds, and then Chapman opened it a crack, peered out with defeated eyes.

'I got the book. It wasn't easy. I'll fetch it for you.' He made to close the door again.

Paxton pushed it open, walked into the untidy kitchen. 'I'll wait here.'

The man rummaged in a drawer under the table. He passed it over, an uninteresting-looking volume in faded green cloth. Was that it? The one Guren was so interested in? Weird.

Paxton took it, put it inside his jacket. 'Now the money.'

Chapman was sweating again. 'I've got together as much as I can. I took out a loan. Here, six hundred quid. And that's with everything in the till. I even took fifty quid from my daughter's savings account.' He held out the notes in a brown envelope.

Paxton's lip curled. Pathetic creature. How could he do that, nick money from his own daughter? Paxton would never steal from his kid. The girl would be better off without him. That was the best way to think about it.

'Where is she?'

Instinctively, Chapman glanced towards the stairs, before trying to pretend. 'Don't know. She went out with her friends, first thing.'

'Really?' Paxton took a step towards the staircase. 'Not sleeping in late, like your usual teenager, then? I wouldn't find her if I went up to the flat?'

'Look, please. Just take the money and the book. I've done everything I can. She doesn't know about any of this.' Sweat pooled on Chapman's upper lip.

Paxton sighed. 'You disgust me. It's not about the money. It's the principle of the thing, see? We let you get away with it and everyone else gets arsey. We can't have that.

'And then last week, you threatened to talk to the police. That's a big problem for us. We've got friends in the police. They keep us informed when someone spills the beans.'

'I didn't mean it. I haven't said anything. I won't tell anyone. I promise, I absolutely promise. You have to believe me.' The man was looking upstairs again, speaking in an urgent whisper.

This was pitiful. Paxton hadn't even needed the knife. Cooper jumped around his feet, giving excited little yelps.

He shushed the dog. Best not to wake the daughter. He didn't want to have to deal with her, too.

'What do you want?' asked Chapman. His lips were dry. He licked them, and a bubble of saliva popped at the side of his mouth.

'Nothing else,' said Paxton. 'Too late. Time's up.' He sat Chapman down at the kitchen table. 'Now, you're going to write a letter. To your daughter. How old is she? What's her name?'

'Sophie. She's sixteen.'

'Sophie. Write to dear Sophie and tell her about your money problems. Say you tried to hide it from her, but you can't keep it secret any longer. Tell her you're sorry.'

Chapman ripped a page from a ledger on the table, found a pen in the drawer. He put on his glasses, began to write; held it for Paxton's approval.

'Good. Now tell her she's better off without you. That she won't see you again.'

'No!'

He slid the knife from his pocket, prodded it against the man's damp cheek. 'Really? You'd rather that she was here, too, would you? Sweet sixteen Sophie? I could give her a shout, get her to join us. Or shall we go upstairs, see if she's still tucked up in bed?'

The man sobbed, gripped the pen again. Wrote.

'Now, how do you usually end letters to her? Don't mess me around, I warn you. I'll know if you try to slip in a hidden message.'

Chapman looked up at Paxton, as if trying to guess whether he really would know. But he was too scared to take the chance, Paxton could see that.

'All my love, Dad.' Three kisses.

Paxton nodded his approval. 'That's it. Now, we're going out. No noise. You're going to get into my van, nice and quiet, and we're going for a drive.'

# Chapter 25

'There she is!' Helen pored over a playbill on yellow paper, capital letters proclaiming the attractions at the Surrey Theatre, March 1824.

'*A Desperate Passion; or The Remorseful Woman*, featuring Miss Love,' she read. Disappointingly, there was no drawing of Nancy, but presumably the punters viewing the advertising bill would be expected to know her name.

'Let me see.' Gus had put on reading glasses, which gave him a more serious, scholarly air that Helen rather liked. He'd picked her up in Deptford early that morning in a shiny dark green Range Rover and driven up over Blackheath, taking the A2 all the way out of London and into Kent. The traffic had been light and they'd made it to Canterbury by ten.

The university campus perched on a hill above the city, its green meadows and modern buildings offering breathtaking views of the cathedral. Canterbury Cathedral held disturbing memories for Helen, from bloodshed in the crypt to a desperate fight for survival in the bell tower. The city was also where she'd met Greg Hall, where their relationship had begun. All in all, Helen was content to keep Canterbury at a distance.

They headed straight to the university library. Helen had

phoned ahead from the car to request access to the collection of theatrical documents, specifically the playbills and scripts from the Surrey Theatre.

'*The Desperate Passion*. That sounds fun,' said Gus. 'Why were the Victorians so obsessed with fallen women?'

Helen looked up. 'Because they were such a bunch of hypocrites, I suppose. You never hear them lamenting about fallen men. Anyway, this was pre-Victorian. King George IV, Victoria's uncle, was on the throne.'

'Of course.' Gus turned to the index of holdings. 'They've got a prompt copy of the script. Shall we have a look? Find out what happened to the remorseful woman in the end?'

The narrow book had a functional brown cardboard cover, tatty with use. On the inside cover, someone had pasted a hand-written list of the cast, including Nancy Love as Letitia Lovelace, the remorseful woman of the title.

Helen turned the pages, fascinated to see the scribbles in the margins. There were crossings-out where the company had cut lines, arrows indicting the point when lights should be turned off or on, hashes where someone had to make a sound like a door banging.

'This is brilliant,' she said. 'I suppose this was what the back-stage crew would use to keep track of what was happening on stage and any effects they had to make. And to prompt the actors, of course.'

She began to read. Letitia Lovelace, a maidservant in a grand house, had allowed herself to be seduced by the Duke's son, dazzled by promises of wealth and luxury. For a time, she lived in his London house, lording it over the other servants, although shunned by polite society. Then the Duke died, the son inherited and married a proud society lady. Letitia was cast aside, thrown out into the London streets. In the final scene, she stands on a bridge across the Thames, threatening to throw herself to her death.

Helen shook her head. 'This is all a bit freaky,' she said. 'Everything seems to lead back to London Bridge.

Gus took the book from her and read aloud in a high-pitched voice: '"Look down to that dark water. Why should I not spring into the tide, with no living creature to bewail me?" It's very dramatic, isn't it?'

'Say that again.' Helen rummaged in her backpack for her copy of *Oliver Twist*.

Gus re-read, while Helen rifled through the pages. 'Gus. Listen. It's practically the same.' She read the passage from *Oliver Twist*: Nancy meeting Rose Maylie on the steps of London Bridge. '"Look at that dark water. How many times do you read of such as I who spring into the tide and leave no living thing to care for or bewail them?"'

She pushed the chair back. 'That's extraordinary. Dickens must have seen this play as a boy. He must have seen Nancy Love playing this role. And he remembered it and gave those words to his fictional Nancy, ten years later.'

Gus turned the page and read on. 'She doesn't do it,' he said. 'Look. Letitia's sister Rose arrives at the last minute and persuades her to return to their humble cottage in the countryside. Where she lives remorsefully ever after.'

Helen realised there were tears in her eyes. She brushed them away, wondering what had moved her so much.

'I'm glad,' she said. 'If only all remorseful women got happy endings.'

Gus dropped the book and took her hand. 'You old softy,' he said. 'Let's have a coffee. I could do with one. There was a cafe downstairs.'

Helen laughed. 'That's a good idea. I'm getting sentimental. I worked too late last night. Need more caffeine.' She tidied the papers. 'I'll give these back to the librarian. You go ahead.'

Gus went. Helen reached for the prompt book, then stopped. A page was sticking out of the end of the book. Not a page from the prompt book, from the play; a scrap of paper, covered over in faded black-ink handwriting.

Helen picked it up. It was written and cross-written, making use of every inch. She turned it sideways, deciphered the first few lines of spidery writing.

'Surrey Theatre, Thursday,' she read at the top. 'My dear Sister.' Heart banging hard, she turned the paper over, looking for the signature. There was none – the letter broke off, as if the writer had been interrupted or forgotten to finish it. Tucked it into the script she was studying, perhaps, and lost it.

Helen was still working on deciphering the writing half an hour later when Gus came back.

'What happened to you? I got you a cappuccino,' he said.

'Look. There was a letter in the back of the book. I think it's from Nancy,' said Helen. 'And it gets weirder,' she added. 'Forget the remorseful woman being seduced by the Duke's son. Nancy was having an affair with a Duke. And she doesn't sound remorseful at all.'

Gus sat down. 'What?'

Helen was half-way through transcribing the letter into her laptop. 'Give me a minute. It's not that easy to read. But I think I've got the gist of it.' He waited while she finished her task. She then sat back, read the transcript as far as she had managed.

'My dear Sister,

'I take this opportunity to write you a few lines from the back of the stage. I hope you are quite recovered from your late illness and that William's good fortune in the glass manufactory continues. Please convey a kiss to my Nephew and Niece from their loving Aunt Nan.

'My dear Frances, you will have heard I am sure what they say about me. And – as the one who shared my pillow and whispered late into the night with me so many times – you know I cannot lie to you. It is true. Not the bad names they call me. I am not, as they accuse me, profligate. But it is true that One who has seen me on the stage, who has found his way to our little Theatre despite his own Greatness, has become very dear to me.

'He is, sister, a Kind man as well as a great one. The Duke is generous and careful of my person, and my reputation. Mother worries for me. But she made her own choices freely with our dear Father, despite all the obstacles put in their way. She cannot begrudge me my chance of happiness with One who is far above me, yet who reaches down and raises me up, and I believe will not let me fall.

'Frances, I wish you could meet A. You would like him; I am sure of it. He has nothing of the harshness of his brother the King, or indeed his late father. Although he is much above me in years, he has a type of youthfulness, a frankness and honesty that would commend him to all who met him, regardless of his station. He takes an interest in the affairs of those less fortunate than himself and has been a Champion of the cause of Abolition, so close to the heart of our dear father.

'The Duke confides in me, sister, as I confide in you. And there is something – a matter of importance to everyone in this country. It is, I believe, something that should be more widely known, and that would indeed be advantageous to my dear A. I hope to persuade him of this. One day, I will speak freely to you about it.

'I am sending this by a boy who has become a great friend of mine in recent weeks. Poor child, his family is all in the Marshalsea and he lodges in the next house to ours and gets his living in a manufactory over the river. He amuses me greatly with his stories, and I have sometimes given him a penny to watch the show of an evening. Then he walks me home from the theatre, all puffed up as if he is protecting me from ruffians. Frances, he reminds me of our Tom. He's about the age that Tom was when he passed. His name is Charley, and I would be pleased if you could give him a bun and a warm welcome, and something for his trouble.'

The letter broke off with no signature.

They stared at each other in silence for a moment.

'Whew. You think that's our Nancy?'

'Yep. And Charles Dickens was her messenger boy. He didn't just know Nancy Love; he was her friend.' Helen flipped through her notebook for her notes on the Love family. 'Tom was Nancy and Frances's younger brother. He died in 1816, aged eleven, and was buried the same day as their father.'

She picked up the letter again. 'I wonder who he was. The Duke, I mean. It says his brother is the King…'

Gus leant close to her and re-read the text. 'Sounds like Augustus, Duke of Sussex,' he said. 'Sixth son of George III. Proponent of liberal causes like abolition of the slave trade and Catholic emancipation.' Gus looked like he was enjoying some private joke.

'How do you know all that?' asked Helen. 'I didn't know

146

you were so interested in history.'

He laughed. 'Come on. Let me take you to Vylands. All will be explained.'

# Chapter 26

The Range Rover bumped down the path through an avenue of tall lime trees. The bare branches produced an elegant silhouette against the pale grey sky, like slim ballerinas holding their arms aloft.

'There it is,' Gus said, with quiet pride. 'The family pile.'

Bright white stucco gleamed in the afternoon light. Vylands was a pleasingly square Georgian building. Six slim pillars held aloft a balcony running the length of the front of the house, framing an imposing door with a double staircase leading up to it.

'It's glorious,' said Helen. It was the sort of place you only saw on National Trust visits, or Sunday night adaptations of Jane Austen. The house looked almost too perfect to be real.

'Glad you like it.' Gus parked, then crunched round the gravel to open Helen's door. 'Leave your bag. We'll bring the stuff in later.'

As they approached, the shiny black door swung open. A middle-aged woman with shoulder-length fair hair wearing a plum-coloured dress walked out on to the steps. Her face was square as the house, but not as welcoming.

The woman's face split into a smile.

'Hello! It's been so long.' She hugged Gus tight.

'Helen, this is my sister Charlotta. Lottie, this is my friend Helen Oddfellow.'

The woman offered a cheek for air kisses. She had Gus's bright blue eyes, if not his grace.

'I rarely get to see Gus's friends from London,' she said. 'I'm glad our visits have overlapped.'

Helen was trying to place her accent. It was clipped, upper class, but didn't sound completely English.

'Charlotta and her children live in Germany,' explained Gus. 'She married into the German side of the family. Has Karl come with you, Lottie?'

She shook her head. 'Too busy. But the boys are here, somewhere. They went out to see the ponies. They will come and say hello later.'

She looked Helen up and down, apparently finding nothing to object to or particularly like in her grey jumper and jeans.

'Mama is in the drawing room. It's warmer in there. Come on through and I'll arrange some tea.'

She led them through the entrance hall with its black and white chequered floor, down a wainscoted corridor and into a big room with three tall windows on to a formal parterre garden. The room was indeed warm; Helen began to sweat. A fire was roaring away in the grate, supplementing the radiators pumping out heat from the walls. A large portrait of a man in powdered wig and silk brocade hung above the white marble fireplace. At the windows hung swagged duck-egg blue curtains, which matched the silk panels on the walls. Three primrose-yellow sofas faced the fire, around a coffee table laden with silver-framed photographs. A baby grand piano sat by the window, lid open and music on the stand.

In an armchair pulled right up to the fire sat a woman swathed in a cream pashmina, her still-dark hair arranged in an elegant chignon.

'Mama.' Gus leaned to kiss her. Helen stood back, intimidated. The woman's olive-black eyes and pronounced cheekbones showed that she had once been incredibly beautiful – and indeed still was. No question where Gus had got his looks from, if not his colouring. Helen glanced at Charlotta, who was watching, and dropped her eyes. The contrast was almost too stark.

'This is my friend Helen Oddfellow. Helen, this is my mother, Lady Maria Cumberland.'

Helen did a sort of bob with her knees. The woman turned her huge eyes on her and reached out her hands.

'Come.' Awkwardly, Helen ducked down. Lady Maria took her face in both hands and scrutinised her for an agonising minute.

'Good bones,' she remarked, letting her go. 'That's something.'

Gus smiled and rolled his eyes at Helen over his mother's head. 'Tea, Lottie?'

His sister disappeared, making a noise that Helen could only interpret as a snort.

They sat, Helen picking the sofa as far as possible from the fire. She noticed a black-and-white photograph on the table. A glamorous young woman with clouds of black hair, wearing a white trouser suit, on the arm of a fair-haired man who gazed at her with adoration. She looked a bit like Bianca Jagger.

'That's you, Lady Maria, isn't it?' Helen said, taking a closer look.

The woman smiled a sad smile, as if remembering a lost love.

'It was. And my husband, Ernest, just before we were married. Nineteen seventy-six. That was taken at the Parthenon, after a dinner to celebrate our engagement.'

'My mother is from Greece,' said Gus. 'She's related to Prince Philip, on her mother's side.'

'Ah, now he was a handsome man,' said Lady Maria. 'Much too old for me, of course. I was the baby cousin, admiring from afar. Otherwise, who knows? History might have been different, again.' She sat back in her armchair, complacently. Helen decided to wait for tea before asking any further questions. Royal connections were somewhat outside of her own family circle.

'We've been to Canterbury, at the University of Kent,' Gus said. 'Helen is looking into the history of a woman featured in a Charles Dickens novel. Nancy Love.'

There was a clatter at the door. Charlotta had returned, carrying a laden tray, and the china was in danger of sliding off.

'Let me help.' Helen jumped up from the sofa.

'I've got it,' said Charlotta, her voice tight.

Helen saw a neatly dressed woman in a navy skirt hovering behind her. She gently took the tray and piloted it to the table. Charlotta, red in the face, sat down with a thump next to her brother, as the maid set out the bone china cups.

Lady Maria laughed. 'Poor Lottie. Always the bull in the china shop, hey?'

Helen looked down, feeling bad for Charlotta. Her height often made her feel awkward and ungainly. She suspected Lady Maria had not been the most comfortable of mothers.

'Have you been back from Germany for long?' she asked.

Charlotta pressed her lips together, composing herself. 'For one week. We return to Munich in one more week and the children will go back to school. But it has been difficult to visit in the past two years, and it is important for the boys to see their English family,' she said.

Helen nodded sympathetically. 'It's been hard for everyone,' she said. 'Even in London, I didn't see my two little nieces for months. I really missed them.'

Charlotta smiled. 'I'm sure. The little ones change so quickly. Don't you want children of your own?'

Helen's sympathy drained fast. 'Perhaps one day,' she said. As if it was that simple; as if you could just wake up in the morning and decide to meet a man and get married and have kids. Maybe you could if you had pots of money and didn't mind marrying your cousin.

'How old are you?' called Lady Maria. 'Don't leave it too long. All you young women leave it too late. Why are you not married yet?'

'Mama,' remonstrated Gus. 'Don't interrogate my friend. She is an academic, like I was telling you. She does amazing research into history and literature. And she writes poetry.' He smiled at Helen, who wished he hadn't jumped to her defence in such an obvious way.

'We're not exactly intellectual in this family,' said Charlotta. She made it sound rather indecent. 'But tell us more about this Charles Dickens research. I know Gus is very interested in him, for some reason.'

'Early stages,' said Helen. She wasn't in the mood to explain it all to this prickly woman.

'I forgot to ask about the shorthand in that book,' said Gus.

'Have you found out anything more about that?'

Helen looked from his eager face to his sister's hostility. 'Not yet,' she lied. 'There's a website. I'll get in touch with the researchers.' She thought uncomfortably of the notebook in her bag with the half-deciphered message. She'd show him later when they were on their own.

'Go on,' said Lady Maria. 'Let's hear the story.' She sat back, hands folded, like a child wanting to be entertained.

'Well, I found a reference to a young woman who Dickens might have known when he was a child,' said Helen. 'I think she could have been an inspiration for Nancy in *Oliver Twist*. She was an actor, so we've been at Kent University, looking up playbills from the theatre where she worked.'

'I wanted to be an actress when I was a girl,' said Lady Maria. 'But my parents said I might as well be a prostitute and have done with it. I got married, instead. Perhaps that was a mistake.'

Helen caught Gus's eye and couldn't help but laugh. 'I'm sure you'd have been a great success as an actress,' she said.

'Wasn't Nancy in *Oliver Twist* a prostitute?' asked Charlotta, distaste in her voice.

'You see?' said Gus. 'That's what I thought. But apparently not. This Nancy Love that Helen's been researching was brought up in a pub, though. And we've discovered that she was the mistress of someone in the royal family. You can see how the confusion arose.'

'Which someone?' Lady Maria sat upright, attention caught by the royal reference.

'The Duke of Sussex. He was one of George III's sons,' said Helen. 'At least, Gus thinks it was him. We found a letter that suggested as much. He'd have been fifty by the time of their affair, although that didn't seem to worry her too much.'

'Ooh. He's one of ours,' said Charlotta.

'Augustus was younger,' said Gus. 'The sixth son, between Ernest and Adolphus.'

Helen looked between them, confused. What did Charlotta mean, one of ours?

Lady Maria leaned back in her chair. 'He hasn't told you, has he? My little prince. Gus, you are a naughty boy.'

'Told me what?' Helen looked between the two siblings, who were laughing at some private joke.

'Gus, you explain,' said Charlotta. 'I get muddled.'

Gus got to his feet and stood in front of the fireplace. 'See the old boy in the picture up there?'

Helen gazed up at the painting. A haughty aristocrat in satin breeches, his hand on the head of a faithful hound, sneered down at her over an enormous military moustache. The style was like Reynolds or Gainsborough, although the technique was not as fine.

'That's Ernest Augustus, Duke of Cumberland and King of Hanover. The fifth son of George III. The head of what became the German side of the family.'

Helen looked from the hawkish face on the portrait to Gus. Augustus Cumberland, son of Ernest.

'Wait – are you telling me he's your great-grandfather or something?'

'He's our father's great-great-great-great uncle,' said Charlotta, counting on her fingers. 'And he should have been King of England, never mind Hanover.'

'The Duke was robbed of his rightful position,' said Lady Maria, 'by that scheming woman.' She looked at Helen, eyes shining. 'And instead of being a cousin of the monarch, my

154

poor husband is left to struggle in obscurity. No wonder the poor man has his difficulties.'

There was an awkward pause.

'Gosh,' said Helen.

'Come on,' said Gus. 'I could do with a walk. I'll show you around, before it gets too dark.'

# Chapter 27

Helen was relieved to get out of the stuffy sitting room.

'I can't believe you didn't tell me you're royal,' she teased him. 'I suppose that's how you knew about the Duke of Whatsit. And what did your mother mean about "that scheming woman"?'

Gus laughed. 'We're not royal. Although my mother and Charlotta would love it if we were. She means Victoria's mother.'

He strode across the smooth dark-green lawn towards a beech hedge. Helen was having trouble keeping up with his pace or the conversation.

'What – Queen Victoria?'

'Yeah. There was a rumour about her legitimacy, whether she was truly her father's child.'

Helen stopped. 'You're telling me that Queen Victoria was illegitimate? That'd disinherit half the royalty of Europe.'

He grinned. 'I know. But it was just a rumour, no proof. Anyway, it's a long time ago. My family is a bit mad when it comes to the whole royalty thing. My father became obsessed with it. Claimed he was the rightful heir to the throne. Which wouldn't even be true if old Ernest Augustus had been made King. Most of the titles and so on were revoked during the first world war.'

'Your poor father,' said Helen. 'Can't the doctors do anything?'

He shrugged. 'He's on medication that keeps him stable, most of the time. But every now and again he stops taking it and things get a bit out of hand. Everyone around here knows about him, so the police usually pick him up and bring him back without too much damage done. Then we call the hospital.'

Helen reached for his hand. 'That must be so tough.'

They passed through a gap in the hedge at the end of the formal garden, then climbed over a stile into a field. The ground was lumpy with tussocky grass. Gus looked at her feet.

'Are you OK in those boots, or do you want to borrow some wellingtons? It's pretty muddy down by the river.'

Helen had changed into her hiking boots. 'These are fine.' She felt comfortable in her old boots, which had seen her through worse terrain than this.

She lengthened her stride, relaxing as her arms swung loose, unlocking the tense muscles in her shoulders. Even on a chilly, grey day, she always felt better on the move.

'This all used to be sheep,' said Gus, gesturing around the field. 'Nature's lawn-mowers. They eat everything down to the ground. So, I sold them, brought in a few ponies, let the hedgerows grow out. Next year I'm going to start work on a wildflower meadow, on the far side of the river where it's mostly chalk. And I'm getting permission for some beavers, to sort the river out.'

They strolled down to the water's edge, where a few scruffy-looking piebald ponies stood, fetlock-deep in water.

'What needs sorting out?' The river looked all right to Helen. It flowed along the valley bottom, carving deep channels in the chalky soil.

'Too straight and too fast,' said Gus. 'It was straightened in my grandfather's time, the idea being to stop these fields from flooding. The water just gets dumped on the village downstream. This is a water meadow; it should flood.

'Beavers would create dams and islands, make it meander and slow down. Then it could absorb flood water and save the villagers from pumping out their basements every couple of years.'

He looked more animated, thought Helen, striding along sketching out plans, his eyes alight. He really cared about the place. And she could see it would be lovely, especially in the summer.

'That sounds great,' she said. She wished she could summon up more enthusiasm for his plans. How could beavers and wildflower meadows work as a strategy to keep the house and estate solvent? Would sheep not have been more practical?

'The neighbours aren't keen, though,' he went on. 'Farmers are obsessed with beavers and badgers. They're worried about beavers flooding their crops and badgers giving the cattle TB. Not that there's any proof that culling makes any difference.'

He launched into the benefits of older rare-breed native cattle, which apparently were better adapted to the land and had more resilience to disease. Helen's mind wandered back to the day's discoveries. The sky turned mauve as the sun dipped behind the wooded hills. Gus stopped talking, took her hand, and pointed.

'Look.' His voice softened. A cloud of starlings swirled high in the sky, shifting and swelling. 'A murmuration. They roost in the west woods.'

Helen watched as the chattering birds settled briefly on the meadow, then lifted again as one, soared into the air like smoke and disappeared into the trees.

'How beautiful,' she said, enchanted.

'It is. I love it here.'

He pulled her closer, smoothed her hair away from her face. Helen tried to banish the memory of his mother grasping her cheeks. He was going to kiss her. She tried to un-tense her jaw, relax into it. He was handsome, kind, cared about wildlife and his family. And he liked her. What more did she want?

Richard. But Richard was dead.

Helen reached her arms up around his neck, pulled him closer. Don't you dare spoil it, she told herself. She kissed him back with determination. She would make a success of this, would not throw away another chance of happiness.

Lady Maria's voice trilled in her head: 'Don't leave it too long!'

Gus was the one to break away. 'Damn,' he said. 'I've been wanting to do that all day.'

She laughed, a little shakily. 'That's good, then.'

He held her close, warm against the chilly afternoon. 'It's getting dark. Come on, I'll walk you back to the house and take your bag up to your room. You'll want to get changed for dinner.'

Her room was lovely: a well-proportioned cube papered in delicately patterned eau-de-Nil. Russet silk curtains hung at the four-poster bed. Gus pulled the matching window swags shut, set Helen's bag down and took her in his arms again.

'Don't let my family scare you off,' he said. 'I'm honestly quite sane.'

This time, his kiss was deeper, more purposeful. Helen began to worry about whether there was a lock on the door. His hands slipped under her jumper.

'Wait.' She didn't want to get all sweaty again. She pulled the polo-neck over her head, flung it on the bed. She'd brought her fancy silk knickers and camisole, but they were still in her overnight case, ready to change into for the evening. Never mind. Her everyday cotton would have to do.

Gus circled her waist with his big hands, rested his forehead against hers. 'I knew you'd be lovely,' he said. 'I wanted you the first time I saw you, when you rescued me from that boring old professor.'

Helen closed her eyes and pressed her mouth to his. After two years of hibernation, her body was coming back to life, nerves tingling and senses expanding. It seemed to know what to do, even if she wasn't sure. She unbuttoned his shirt, ran her hand over his firm chest and stifled the voice of caution in her head.

# Chapter 28

Helen felt sure the whole family knew exactly why she didn't arrive till ten minutes after the dinner gong, face bare of make-up and her hair still damp from the shower.

It had been nice. Better than nice, good. She'd worried she might have forgotten how, but Gus was pleasingly ardent, if conventional. That was OK. Helen was quite conventional about these things herself.

Somehow Gus managed to look cool and relaxed, smiling at her across the drawing room as she gulped down a gin and tonic before dinner. At least Crispin would be cheering her on, she thought.

Helen realised her velvet trouser suit was both too glamorous and not conventional enough. Lady Maria, clad in a well-cut dark green wool dress which displayed a dramatic ruby necklace, looked at her in surprise, then declared her outfit 'very original'. Helen didn't think that was a compliment.

Charlotta, who didn't seem to have changed her clothes, avoided looking at Helen at all. She monopolised her brother, reminiscing about childhood holidays in the Black Forest, laughing extravagantly at everything he said. Helen was left with Charlotta's sons, typical teenagers with baggy jeans who were inseparable from their phones even at the dinner table. The elder, Hans-Karl, deigned to lift his eyes long enough to answer her questions. He was studying science and languages at boarding school, he said in precise but accented English. He planned to move to England and enrol in Sandhurst after school. There was no point in university. There was no point in studying literature or history. He would become an officer, then later a politician like his father, or a diplomat.

He might struggle with diplomacy, thought Helen, bristling at his lordly sense of entitlement and his dismissal of the main interests of her life.

The dining room was gloomy and formal. Helen was almost relieved that Lady Maria's exquisite taste had lapses into heavy Victorian gothic. The panelled walls were lined with dark oil paintings, bloody hunting scenes featuring dead deer and partridges mixed in with more portraits of ancestors, all men and all looking stern. She could barely move her heavy mahogany chair, uncomfortable with carving that dug into her back.

Gus grinned at her across the gleaming table. 'Hope you like venison,' he said. Helen took her eyes off the painting of a butchered stag that hung opposite her and swallowed. 'It's the best meat, ecologically. They live natural lives and need to be culled. It's very lean and healthy.'

'Sounds lovely,' she said. She supposed it was too late to pretend to be vegetarian. She turned to Charlotta, seated on her left, determined to take some part in the conversation. 'Hans-Karl was telling me he would like to follow in his father's footsteps and become a politician,' she said. 'Has your husband been involved in politics for long?'

She caught a flicker of unease from Gus across the table.

'For most of his life,' said Charlotta. 'He was a representative for the CDU for many years, until he began to have serious misgivings about its direction after the Syria crisis. Now he is quite senior within Alternative für Deutschland. But it will be a long struggle to power, I think.'

Helen tried to remember what she knew of German politics. Wasn't the AfD very right-wing? Anti-immigrant? How did that fit with his English wife and children?

'Forgive my ignorance,' she began. 'The CDU is the Christian Democrats, is that right? Angela Merkel's party?'

'No politics at the dinner table,' said Gus, forced jollity in his voice. He was looking anxious.

Hell, thought Helen. I've put my foot in it again.

'Don't be silly, Gus,' said Lady Maria. 'Your father talks politics all the time. We should be proud of Karl's achievements. Someone had to challenge that ridiculous Merkel woman. It's important to stand for what you believe in, Helen, isn't it?'

Helen smiled, awkwardly. 'Of course,' she said.

'Karl is just saying what everyone in Germany thinks,' said Lady Maria. 'There are limits to what a country can do, how many outsiders it should have to accept. It's a pity no-one in England is allowed to say the same. If only your father had been able to continue his political career, Gus.'

Helen took a swig of red wine to wash down the bloody venison.

'We don't take that many refugees, really,' she began. 'And we are quite a rich country…'

'Ha! They'd like us to think that, yes,' said Lady Maria. 'It's all draining away. My husband says that too much charity will finish this country off. You don't become rich by giving it away, Helen.'

Helen remembered her son saying exactly the same thing, as they'd passed under London Bridge and she'd dropped a coin in a beggar's cup. She glanced at Gus, who was tackling his meal and keeping out of the conversation, looking embarrassed.

'No,' she said, wondering if she might have made a bad mistake. 'I don't suppose you do.'

# Chapter 29

The Sunday morning train to Rochester took just over an hour. Helen stared out of the window, barely noticing the passing fields. Gus had offered to drive her, but she'd preferred to travel alone. She wanted time to think.

Gus had seemed nicer, more relaxed in the countryside than in London, especially when he talked about the estate. But much as Helen applauded his efforts, this was not her world. She could not get enthusiastic about beavers, no matter how excellent their flood management potential.

And the rest of the Cumberland family was a complete nightmare. How much of their obnoxious political outlook did Gus share? He'd told her afterwards that he had no interest in politics; that running the business and conservation of the estate took up all his energy.

'Except the energy I intend to devote to you,' he'd told her, back in her bedroom after the seemingly endless dinner was over. 'You and the quest for Nancy Love.'

How did she feel about Gus himself? That was a question she wasn't quite ready to look at in daylight.

The train pulled into the station and Helen jumped up,

almost forgetting her overnight bag. Right, she told herself. Focus. She needed to know where the Robert Mudie book had come from, and better still, where it was now. She checked her watch: half past eleven. When she'd first visited, the bookseller had said they were open on Sundays. They should be open now.

She walked down the High Street, which looked drabber and more deserted than on the sunny Saturday of a week ago. There was litter in dirty puddles, abandoned beer cans and fast food wrappers from the night before. A brisk wind whipped her hair around her face.

The bookshop, as before, had the closed sign on the door. Helen pushed against it and it opened. But the lights were off and no-one seemed to be in the shop. Maybe it was closed this time.

'Hello?' she called. 'Anyone here?'

Nothing, for a moment. Then the door from the back opened and the girl appeared, swathed in a baggy sweater, her feet bare. Her eyes were crusted, her face unfocused. She looked like she'd just woken up.

'I'm sorry. I thought the shop was open and I pushed the door…'

'S'alright.' The girl rubbed her face. 'Give me a minute.' She switched on the lights and flipped the sign on the door.

'I was hoping to talk to your dad,' said Helen. 'I was here last week and bought a book. Do you remember? You sold it to me.'

'We don't do refunds,' she said flatly.

'No, it's not that. I wanted to know more about it. You see – it's rather strange, but someone stole the book from my hotel room, the night I'd bought it. And I'm wondering why.'

The girl perched on the edge of the cash desk. She looked awful, as if she hadn't eaten or slept for ages.

'He's not here.'

'Do you know what time he'll be back? I have to return to London, but I can go for a coffee and come back in an hour.'

'No.' The girl stared at the floor.

'That's a pity. I wanted to talk to him. I don't suppose you know anything about the book, do you? Your dad said it came from a big house clearance…'

Helen tailed off. The girl was trying not to cry.

'Are you OK? Is there something I can help with?'

She shook her head violently and wiped her nose on her jumper. 'Stupid.'

'It's not stupid. Come on, what's the matter?'

The girl rubbed her face again and looked over Helen's shoulder. 'I thought it was him when I heard the door open just now. I've been waiting for him since yesterday morning.'

'You mean… your dad? You don't know where he is?'

The girl went to the front of the shop and looked out through the window at the street. 'I got up yesterday, about this time. He wasn't here. And usually he opens at ten, so that was weird. So, I just opened up and ran the shop. But he hasn't come back.'

Helen joined her in the window. 'That's worrying for you. Is that something he's done before – disappeared for a day or two?'

She shook her head. 'Not without telling me. It's just the two of us. He always tells me where he's going. But then I found this stupid letter last night and I'm really worried.' She turned to Helen. 'Sorry. Shouldn't tell you all this. It's not your problem.'

Helen found a pack of tissues in her bag and passed them over. 'That's all right. What did the letter say?'

The girl pulled it from the pocket of her baggy cardigan, crumpled as if she'd been holding it all night. 'That we've got money problems. Well, I knew that. I'm not stupid, and I've been working in the shop since I was twelve. That he's sorry. That I'd be better off without him, which is crap, and he knows it.' Her face crumpled. 'That I won't see him again.'

Hell. It sounded like a suicide note. 'May I see?' asked Helen. She took the crumpled paper and read, 'Dear Sophie. You probably know that the shop hasn't been making money for some time. I've tried to hide the extent of the problems from you, but I can't do that anymore. I'm so sorry. I've done stupid things, taken out loans I can't pay back. I didn't want to have to write this letter, but I think you will be better off without me now. I'm going away and you won't see me again. Be happy, my best girl. All my love, Dad.' Three kisses.

Helen raised her eyes to the pale-faced girl. 'Sophie, have you called the police? You should report him missing. Show them this letter.'

She shook her head. 'I thought he'd come back. But he hasn't. And I don't want to go to the police. He might be in trouble. I want to be here when he gets back.'

'I'm so sorry.' Helen put her hand on the girl's arm. 'I think it's time to call them. Would you like me to help?'

Sophie nodded, took back the letter. Helen called Sarah Greenley.

'Are you all right?' The policewoman always sounded nervous when Helen called out of the blue.

'I'm fine. But I'm with a young woman who needs to report a missing person. Can you tell us who to speak to?' Helen turned to Sophie. 'How old are you, Sophie?'

'Sixteen.'

'She's sixteen and her dad's been missing more than twenty-four hours. He's left a note, which is a bit concerning. I wondered if someone could come here? She doesn't want to leave the home, in case he comes back.'

'Right. Give me the name and address and I'll pass it on to my colleagues in Rochester. We should be able to send someone round.'

Helen finished the call, satisfied it was in capable hands. 'Let's make a cup of tea or coffee, shall we? While we wait for them to arrive.'

The girl led through to the back room. It was full of junk: dirty mugs and piles of paper, cardboard boxes stacked under the table and around the walls. An empty pizza box balanced on top of the detritus on the kitchen table.

'It's a bit of a mess,' said Sophie. 'Neither of us is much good at clearing up.' She turned a watery smile to Helen. 'I'll find some clean cups. Might be best not to look too closely. I don't think there's any milk.'

They sipped the black instant coffee from chipped mugs, sitting on creaky old mismatched kitchen chairs.

'I found the letter on the table,' said Sophie. 'That's why I didn't see it till last night. Usually, Dad leaves me notes taped to the fridge, so I'll see them straight away. So that was the first weird thing.'

Helen sat up. 'What else was weird?'

'Well, he never calls me Sophie. Not since I was little, before my mum left. Unless it's in front of teachers, and half the time he forgets even then.'

'No? What does he call you?'

'Wiz.' She looked half embarrassed, half proud.

'As in wizard? Harry Potter?'

The girl shook her head. 'It's stupid. Wiz, short for wisdom. That's what Sophie means, wisdom. According to Dad, anyway. He said that's why he picked it. That when I was born, I looked like I knew everything.'

Helen smiled, touched. 'It's not stupid. That's really lovely.' Her own father had named her for Helen of Troy, his love of the classics outweighing the rather ambiguous nature of her namesake. Could have been worse; he'd originally wanted to call her Athena.

The girl took the letter from her pocket again. 'So why does he call me Sophie? I mean, if he's saying he won't see me again, why would he use a name he never uses?'

Helen re-read it over her shoulder. *I've done stupid things. I didn't want to have to write this letter.* She thought for a moment about that last sentence. He hadn't wanted to get to the point where he had to write it? Or he literally didn't want to write it, but was being forced to do so?

'It does seem odd,' she agreed. 'Your dad says in the letter that he's taken out loans. Do you know who from? I hate to ask, but was he involved with anything dodgy?'

The girl shrugged, hunched in her chair. 'Don't know. I mean, it looked like we'd have to sell up last year. The first lockdown, Dad took out one of those government loans. But he was really worried about how to pay it back. And the rates and stuff were frozen for a while, but he was worried about how we'd pay them afterwards. Thing is, we've got a massive mortgage for the shop and the flat above it. If we sold the shop, we'd have nowhere to live. And I know we're behind on the mortgage payments.'

She sighed. 'Mostly, I know all the dealers he worked with. I've known them since I was little. They're all old blokes with beards and dress like they're from the past.

'But there were some new ones, the last couple of years. Younger than the usual dealers. They'd leave a load of boxes, then pick stuff up a few weeks later. And there was more money going in and out through the till. Dad said there was a big collector and he was getting stuff in for him specially. He looked quite cheerful about it at first. But he's been jumpy in the last month or so.'

The shop doorbell rang. Helen went through to find a hefty policeman standing in the doorway, looking unfriendly.

'PC Dangerfield. What's up, then? Some bloke gone walkabout?'

Helen was glad she'd stayed with Sophie. The policeman was brusque, dismissive of the length of time the bookseller had been missing. He read the note, grunted, and folded it into his notebook.

'That's mine!' Sophie was distraught.

'Can't you take a photo of it?' asked Helen. 'It's important to her.'

He looked annoyed. 'It's evidence,' he said, as if that settled the matter.

'So, shouldn't you put it in a proper evidence bag, in case you need to do forensics on it? Not just fold it up in your notebook?'

He rounded on her. 'Been watching too much *CSI*, have we? This,' he brandished the note, 'is what I need to talk to my boss and decide whether you and your friend are wasting our time, or whether there's actually anything to investigate. All right?'

Helen swallowed. 'Sophie is sixteen. Her father has been missing for over twenty-four hours, and it's out of character. We are not wasting your time.' She considered dropping Sarah Greenley's name, but the man was already on his way to the door.

'Someone will call you later today,' he told Sophie. 'Let us know if he turns up, won't you?' He slammed the door shut behind him.

# Chapter 30

'I'm sorry, that didn't go well,' said Helen. Sophie threw herself onto the leather sofa by the till and curled up, wrapping her arms around her knees. Helen went into the back room to make more coffee. A minute later, the girl joined her.

'He was a dickhead,' Sophie said. 'Lev says you can't trust any of them.' She opened the table drawer and pulled out a ledger. 'You wanted to know about the book you bought, didn't you? It should be in here.'

'Oh, that's kind.' Helen brought her chair around the table to look, touched that the girl would take the trouble when she had so much else to worry about.

'S'alright. These are the house clearances we've done in the past couple of weeks.' She showed Helen pages of titles, each painstakingly written out by hand. The sales were all dated, with the name and address of the seller. Didn't they have a computer for that?

'I know,' said Sophie, although Helen hadn't spoken. 'Mad, isn't it? I've been on at him to get a laptop for years. But he says he prefers it this way.'

She flipped over the pages. 'Here it is. Look.' She frowned, read for a moment. 'It wasn't a clearance, though. It came from an auction, a big house in the countryside. He bought quite a bit of stuff. I don't think we've sold it all. There were boxes all over the place, not even unpacked.'

Helen looked over her shoulder at the list of titles and their former address. She gasped.

'Cobham Hall? The book came from Cobham Hall?'

She sat back down. She'd not been back to the hall since the funeral of Lady Joan, the last owner and final descendant of the aristocratic Brooke family.

'Yeah. You know it?'

Helen was adrift in memory. The beautiful library at Cobham with its tall windows, gleaming leather-bound books on every wall, acres of mahogany shelving. She hated to think of it empty, the books all scattered.

'I do,' she said. 'I used to know it very well.'

'Cool.' The girl got up and dragged a box across the floor. 'We both went. The auction was in this big white room with all gold stuff on the ceiling and walls. Massive. It was packed, loads of people.'

The Gilt Hall, thought Helen. She'd read in the press about the sale of the hall to a luxury hotel chain which had promised a sensitive restoration and conversion of the building. She'd wondered what it would be like as a hotel. Her own stay had been brief and uncomfortable. Lady Joan had not been one for modern luxuries like en suite bathrooms and central heating.

'He didn't get all the books. There were lots of collectors there. Some of the books were ancient,' said Sophie. 'But he got quite a lot of stuff. As far as I can tell, we've sold six boxes to a collector, including the one your book was in. But there's another one here.'

174

Wow. Helen woke from her reverie. Treasures from the great library of Cobham Hall, stuffed into boxes in the back room of a Rochester bookshop. What else might she find? And if the Robert Mudie book had come from Cobham Hall, how had it got there?

Lady Joan's family had bought Cobham Hall in the middle of the nineteenth century, around about the time that Dickens had bought Gads Hill. They were near neighbours; only a couple of miles separated Cobham Hall from Dickens' more modest country house. Would the two families have known each other, perhaps even socialised?

Helen had checked the inventory taken for the sale of Dickens' books after his death, as Hester had suggested. To her excitement, it had included *London and Londoners*, although Mudie's name as author was omitted, making it hard to spot. So the book – if it really was Dickens' copy – had been at Gads Hill in 1870, when Dickens died.

Albert Brooke, Lady Joan's grandfather, had collected most of the books that adorned the library. But – she carried out a few quick calculations – Albert would have been a child in 1870. Too young to have been at the sale of the Gads Hill library. Maybe Albert's father, the man who'd restored the family's fortunes, had bought a few mementoes of his illustrious neighbour.

'Let's take a look,' she said, helping Sophie rip off the tape securing the cardboard box. 'Sophie, you are an absolute star.'

The girl looked up and grinned. 'Yeah. You can call me Wiz, if you like.'

Helen's heart squeezed a bit. 'All right. Wiz, you're a star.'

She unpacked a handsome set of leather-bound classic works of literature with gold lettering. Wiz snorted.

'I told him not to bother with those. No-one buys that stuff except posh hotels wanting a backdrop – and they buy leather spines by the metre. Doesn't matter what they are.'

Wiz lifted out a pile of prints. 'These are good,' she said. 'They look pretty old.'

She laid them out on the sofa. They were monochrome engravings of characters from Dickens, pictured in scenes from his novels.

'They're nice,' said Helen. She recognised Fagin in his Newgate cell; Oliver being pulled along by Mr Bumble. 'Do you think these are originals?'

Wiz shrugged. 'I don't know much about prints. But people like them. There are a few collectors I could call. Book illustrations are quite popular, even the more recent ones.'

There were maybe twenty of them in varying condition. They ranged from the earliest characters from *The Pickwick Papers* to Dickens' later autobiographical novels – Mr Murdstone from *David Copperfield*, Miss Havisham from *Great Expectations*. Different artists, different styles, from the rather cramped early works to the freer, more artistic styles of the mature novels.

Could these, like the Mudie book, have come from Gads Hill? Perhaps the novelist had kept his own gallery of illustrations. In which case, they could be valuable. Maybe she should ask Hester to look.

She lined them up. 'Hang on to them for a bit, will you? I'd like to show them to my friend at the Dickens Museum.' She took a photo. 'They might be worth more than you'd get from an average collector.'

'All right. But I can't set them aside for long. We really need the money,' said Wiz. Her voice broke. 'I do, anyway.'

176

'Of course. I'm sorry.' Helen gave herself a kick. The poor girl was facing up to an unknown future, and she was getting excited about a few engravings.

Helen leaned over the almost-empty box. A man's face stared up at her, cool grey eyes with an amused glint, as if he was laughing at himself. He wore a white silk turban, a red tunic, and a quantity of gold braid.

'Oh.' Carefully, Helen lifted it from the box.

'Yeah, Dad bought that painting, too. Don't know why; we don't sell paintings. Maybe he just liked it.'

Helen set it on the sideboard, propped against the wall. 'He has good taste, your dad. This is Sir Albert Brooke de Cobham, painted just before his return to England from serving in India.'

'Do you know him, then?'

Helen laughed. 'I'm not that old. I knew his granddaughter.' She paused for a moment, remembering. The painting had been in the sitting room. She'd remarked on it, in a desperate attempt at conversation with Lady Joan, the night that Richard died. 'And his great-grandson.'

There was a family resemblance. She could see it now: the same intelligent features, the air of amused curiosity with the world. It could have been Richard himself in fancy dress.

There was a rap on the back door, making them both jump. Wiz leapt to her feet, hope lighting up her face for a second. But the pale face outside was not her father's.

Helen pulled the door open.

'Who's there?' she asked. If there were dodgy characters coming and going from the shop, she wanted them to know that the girl was not alone.

'Mind your own business. I'm looking for Wiz.' Helen

recognised him now: the lanky boy who had been reading comics with Wiz on Helen's first visit.

'In here, Lev,' the girl called. 'We're going through some boxes.'

He pushed past Helen. 'He's still not back?' he asked.

Wiz shook her head, looking away.

Tentatively, the boy put a hand on her arm.

'Wiz, they found something down by the river.'

Her head went up, her face frozen.

'What?'

'I think you should come.'

# Chapter 31

Paxton drove north towards the farm. Flat fields on either side the dull brown of ploughed earth patchworked with shining rows of plastic polytunnels. A church spire rose above the fields, guarded by skeletal trees. On the horizon, he could see red lights from the cranes and gantries of the deep-water London Gateway port on the far side of the river.

Now and then a lorry thundered past, going to or from the aggregate yards that clustered along the Thames. There was little other traffic. Beyond the farm was nothing but marshland, crisscrossed by drainage channels.

He took a sharp turn off the main road. You could see the farm in the distance, a dispiriting collection of sheds and metal barns, exposed on all sides. Hiding in plain sight. Better like this, Guren had told him once, when he asked. We can see if anyone tries to leave. And we can see anyone who comes long before they get here. Everyone can see us, so no-one thinks there is anything secret. You see?

He pulled into the entrance and went to open the metal gate. A security camera whirred into life from the top of a pole. He unlocked the padlock, pushed the gate aside and drove through.

Guren and two other men stood at the door of the bungalow. Paxton hadn't seen the others before, as far as he could remember. They were squat, ugly blokes with close-cropped hair, boxers' noses and mean little eyes. Paxton's eyes went to their jacket pockets. Were they carrying? Probably.

He opened the door and Cooper jumped out, barking.

'Stay,' he yelled. He could already hear the farm dogs set up an answering volley. They were usually chained up, but not always. He didn't fancy Cooper's chance in a fight with five security dogs. Not yet anyway.

He jumped out into the muddy yard and fixed the dog's lead. Then he remembered. The stupid book. He found it in the glove compartment and walked to where the men stood in silence, smoking cigarettes.

'There you go. All done.' He held up the book.

Guren took it. 'And the money?'

Paxton reached into his jacket and pulled out his wallet. 'Two hundred and fifty quid. That's all he had.' He put the notes into Guren's outstretched hand.

'You're shitting with me.' Guren closed his hand around Paxton's wrist.

He met the man's eyes without flinching. 'You want to ask him?'

The two other men closed in. Paxton held steady. Guren hesitated a moment and Paxton withdrew his arm, dug his hands into his jacket pockets.

'What would happen if I did?' said Guren.

'He's not very talkative now.' Paxton curled his fingers around the knife handle. Three of them, one of him. It had been stupid, keeping back some of the money. Not even enough to make the risk worthwhile, but he'd had enough of doing Guren's dirty work.

'OK. It's done, yes? No more trouble with Mister Bookseller?'

'It's done.' Paxton's jaw clenched. It hadn't been as easy as he'd hoped. He had a flashback, a memory of the struggle, the man thrashing in the murky water. He banished it.

Guren nodded. 'Come inside.'

Paxton followed warily as the three men walked into the pebble-dashed building. The lino on the floor was yellowed and dirty, the kitchen almost as chaotic as the bookshop in Rochester.

A man he had not seen before was sitting at the table. He was older than the others, about the same age as Paxton. He wore a smart, expensive-looking dark suit and steel-rimmed glasses, his grey hair neatly cut and brushed back from his forehead. Guren slapped the book down on to the table in front of him. He barely glanced at it.

'Who's this?' asked Paxton, swivelling to Guren.

'You don't need to know,' said the man. His voice was clipped, business-like. He looked almost amused. 'Now, take his knife away from him and disappear.'

There were too many of them to resist. One held his arms – unnecessarily, Paxton protested – while the other fished the knife from his pocket. Guren smiled.

'Don't worry, Gary. You get it back later.'

They headed out the door, leaving Paxton with the stranger.

The man picked up the book, flicked through it. Found a newspaper cutting folded in the back. Read it, raised an eyebrow. Then he reached for a briefcase and stowed it away.

'Well done, Mr Paxton.'

Paxton's eyes snapped back to the man's face. He'd been going by his old name, Gary Street. He didn't think Guren or any of his gang knew about his involvement with politics. Their whole relationship was strictly business.

'What do you want?' he asked.

The man raised his eyebrows again, his smile mocking. 'Let's talk about what you want. I hear you have been talking to Sebastian Johansson from the British Patriot Party. He has tempted you, hasn't he? Offered you money to get away from this horrible business you have got yourself mixed up with?'

Paxton was confused, now. 'I didn't tell him anything. I said I was working, earning money. That I wanted to set up a gym. That's all.'

The man tapped his fingers on his briefcase. 'The good captain does not know where the money he was offering you comes from. He is very useful, in many ways, but he is not as clever as he thinks he is.'

He opened the briefcase again, turned it so that Paxton could see the contents. It was stacked with twenty pound notes, neatly packed in brick-like parcels. He picked one out and threw it across the table. Paxton caught it deftly, weighed the heft in his hands. About half a kilo, surprisingly heavy given how light the plastic notes were individually.

'Count it later,' said the man. 'Ten thousand. For your assistance so far. Enough to put towards your gym, yes?'

Paxton nodded. 'Yeah. It's a start.'

'I have two jobs for you.' The man thought for a minute. 'Three, maybe. The first is to finish the job you have started. There is one more box in the bookshop. It was not part of the original deal, but now we want it. You need to get it tonight, before it gets sold off. Get it and bring it back here.'

182

Shit. The very last thing Paxton wanted to do was go anywhere near Rochester, never mind the bloody bookshop. Far too risky.

'Lot of boxes in that shop,' he said. 'How do I know which one?'

'There's a painting in it,' said the man. 'A man with a turban. You'll find it.' His voice left no room for argument. Paxton swallowed. He'd have to find a way. The man's daughter would be there on her own – or maybe she'd have gone to stay with friends, family. Yeah. The place was probably empty.

He nodded. 'What else?'

'Keep talking to Captain Jonnie. Let him think you're going to work with him. Take his money if he offers it. Get to know his friends, his associates in the BPP. There's a leak in his organisation, somewhere. Find it. Then fix it.'

Paxton considered. He'd wanted to get away from Guren and his mates, their dirty business. He'd seen the BPP as a way out. But if he could believe what this smooth operator was saying, there was no choice between the two. They were one and the same. And Jonnie was no more boss of his operation than Guren was of the gang running the farm.

He closed his hands around the notes. If the dosh for the BPP was coming from the organised crime group, then he might as well take from both.

'Yeah,' he said. 'I can do that.' He put the money in his jacket pocket. 'Better get going.'

The man leaned back and rapped on the window. 'One more thing.'

Guren pulled the door open. 'Boss?'

The man stood, stretched. 'Give Mr Paxton his knife back. Then I believe you have a job for him?'

Paxton followed Guren out the door. The man was morose, sulking. Guren liked to be in charge, Paxton thought. He hated being ordered around by the stranger, just as much as Paxton hated being ordered around by Guren. Paxton wondered who the besuited stranger took his orders from. How pissed off he'd been at being sent to a muddy farm in the middle of nowhere to get his shiny shoes dirty.

They crossed the farmyard, went down a potholed path beside a scraggly hedge. In the field beyond, Paxton could see a handful of people, backs bent to the claggy earth. He had no idea what happened on farms in January. Planting potatoes, maybe? Picking cabbages? He was too far away to see if the group included the last lot of migrants he'd ferried here.

They arrived at a row of static caravans, stained green with algae. The workers' accommodation, he supposed. Drab curtains were drawn across the windows. The ground was littered with a few signs of life – a tennis ball; a couple of empty beer cans; a pair of mud-caked boots lined up beside an entrance.

Guren stopped outside one of the caravans. Paxton could see condensation misting the inside of the windows. Someone was in there.

'She's been giving us a pain. Won't let anyone near her; screams her head off if you open the door, even. She keeps asking for you. So, here you are. Sort her out, Gary.'

Guren unlocked the door and Paxton walked up the steps. Curled in a corner, looking up at the two men like a terrified stray dog, was Aisha. She rubbed her eyes, swollen with tears. Dredged up a smile from somewhere.

'Hello, Gary,' she said. 'Have you come to help me?'

Paxton's chest hurt. What had the arseholes done to her?

'All yours,' said Guren, with a smirk. He closed the door behind him.

# Chapter 32

Helen ran to keep up with the teenagers, who glided ahead on their skateboards. She hadn't run for ages, but the action felt good after all the time spent inside. Lev had refused to say what he had seen – only that Wiz should come. The girl had turned to Helen in mute appeal, and she'd gone with them.

It was a dirty sort of afternoon, the light casting a sickly glow over the cathedral as they made their way along the High Street. Lev turned down a quiet side-street lined with pretty old houses, winter clematis splashing red and pink. Helen caught up as the teenagers carried their boards down steps at the far end, which took them to the busy main road.

They crossed beside the train station and went through a tunnel under the rail tracks. The land beyond was all new developments, boxy blocks of flats and brand-new open spaces, the newly laid turf still a vivid green. The Medway river, a wide ribbon that curled around the peninsular, was the colour of milky coffee, its opaque depths mirroring the heavy sky. Near the shore, mud flats lay exposed by the tide, a dull gleam like pewter streaked with green weed. It smelt of salt and decay.

The land on either side of the river stretched flat and wide, the wind whipping down the shallow valley, blowing Helen's hair into her eyes. Ahead of her, Wiz and Lev had reached a long wooden hoarding with brightly coloured pictures showing families walking hand-in-hand along an idealised riverside, people cycling, roller-skating, and laughing in the sunshine. Rochester Riverdale Park, according to the developers, would offer 'prestigious waterfront living'.

Helen speeded up as the teenagers turned the corner at the end of the hoarding. A padlocked chain-link gate allowed a glimpse of the site. The chain-link had been cut and was pulled half-open. Lev pulled it further.

'Come on. In here.'

A security notice outside warned against trespass, but Lev and Wiz were through before Helen could reach them. She ducked to squeeze through the gap, hoping there wouldn't be guard dogs. Inside, the ground was claggy with trenches for utilities, the foundations for new buildings pegged out.

'Wait,' she called. But the teenagers were running now, across to the low river wall. Helen sprinted the last few yards, filled with dread.

Wiz let out a piercing wail. She scrambled on to the wall, as if planning to hurl herself over.

'Stop!' Helen grabbed her jacket, then threw an arm around the girl's thin torso. She felt her ribs heaving, the racking of her sobs shuddering through her body. The girl dropped to her knees on the top of the wall, dark hair falling over her face like a shroud.

'Shit,' said Lev. 'Thought so.'

Helen looked down. A muddy bundle, the same colour as the silt surrounding it. Like a chrysalis, except that no living thing would ever emerge from it. At first, she could see nothing to identify the man. His face, abdomen and hands were puffed up, grotesque, unrecognisable. He was clothed, but the clothes were covered in the same layer of mud that coated his face. Then she saw it. A glint of silver, light flashing off glass. The dead man's spectacles, still somehow on the chain around his neck.

'Call the police,' Helen told Lev, her arms still tight around Wiz.

He backed away. 'Can't do that.'

'Don't be stupid.'

He looked around, desperate. 'They'll want to know why I was in here.'

'Why were you in here?'

He grabbed his board. Made a gesture partway between a shrug and a plea.

'I gotta go. Wiz... I'll call you. Sorry.' He ran, squeezed through the gate and was away.

Helen took a deep breath. 'OK. Wiz, we need to call the police. Can you get down from the wall? Come on, that's it. Sit down here, next to me.'

They sat on the wet ground, backs to the wall and the horror of the mud-encrusted body. Helen kept one arm around the shivering girl. With the other hand, she extracted her phone from her coat pocket and made an emergency call.

They were still sitting there, twenty minutes later, when a police car arrived, along with a red-faced man in a yellow high-vis jacket and hard hat, who unlocked the gate, tutting at the damage.

'You've got to wear one of these,' he was telling the officers in the car, waving a brace of hard hats. They drove past, headlights dazzling as they drew up to where Helen and Wiz were sitting. A middle-aged police officer got out and looked over the wall for a long minute. Then he crouched down next to them. To Helen's relief, it was not the man who had come to the shop earlier.

'I'm PC Norbury. What's happened here, then?' His voice was gentle.

'She thinks it may be her father,' said Helen. 'He's been missing for two days. Her name is Sophie.'

'All right, Sophie. Let's get you looked after,' said the policeman. He raised her up and wrapped a silver thermal blanket around her shaking shoulders. The site manager unlocked a cabin, switched on lights and turned on the heating. Wiz sat in a chair, staring into space, while he made them cups of sweet, strong tea.

Helen stepped outside to talk to the second officer, who was erecting a line of blue and white tape around the river wall.

'How long will it take to find out if it's her father?' she asked. She was clinging to a hope that it might not be, that Wiz's dad was still out there somewhere, alive.

'Well, we'll need to recover it first,' the officer said. 'The tide's coming in, so we'd better get a move on. Then we'll need DNA or dental records to identify the body.' She looked up at Helen. 'You're not the wife or something?'

Helen shook her head.

'Pity. That would speed things up. You get these washed-up bodies, from time to time, in this part of the world. Identification can be a challenge. At least we have a lead on this one.'

Helen felt she could have been less enthusiastic. 'But it might not be him? How soon would you know?' she asked.

'A day, maybe two. Depends how quickly we can get the records. Do you know who his dentist was?'

Helen shook her head. 'Sorry. I don't really know him – I only met them a week ago. But we reported him missing this morning. Your colleagues should have the details.' She hesitated. 'I suppose… I suppose it looks like suicide? If it is him, I mean. He left a note.'

The woman looked up from her notebook. 'Who knows? To be honest, drowning is quite unusual for suicides, more so than you'd think. But we don't know how he got in the river. Maybe he got drunk and fell in; maybe he jumped from the bridge. Maybe he was already dead when he went into the water. The post-mortem will tell us more. Now, can you accompany the girl back home? I might as well drop you off. We can take your statements, pick up his toothbrush for DNA; save a bit of time. Derek will stay here and see to the body.'

Wiz sat silently in the back of the police car, eyes pressed shut. Only when they arrived back at the shop did she open them.

'Thing is,' she said, 'Dad hated the water. No bloody way did he go in deliberately.'

Helen thought again of the police officer's words. Maybe someone pushed him. Maybe he was already dead. And what about Lev – how had he found the body? What had he been doing on the building site? She remembered the boy's words when he arrived at the shop: they've found something. He hadn't been alone. Who had Lev been with?

# Chapter 33

Inside the shop, Helen switched on all the lights while Wiz fetched her father's toothbrush for the policewoman. Once she'd gone, they retreated upstairs to the living room of the flat above. Helen drew the curtains on the darkness. Wiz slumped in an armchair, clutching her skateboard as if it was a teddy bear.

'Tell me about Lev,' said Helen. 'Is he your boyfriend?'

'God, no,' said Wiz. 'Why do people always have to put a label on things? It's so binary.'

Helen felt very old and wondered what that meant in practice.

The girl started to plait her dark hair into a long braid. 'I met him at the skate park,' she said. 'I used to go there on my own to practise. Some of the boys were being wankers. Giving me a hard time and that.

'Lev told them to leave me alone. He's one of the best skaters there, so they listen to him. He could see I'm good. He respects that.'

They had started to spend time together, she said. Lev had been in care; now he was in what the council called a half-way house, too old for foster parents but too young to be on his

191

own.

'It's basically a hostel. Pretty crappy. He started to come here with me, hang out. Dad doesn't mind.'

She broke off, looked stricken. Present tense, Helen noticed. She hasn't given up hope.

'He's supposed to go to college, but he doesn't bother any more. Says he can get by selling stuff for people.'

'Stuff?'

'Don't ask me. I don't get involved. I don't even smoke that shit. Rots your brain.'

Helen didn't feel she could leave her alone, not that first night. Wiz seemed to have few responsible adults in her life. She'd given the policewoman the name of an aunt in Dublin, who she said might come over. Pressed, she'd added the name and phone number of her mother.

'But she won't care about Dad,' she'd said, her voice bitter. 'And I'm not going to Ireland with her. I'm staying here, where my friends are.'

Helen ordered a pizza and tried to get Wiz to eat. The girl nibbled at half a slice, then pushed the rest away.

'I'm knackered,' she said. 'Going to bed.' She went to her bedroom, taking the skateboard with her, leaving Helen in the scruffy living room, alone.

The sight of the mud-encrusted body kept rising in her mind. Looking for distraction, she pulled out her copy of *Oliver Twist*, reading over every scene that featured Nancy, thinking about the young actress on stage; the star-struck boy watching from the gods. She hadn't told Gus about the shorthand, she remembered. She searched in her bag for her notebook, frowning. Where was it? She felt sure she'd zipped it into the inside pocket. Eventually she found it in the back section, tucked behind her laptop.

'My poor Nancy. Forgive your Charlie for a frightened, foolish boy…'

Why had he been writing to her, all those years after her death, asking for forgiveness? Perhaps the writing of *Oliver Twist* was intended to exorcise her memory as much as pay tribute to her. If so, it didn't seem to have worked. Dickens had returned to the fictional Nancy's death time and again in public readings from his works. Right at the end of his own life, he'd almost collapsed on stage while giving a dramatic reading of the murder scene. He'd performed it obsessively, ignoring the warnings of his doctors that it put too great a strain on him. A guilty conscience, perhaps?

Helen turned again to the note. 'I will give it into the safekeeping of Mr Pickwick.'

She sighed, too tired to think any more. She bedded down on the sofa, her knees bent up and her neck cricked against a cushion, a grubby-looking throw pulled over as a blanket. Despite her tiredness, she didn't expect to sleep.

She listened. She could hear no sounds, no sobbing from Wiz's room. Maybe she was asleep. Grief and worry were exhausting, after all.

The silence pressed in. Helen was about to turn the light back on and reach for her book again when she heard it. Footsteps, quiet but definite, outside the back window. Leaving the light off, she got up and looked out into the dark. She could see nothing in the shadowy yard. She waited, listened hard.

A creaking sound, a rattle. Someone was trying the handle of the door that led into the shop's back room downstairs. Helen held her breath. She was sure she'd locked it, and the front door, after the police had left.

Quietly, trying not to make any sounds or wake Wiz, she crossed to the stairs leading down to the shop, tiptoeing on bare feet. Had she remembered to lock the door at the bottom of the stairs, between the shop and the flat?

She was halfway down the stairs when she heard the glass break. The sound was muffled, as if the brick or whatever it was had been wrapped in cloth. A jangle as the pieces of glass hit the floor. Helen could see the door from the stairs into the back kitchen standing ajar. Damn. She'd forgotten.

She inched her way down. Only a few more steps, then she could lock them in, run back up the stairs and call the police.

More glass fell to the ground. Helen could hear shallow breathing. She reached the door, took hold of the handle. Close it, her brain urged. Keep safe.

She peered around the door. A slim figure in a baseball cap was squeezing through the broken pane in the back door. He landed with a thump, then groped on the shelf beside the door for the key.

'Got it,' he whispered.

Helen knew that voice. She found the light switch next to the stairs and flicked it on. Bright light flooded the room and the boy yelled.

'Lev. What the hell are you doing?'

'Nothing... I got locked out...' He was scrabbling with the key, trying to unlock the door and make his escape. Helen crossed the kitchen in two paces, grabbed his wrist. Then she saw where his panic-stricken gaze was fixed.

Staring back through the broken window, his face transfixed with shock, was Gary Paxton.

The man recovered before she did. He turned and fled. Lev

194

yanked his wrist free and pulled open the back door.

'Stop!' Wiz had appeared at the bottom of the stairs, wrapped up in a man's dressing gown. 'What's going on?'

'Sorry.' Lev flung himself out of the door, slammed it behind him, and ran.

Helen stepped forward, then swore as pain lanced through the sole of her foot.

'Shit. Careful, there's glass everywhere.' She looked down, saw bright red blood drip on to the vinyl floor. She grabbed a chair, sat down, and pulled out the shard of glass. It hurt like hell.

'Here.' Wiz, face white, passed her a roll of kitchen paper.

'Call the police.' Helen pressed a wad of paper down on the wound, teeth gritted.

'No! That was Lev. He didn't mean anything.'

'It wasn't just Lev. Did you see the man he was with?'

Wiz shook her head.

'I did. He's a vicious thug.'

Wiz sat down. 'How do you know?'

'Because I've met him.' Helen pulled aside her t-shirt and showed Wiz the puckered scars that circled her neck. 'He did this. With a lit cigarette. And he stabbed my friend to death.'

Wiz was looking bewildered.

'What's he doing here? And why is he with Lev? What was he breaking in for?'

'I don't know.' Helen thought. 'He must have wanted something. Like someone wanted the book that was stolen from my hotel room.' She remembered how she'd suspected Wiz's father of stealing the book. Had he been working for Paxton?

Her eyes lit on the box they'd been investigating earlier.

'That box. The one from Cobham Hall. You said that was the last of them?'

Wiz nodded. 'Yeah. The others all went. Dad said some bloke came to pick them up for a collector.'

They carried the box up the stairs to the living room, Helen limping on her cut foot. She made sure the downstairs door was locked.

'Listen, Wiz, I need to call the police now. We need to get the shop secured and keep you safe, especially if there's something in that box that Gary Paxton wants. We have to tell them Paxton is involved in this. It might be why your dad is missing.'

'You think that man killed Dad?' asked Wiz, eyes wide.

'I don't know. But he's incredibly dangerous. And if Lev is involved with him, he needs protecting too.'

Wiz still looked dubious. 'Can't we say it was that Paxton man who broke the window? Do we have to mention Lev?'

Helen reached for her phone. 'Sorry. I think we do.'

# Chapter 34

N ick sat up in his narrow bed in the Dover hotel, laptop propped up on his knees. He'd give it one more night, then he should head back to London. He'd clocked Paxton walking into the bail hostel at quarter to eight, well before curfew, stopping to chat to the warden on his way in.

After watching the meeting on the cliffs from the borrowed laundry van early on Saturday morning, Nick had followed Paxton's van west from Folkestone, up the motorway towards London. It had turned on to an A-road heading north, the Rochester turn. To Nick's frustration, he'd lost Paxton there, caught up in the one-way traffic entering the town.

Nick had given up, returned the laundry van to its indignant owner – along with fifty quid for the loan – and spent half of Saturday trying to source a new tyre for his vandalised bike.

Paxton had been back on time on Saturday evening. On Sunday, he'd left the hostel late in the morning, gone running along the seafront with the dog. Then he'd taken the van out after lunch, heading west on the motorway. Nick had followed for a while, careful not to get too close. It looked like he'd been heading for Rochester again, but he'd bypassed the town, gone over the bridge and north of the Medway river.

Then he'd disappeared, somewhere in the farmland leading up to the Thames estuary. The place was weird. It reminded Nick of the flatlands to the west of Liverpool, ringed by stretches of mud washed bare by the Mersey and the Dee. Deserted bleak places with no human warmth. He'd driven around for a while, then headed back to Dover.

Nick was back in the hotel room by mid-afternoon. At half past six, Amy brought up a plate of egg and chips for his dinner, then sat on his bed for a gossip. He was the only guest, she said. No point in opening the dining room.

Stake-outs were boring. But he'd made progress: a solid few hours online had advanced his knowledge considerably. He'd identified the man Paxton had met on the clifftops, for a start. Nick had grabbed a decent photograph of him as he walked back to his car. Online image searches had turned up a particularly unflattering police mugshot of an Albanian man named Guren Hasani, charged with an assault outside a nightclub in Rochester three years previously. He wasn't on the electoral roll, but the newspaper report gave his address as Gravesend.

It was an uncommon name. A search threw up a few Guren Hasanis, none of whom seemed very likely. A banker at Credit Suisse, according to a networking site which had a photograph of a sleek-looking man in his twenties with perfect teeth. Not him. Someone of the same name had presented a paper about recent advances in ophthalmic imaging at a conference in Birmingham. That Guren Hasani was also registered as an ophthalmic optician with a practice in Solihull. Companies House had a Guren Hasani named as a director of a company called Agriland, based in Leicester. But there was nothing for

Guren Hasani, night-club brawler and associate of low-life scum from Gravesend, Kent.

Since then, Nick had been delving into the finances of the British Patriot Party. As a registered political party – at least until the ban – it had been required to declare donations to the Electoral Commission. It had declared half a million in the last quarter, from company and individual donations – a huge increase on the previous three quarters. He clicked through to look at the donors list.

There were two companies listed, neither of which he'd heard of, and thirty-eight names of individuals. One was Sebastian Johansson, who had donated ten thousand quid the previous quarter. Nick frowned. Surely, as a listed candidate for the party, Captain Jonnie should be taking money out, not putting it in.

He clicked back through the four years that the party had existed. The same handful of names were repeated, ten to twenty grand here and there, every quarter until the last. Then a big increase in the number of individual donors, donating larger sums.

Nick checked out the companies. Both had bland-sounding names that didn't tell you what they did: Buckingham Property Services; Landbanking UK. Both had donated hundreds of thousands of quid. He'd go to Companies House later, do a proper search.

He moved on to searching the individual donors, grinding through tedious electoral roll lists and social media sites. Some, like Johansson, had angry rant-filled accounts that made no secret of their politics. Others, potentially more interesting, had barely any online footprint at all.

He glanced at his watch, saw to his surprise that it was after midnight. He yawned. Time for bed. Just as he was shutting down his laptop, his mobile rang.

'Helen? Are you OK?' She never rang this late unless there was something badly wrong.

'I've just seen Paxton. Right here. He tried to break in.' She spoke fast, sounding as panicked as he'd ever heard.

'What? Are you sure?'

'Yeah. He was looking right at me. He ran off when he saw me. But the girl I'm with – her father has disappeared. They've found a body. And then Paxton tries to break in tonight – I mean, he must be involved.'

Nick was already pulling on his jacket. How had he missed the man?

'That's weird – I thought he was safely under curfew. He must have snuck out. Where are you? I'm coming over. I can be in London in a couple of hours.'

'Rochester. At a bookshop on the High Street. Chapman and Daughter. Call me when you get here – we're barricaded in. The police have been, but they're treating it as a standard burglary.'

Rochester. Where Paxton had driven yesterday, and on Saturday morning. Nick didn't bother asking what on earth Helen was doing in a bookshop in Rochester with a girl whose father had disappeared. She had an uncanny knack for finding trouble wherever she was. Much like himself.

'I'm in Dover. I should be with you in an hour. Stay safe.'

He grabbed his bike helmet and scribbled a note for Amy. He felt great. Helen was in danger and she'd called him. He allowed himself, just for a second, to feel like some kind of knight in shining armour, off to rescue a damsel in distress. He imagined Helen's reaction if she'd known what he was thinking and grinned. On most of their adventures, Helen had been the one doing the rescuing.

He kick-started the bike and roared along the narrow street, up on the ramp that took lorries out of the port and on to the deserted motorway. By two o'clock, he was puttering down Rochester High Street, looking for a bookshop. He soon found it, with the lights on in the flat above the shop. A pale-faced girl looked out of the window, then Helen joined her and waved.

She let him in to the book-lined shop and locked the door behind them. She looked knackered, hollow shadows beneath her eyes betraying lack of sleep. Her hair, cropped short for years, had grown longer and was tucked behind her ears. Her cheekbones were sharp as ever, her eyes the same clear blue.

'Hey. How's it going, girl?' Nick held his arms out. After a moment's hesitation, she leaned in for a hug. He always forgot how tall she was. His chin barely reached her shoulder. She set him back firmly at arm's length.

'Good to see you. You didn't have to come, though. We could have talked on the phone.'

So much for his mercy dash. 'No problem. I was awake, anyway. What's all this about?'

'Tell you in a minute. Come upstairs and meet Sophie. Careful in the back room, though. There's broken glass all over the place.'

They crunched through the kitchen. Someone had boarded up the broken window in the door and swept aside the bigger shards of glass. He followed her up the stairs and into a living room so scruffy it could have been his own. Curled up in the corner of the sofa was a huge-eyed teenage girl, black hair scraped back in a braid, her face goth-pale. She stared at him with suspicion.

'Hi, Sophie. I'm Nick. Is it OK if Helen tells me what's going on? I'm a journalist. We've worked together before.'

She shrugged. 'I'm not saying anything.'

'That's all right. You don't have to.' He took his notebook and pen from his bag. Most people recorded interviews these days, but old habits die hard and Nick liked to have his notes to rely on.

Helen told her story from her arrival at the shop on Sunday morning, taking in the link to the books from Cobham Hall's library and the discovery of the body in the river at Rochester.

'I stayed over. And I heard the glass break downstairs. A boy climbed in through the window.' She glanced at Sophie, who was staring at the floor. 'I tried to grab him. But then I saw Paxton, looking right at me, staring through the window. They both got away.'

Helen was shivering, he noticed. He knew what she'd been through at Gary Paxton's hands. It made him sick with rage.

'Sophie.' The girl looked up, unwillingly. 'When did you last see your dad?'

She shrugged. 'Friday night, I suppose. I told the police all this. I got back about ten. He was drinking whisky and reading a book. I went to my room. When I got up in the morning, he was gone.'

'What time?'

She shrugged. 'About half ten, eleven.'

'OK.' Nick leaned forward, flipped through pictures on his phone. 'Here. This is Paxton's van, heading into Rochester at six minutes past eight on Saturday morning. I followed him here from Dover. I lost him in the one-way system in the town centre, but he was here.'

Helen smiled for the first time since he'd arrived. 'That's brilliant, Nick.'

He swiped backward. 'He met a guy up on the cliffs near Folkestone, seven o'clock. This is him. Guren Hasani.'

Sophie sat up and leaned over to see the picture. 'I recognise him,' she said, stabbing her finger at the screen. 'He came here. Ages ago. Dad said he was a dealer. But he didn't know anything about books. He left boxes here.'

'Right, right. He's involved, then.' Nick turned back to his notebook. Helen was pressing her fingers into her temples, the way she always did when she was thinking.

'So, what do we think – Paxton is working for this Hasani guy?' She turned to Sophie. 'You said your dad had been worried about money. And he said in the letter that he'd taken out some loans. Paxton used to work in security, remember, Nick? And we know what he did for his clients in the old days. Loan shark – or collecting on loans – would be right up his street.'

Nick jiggled his legs up and down, excited. 'I haven't even told you about how I found him in Dover. I was asking around in a pub. This guy said Paxton had been working for some dodgy people, dangerous. That they target people in prison, then get them to work for them when they come out. And that they'd kill me if they knew I was poking my nose into their business.'

Sophie let out a whimper. Helen frowned at Nick.

'Sorry. I thought it was just a figure of speech.' He hadn't, though. The man in the pub had been deadly serious. And if Paxton was working for these people, killing was not a remote possibility. He remembered something else, flicked through his notebook until he found his notes from Friday night.

'But it's not just them. You remember those men from the anti-refugee protest who torched the building in Dover? One of their leaders went to see Paxton at his hostel on Friday. Offered him money to work for them, instead of whoever he is working for. He said they had loads of dosh. Said it would be better than, quote, working for "those bastards out on the farm".'

Helen leaned forward. 'Wow. What did he say?'

'I never found out. His dog barked at me and I had to leg it. Paxton almost caught me, halfway up the fire escape to my hotel.'

Helen was staring at him as if he was mad. 'And you didn't tell me when that happened? What about the police? Please say you've reported it.'

He shrugged. 'Tell them what? A bloke chased me off because I was ear-wigging on his conversation? It didn't seem worth wasting their time.'

# Chapter 35

Paxton curled up next to Cooper in a corner of the van. Helen Oddfellow. He couldn't believe it. What in God's name was that woman doing involved in all this?

She was one of the few people who'd got under his skin. Maybe it was the way she'd fought back at every opportunity. Even when he'd thought she was broken, she'd found a way to deceive him and escape. And then she'd stood, tall and pale as a lighthouse in the courtroom, giving the evidence that sent him down. She'd refused a screen and he'd watched closely as she coolly dismissed every suggestion the defence lawyer put to her, speaking directly to the judge or jury, never glancing his way.

As she left the witness box, she'd turned and looked at him, just once. A long, penetrating gaze full of contempt. He had not expected – or wanted – to see her again.

And now here she was, materialising in the Rochester bookshop in the middle of the night like some kind of avenging angel. If Helen Oddfellow was involved, then there was more to the business with the bookshop than Guren had been letting on.

He thought of the book that he'd been told to find, the box with a painting. The cool customer at the farm with his suitcase of cash. No messing around with gift cards for him. What was the big deal? The book hadn't looked anything much. And he knew paintings could be expensive, but art theft was hardly Guren's usual line of work. Helen Oddfellow was an academic, a researcher. There must be a secret involved, something that the people in charge wanted to know. Or to suppress.

After his trip to the farm, he'd gone back to Rochester. He'd been round the back of the bookshop, planning his entry, when one of the county lines kids came up on his skateboard, warned him off. They'd found the bookseller's body, down by the river. The police would be here any minute.

He'd set the kid to watch and retreated to the hostel, making sure the warden saw him arrive. After ten, the kid had called and reported no more sign of movement. The lights had been on upstairs, but then switched off. He waited an hour.

Then he slipped out of the hostel, through the back door he'd unlocked before going to bed. Everyone was asleep; no-one would look for him until the morning.

He'd called the kid when he arrived in Rochester, around midnight.

'You're skinny. I'll break the window; you can climb through and open the door.'

He'd protested, of course. But word had got around of what Paxton had done to the last kid who tried to get out of the county lines network. He'd agreed – only to mess the entire thing up by making too much noise.

And now Helen Oddfellow knew Paxton had been trying to break into the shop. She would immediately know he had something to do with Chapman's murder. Which meant Paxton would be back inside as soon as the police caught up with him.

He'd taken the van up on to the marshes, parked down a lane not too far from the farm. Not too close, either. He wanted time to think before he told Guren what had happened.

He had to get rid of her. That was clear. Helen and the journalist, Nick Wilson. Were the two of them working together again? Of course they were. That must be the link. Somehow, Wilson had found out that Paxton had something to do with the Rochester bookshop and he'd got the Oddfellow woman involved. They both had to go.

But the woman first. She'd seen him at the bookshop with the kid. She was the only one who could identify him, place him in Rochester. He shifted, closed his hand around the handle of the knife. Cooper whimpered in his sleep. There would be blood. But it would be quick; he'd make sure of that. He knew how to angle the blade, how to press it home. The force – the surprising force – needed to slice through clothing, skin, muscle, and fat. How to avoid the ribs, twist the blade up and into the heart.

He needed her on her own, somewhere he could clear up the mess and dispose of the body. He preferred to work alone, but he couldn't risk picking her up on the street. There'd be a warrant out for him by morning, he supposed. The hostel would have been alerted already and found his empty bed. He couldn't go back. He'd have to call Guren. Much as he hated the idea, this was not something he'd be able to do alone.

He sighed, tried to get comfortable. He'd call the farm early, see what they could sort out. The kid, maybe: Levi. He could use him as a messenger, lure her away to a meeting somewhere.

Promise to tell her a secret. If he knew Helen Oddfellow, she'd be too damn nosey to resist.

He shivered, pulled the sleeping dog across his legs for warmth, closed his eyes. Why did she have to get caught up in this? The woman was like a heat-seeking missile for trouble. She didn't back down, never looked the other way. A dangerous woman. It almost seemed a pity. He tried to imagine another world, an alternative universe in which Helen Oddfellow stood beside him, using her cool intellect to further his own goals. The two of them working together, instead of her and that runt of a reporter.

Cooper groaned, shuddered, and let out a disgusting fart that smelled of boiled cabbage. Christ. Paxton looked at his watch. Almost five o'clock. He'd get out of this foul-smelling van, wake himself up with a run, then call Guren. Time to put a plan into motion.

# Chapter 36

At first, Helen couldn't think where she was. Her neck was cricked by the sofa cushion, her legs dangling off the end. Her foot hurt.

'Morning. I brought you some tea.' Nick walked up the stairs with a couple of mugs, cheerful and far too wide awake. He'd insisted on sleeping on the sofa in the shop downstairs, in case of further incursions overnight.

Helen sat up, rubbed sleep out of her eyes. 'What time is it?'

'Half eight.' He pulled the curtains and let in bright sunlight. 'Nice day.'

'Thanks.' Helen raised her arms above her head to stretch out her stiff back and yawned. They'd talked until Wiz had fallen asleep. She and Nick had carried her through to her bedroom. Helen wondered if she should wake her. It was Monday morning, a school day, she supposed. But perhaps Wiz would want to stay home and wait for news from the police.

Helen took the chipped mug. Black tea. No milk, she remembered. She should get some shopping in.

Yesterday morning, she'd woken in luxury, cocooned in a downy four-poster bed with views over the parkland at

Vylands. Her morning tea had been delivered in bone china on a silver tray, by a maid who pretended not to notice Gus's jacket and tie hanging over an armchair. He'd disappeared early, muttering something about needing to talk to someone about the cows.

'What?' Nick had his laptop open, perched on the arm of the sofa.

'Hmm?'

'You're smiling. What's funny?' he asked.

'Oh…' Helen felt herself blush. 'Nothing. I stayed at a posh country house on Saturday night. They brought me tea on a silver tray in the morning. I was contrasting the levels of service.'

He laughed. 'Apologies, Lady Muck. I'll find you a cup and saucer next time. What were you doing there?'

Good question, Helen thought. She'd not processed her relationship with Gus yet. If indeed that's what it was. On cue, her phone rang.

'Hello, sorry to ring so early. Are you up?'

'Yeah, sure. How're you?' Helen got up from the sofa and walked to the window. She didn't particularly want to talk to Gus in front of Nick.

'I've had an idea. About Nancy Love, and Dickens?' He sounded excited, his usual drawl more animated and nervy.

'OK. What sort of idea?'

'Well, she said she would use him as a messenger, didn't she? If there was another message – this big secret she hints at – she'd have given it to Dickens. But then she goes missing and her body is found. So he gets scared, worried about delivering the message. And he keeps it. For years, maybe.'

'It's possible,' Helen agreed. How had he guessed there was

another letter?

'Or maybe he tries to get rid of it or hides it. Puts it somewhere he doesn't think anyone will find it. Gives it to someone else to look after.' He paused. 'Have you got any idea about where it might be?'

Helen thought guiltily of the shorthand note. 'Not really.'

'OK. That's a shame. Well, I had a thought.'

'Go on.'

He took a deep breath. '*Great Expectations*. The bit at the beginning, with Pip's brothers and sisters and parents all buried in the churchyard where he meets the villain. What's his name?'

'Magwitch.' Helen frowned, her tired brain trying to follow his logic.

'That's the one. Well, Dickens writes about a young boy, Pip, helping a criminal and keeping his secret, doesn't he? And it's a real church, St James's, out on the marshes at Cooling, near the Thames estuary. It's close to where Dickens lived at Gads Hill.

'The graves are in the churchyard. There's a chapel inside the church, all decorated with shells. I've been there a few times with my father.'

Helen remembered the map she'd found in the bookshop on her first visit. 'I know it.'

'Anyway, I thought we could have a look. I remember there was a sort of hatch in the chapel wall, like a little cupboard. It'd be a good place to keep a secret, don't you think?'

Helen hesitated. She didn't want to pour cold water on his theory, but it was tenuous, to put it mildly. And any cupboard in a chapel would have been opened hundreds of times since Dickens lived in Rochester.

'It sounds intriguing,' she said. 'When are you thinking of going?'

She heard a noise and turned to see Wiz emerge from her bedroom, dressed in her school uniform. She looked different, much younger, with her face clear of black make up and her hair tied back.

'Today. This morning, if you're free. Are you still in Rochester? I could pick you up on the way. I'm driving back to town anyway.'

'Um… I don't know if I can. I'm with some friends. We might have stuff to do,' she said, looking at Nick. He shrugged and handed Wiz a mug.

'Go on.' Gus was almost pleading. 'I can't wait to see you again. Please, Helen.'

She covered the phone with her hand. 'What are you two doing this morning? I might need to go somewhere. But I can be back by lunchtime.'

Wiz picked up her skateboard. 'I'm going to school. You can do what you want.' Her face was pale and set.

'I can hang around here this morning, make sure no-one tries to break in again,' said Nick. 'I have some more digging to do online.'

Helen thought. School was probably the safest place for Wiz. If there was any news, one of them could ring her. And Cooling wasn't far away by car. She could pick up some groceries on the way back, relieve Nick and be there when Wiz got home. She'd need to get back to London, but not until tonight for lectures tomorrow.

'OK,' she told Gus. 'I'm in Rochester High Street, Chapman and Daughter booksellers. Ring when you get here and I'll come down.' Something told her that Nick and Gus would not be likely to get on.

# Chapter 37

Gus drove silently across the bridge over the Medway. His good humour seemed to have dissipated on the journey. The road took them out of town, through winding suburban streets. Smart new riverfront apartments gave way to terraced houses with unkempt front gardens, rubbish bags piled in the gutters. The houses thinned out, replaced by scruffy paddocks with a few sad-looking horses in them, then bare fields.

He parked by the stone wall that ringed St James's Church and turned off the ignition. The old church was surrounded by flat, ploughed fields. Plastic polytunnels marched across the landscape. There was a pile of bright blue plastic tubs by a metal gate, the mud beside it churned into deep trenches. The sun gave the cold air a sharp edge, an almost-painful clarity.

They walked through the grassy churchyard.

'Here,' she said. The row of graves – not the five of Pip's brothers, but thirteen – was neat, the stones heartbreakingly small, overgrown with moss and yellow lichen. She crouched, trying to read the inscriptions on the parents' headstones. The words were illegible, crumbled away by centuries of weather, rain and wind whipping mercilessly across the open ground. 'No names.' Just a headstone and a row of little graves, anonymous witness to an everyday tragedy on the marshes.

Helen thought of Dickens' novel, Magwitch appearing in the churchyard, frightening young Pip out of his wits. The convict, escaped from the prison hulks moored on the river. She straightened up, suddenly afraid that Gary Paxton would loom up from behind a gravestone.

'Let's go inside,' she said.

They went through the porch into the stone and flint building, simple and ancient with whitewashed walls and tiled floors, the dark rafters arching above like an upturned ship. Ahead was a massive stone font, its interior bowl worn smooth. Beyond stood the remains of a big wooden door, hanging askew on its hinges with an enormous iron lock. Helen crossed to look. The door marked where the entrance to the church had once been, she read, and had been left in place in front of the walled-up space when the Victorian porch was installed.

The church was cold and she wished she'd brought her coat from the car. Maybe she should go and get it.

'Here,' said Gus. 'This is the place I was talking about.' He opened a wooden door.

It was a vestry, not a chapel, with a gothic pointed archway. Inside it smelled chalky, like a limestone cave. Helen reached her fingers out and touched the walls.

'Amazing.' They were almost completely covered in cockle shells, pressed into the plaster. 'Saint James, of course.' The saint's emblem of a shell, worn by pilgrims on their journey to the Spanish cathedral of Santiago de Compostela. A walk Helen herself would love to do, one day. 'Where's the alcove you were talking about?'

215

He followed her in. 'Over here, somewhere. Look, that's it. Next to the door.'

He reached his hand into an arched space, just above head height, and scrabbled around.

'Ah, well.' He smiled. 'I suppose it was a bit of a long shot.'

'Let me see?' Helen stood on tip-toes to peer into the empty space. Her fingers met nothing but chalky plaster and dust, came away white with residue.

'Never mind,' said Gus. He leaned against the wall, watching her. 'What do you think, though? Where would Dickens have hidden a letter? And what do you think it might tell us?'

Helen shrugged. 'I wish I knew.'

From outside, a car horn started to blare repeatedly.

'Damn,' said Gus. 'That's the Range Rover. I'd better sort it out. The alarm's over-sensitive. Why don't you carry on exploring in here?'

Helen checked her watch. She'd said she would be back by lunchtime, but it was only just after eleven o'clock.

'Thanks. Could you get my coat? It's cold. I should have put it on.'

His footsteps receded through the empty church. Helen left the little chapel and wandered back through the pews towards the altar. She stopped to read the brass plate of a grave memorial set in dark stone.

There was an image of a woman, her head covered with a wimple. The gothic lettering beneath asked people to 'Pray for the soule of Ffeyth Brooke, wife of John Brooke, Lord of Cobham'. She smiled. The Cobham connection seemed to get everywhere. She remembered that the family had once owned the nearby Cooling Castle, now ruined, as well as Cobham Hall. Helen thought of the portrait of Albert Brooke

216

she'd unearthed from the box in Rochester, the quizzical smile which reminded her of Richard. Both descendants of the woman commemorated in this modest brass effigy.

The car horn stopped blaring. Then Helen heard Gus yell, in surprise or protest. She hadn't made out his words. He shouted again, and this time it was clearer.

'Get off me!'

Helen ran out of the church, around the tower and towards the road where they had left the car. As she rounded the corner, she saw two men dressed in black with balaclavas over their heads. They had Gus between them and were forcing him into the back seat of the Range Rover, pushing his head down. Another hooded man sat in the driver's seat.

'Stop!' Helen ran towards them, stumbling on the uneven grass. The men jumped into the car, one either side of Gus. As she vaulted over the low wall around the churchyard, the car started up and reversed towards her, fast.

Helen threw herself back over the wall, landing on the ground inside the churchyard just as the vehicle smashed into the stones. A heavy capstone crashed down beside her, catching her shoulder.

The shock of it kept her conscious through the wave of pain. She rolled away from the wall, forced herself to her feet, clutching her right arm. Something felt wrong – it wasn't working properly.

Swallowing down nausea, Helen turned to see the Range Rover accelerate away.

# Chapter 38

Helen stared after the receding car. Her shoulder hurt like hell. Her brain raced to process what had just happened.

They'd tried to kill her. If she hadn't moved fast, she would have been crushed between the car and the wall. And Gus – what on earth did they want with Gus?

She cradled her right elbow with her left hand to take the weight of the arm. It felt too heavy for her shoulder, dragging on it. She could feel bones grinding. Her breath was coming in quick gasps and she had begun to shake.

She tried to slow her breathing, keep calm. She had to find help, get someone to rescue Gus. Where was her phone? She cursed. Her bloody phone was in her coat pocket, in the car.

She looked along the empty lane, gazed over the deserted muddy fields.

Shivering with cold and shock, she climbed over the broken-down wall and started walking along the road in the direction the car had disappeared. A signpost pointed the way to Cliffe village, two miles. She'd have to walk it; hope that the men who'd stolen the car didn't decide to come back and finish the job.

At first, she tried to run, but the jarring was too painful. Cold sweat bathed her face and she had to stop, dizzy. She bent forward, took deep breaths, willed herself not to pass out. Two miles. If she went at a decent speed, she could walk it in half an hour.

She straightened up, jaw set. She heard an engine and pressed herself back into the hedge. Had they come back? But no, it was from the other direction and the engine was different – noisier, a diesel engine with a low thrum. Thank goodness.

A tractor came around the corner. Helen stepped out into the lane, waved it down. A young man in a baseball cap leaned out of the cab.

'Are you OK?'

'Not really. Have you got a phone?'

The man jumped down. 'Yeah, but the signal's awful out here. Let me check.' He looked, then shook his head. 'Nothing. What's up? Are you hurt?'

Helen tried to explain. 'My shoulder. I think it's dislocated or something. These guys tried to run me over. And they've stolen my friend's car and taken him with them. I need to call the police.'

'Shit.' The man shook his head, eyes wide. 'Come on, then. I'm on my way back to the farmhouse. You can call from there.'

Almost weeping with relief, Helen climbed up into the cab beside him. 'Thank you. Thank you so much.'

'It's going to jolt about a bit. Sorry, I'll be as careful as I can,' said her rescuer.

Helen closed her eyes and braced herself against the movement. The whole cab vibrated, but if she sat up straight and didn't touch the door, it wasn't too bad. When she opened her eyes again, they were going past a turning to Cliffe.

'Would it be quicker for me to call from the village?' asked Helen, raising her voice to be heard over the chugging engine.

He shrugged. 'We're almost there.'

The road was a little wider now. Twice they had to pull over to let lorries loaded with gravel go past. The fields stretched wide on either side of the lane, a patchwork of plastic polytunnels shining silver against the dark, bare earth. The rooftops of Cliffe village receded into the distance.

Finally, as Helen was starting to feel uneasy, they took a sharp turn off the main road. Another turn, then the man jumped out and opened a padlocked steel gate across a driveway. A security camera swivelled towards them as they drove through.

'Here we are,' he said. 'We'll have you all sorted out in a minute.'

The farmyard was almost deserted, a muddy expanse populated not, as Helen had imagined, by free-ranging chickens or ducks, but by a brooding pair of German shepherd dogs who set up a cacophonous barking as soon as the tractor stopped.

'Don't worry. They're chained up,' said her rescuer.

To their left was a pebble-dashed bungalow. Ahead and to the right stood two vast aluminium barns, with rows of caravans beyond. Helen shivered, wishing once more for her coat.

He helped her climb down and pointed her to the bungalow. 'Wait in there. I've got to put the tractor away. My missus will show you the phone and get you a cuppa.'

Helen turned the doorknob. The door was unlocked. She walked into a kitchen with yellowing lino, dishes piled high in the sink, a smell of dog food. There was a table in the middle of the room. Behind it sat a man with cropped dark hair wearing a green Barbour coat, his shoulders bunched and heavy. He smiled in a peculiarly insinuating way, exposing teeth stained yellow with tobacco.

'Helen Oddfellow?' he asked.

# Chapter 39

S he tried to run, but the door had been locked behind her. The man watched as she pulled uselessly at the handle with her good arm. She turned, desperate, and started towards the open door on the other side of the room.

Two men dressed in black, wearing balaclavas and holding baseball bats, walked in and stood on either side of the door. Defeated, she turned back to the man at the table.

'What do you want?' she asked. 'Where's Gus? What have you done with him?'

'Sit.' He gestured to the chair on the other side of the table.

Reluctantly, she obeyed. 'Someone will find us,' she said. 'He's an important man. People will be looking for him.' She hoped that was true. And what about her – would someone be looking for her? She thought of Nick at the bookshop in Rochester. When had she said she'd be back?

'No-one will find you,' he said. 'No-one finds anyone here.'

She turned to look out of the window at the muddy farmyard. 'Nothing to stop people from coming here. It's not exactly hidden.'

He smiled again. 'But nobody does come here. They can see – it's just a farm. Nothing interesting. Why would they be looking for Helen Oddfellow, a university lecturer from London, on a farm in the middle of Kent?'

'People know where I was going,' she said, trying to remember. Had she told Nick and Wiz about St James's Church? She wasn't sure.

He shook his head, confident. 'No. Because you didn't know this was where you were going, did you?'

She said nothing. He was right – no-one would look for her here. Her shoulder throbbed, the pain settling into an intense ache. The room was so cold she could see her breath misting in front of her face. She longed for warmth, a blanket, or a hot drink. From the look of her captors, that would not be forthcoming.

What did they want? Gus was rich, he had money. She could understand why they might kidnap him, send a ransom note to his family. She didn't imagine his mother would hold out for long if her darling son was in danger. Was he on the farm, too? Maybe in one of the rooms beyond the kitchen. Had she been taken just because she'd seen the men kidnap Gus?

'I wanted to see your face,' said the man. 'The famous Helen Oddfellow. The woman that our friend Gary is so frightened of.'

Her head jerked up. 'Gary?' Christ, was she in the hands of Gary Paxton's mates? That was even worse.

'You are here as his guest,' he said, smiling his horrible smile. 'We will look after you until he gets here.'

Helen tried to remember what Nick had said. Something about Paxton working for a bunch of people out on a farm. He'd seen him meeting a man up on the cliffs. What was his name? Hasan, Hasani, something like that.

Her captor stood. Was this Hasani? She tried to remember the photo Nick had shown them on his phone. It could be, she thought.

He waved over the two men with baseball bats. 'These guys will take you to your accommodation. Don't give them any trouble.'

He spoke to them in a foreign language, something Eastern European that Helen did not understand. Polish, maybe, or Russian.

One grabbed her by the bad arm and pulled her up from her chair.

'No!' She screamed with pain.

'Bej kujdes,' said the boss, tutting. 'Careful. What would Gary say?'

They marched her across the farmyard. The dogs, loose now, bounded up to them, baring their teeth. Helen shuddered. Her guards shouted at the animals, brandished their bats at them. The dogs slunk away, growling. Helen wondered if the demonstration had been for her benefit. The dogs will have you if you make a break for it.

They passed in front of a barn. The door was ajar, an electric light on inside. Helen peered through and saw with surprise a big group of people intent on some task, backs bent over a long table.

'Hey!' she called. 'Help me!'

The man on her right grabbed her arm again, twisted it. She gasped as the pain lanced through her shoulder.

'Shut up,' he shouted. They pulled her past the barn and through a gap to a field. Lined up by the hedgerow was a long line of old static caravans propped up on bricks. One man took keys from his pockets and opened a door. A fug of stuffy air emerged, smelling of unwashed bodies. At least it was warm.

Helen, fight gone out of her for now, climbed the steps into the van, its flimsy floor shaking under her feet. Two women looked up from the bunks on either side of the narrow van. A small gas fire hissed at the end of the room.

'Hello,' said the younger of the two women, a girl with dirty blonde hair. She sat up and crossed her legs. 'I am Aisha.' Her voice was strongly accented, with an eastern European inflection.

Helen sat on the bed next to her, trying not to wrinkle her nose at the smell of sweat. She heard with resignation the key being turned in the door.

'Hello, Aisha. I'm Helen.' The girl was a teenager, she saw with shock, even younger than Wiz. The older woman was watching, her eyes suspicious, saying nothing. They were both dressed in cheap, thin clothes: leggings and t-shirts that looked as if they had not been washed for a while. 'Aisha… I just got here. I'm trying to find my friend. And I don't understand anything. Can you tell me what's going on?'

The girl smiled, a wide and guileless smile. She patted Helen's hand.

'Don't worry,' she said. 'You are too old. They only want young girls like me.'

'What?'

The girl shrugged. 'But we stop them. Elira didn't let them take me. And Gary, he told them I am too young. He said they should make me work in the barn, but I won't go without my sister.'

Helen looked at the older woman slumped on the divan, defeat on her round face. She started to put the pieces together: the barn full of people working; the caravans; the locked-in women. She'd been brought to a people-trafficking site. And Gary Paxton, the evil bastard, was up to his neck in it.

'How did you get here? Where are you from?' asked Helen. 'How long have you been here?'

The sister started speaking in a language Helen didn't recognise, her voice rapid and low. She glared at Helen.

'Elira thinks I should not answer questions. But we have been here for almost two weeks. Tomorrow it will be two weeks.'

Helen already knew the answer to the next question. 'And can you leave?'

Aisha laughed. 'No, of course not. They lock the door. And there is no place to go. One man, he tried to fight when we first got here.' She made a slicing gesture across her face. 'Gary cut him. His eye is gone. They are all so scared of Gary. But I think he is not so bad.'

Another rapid stream of speech from her sister, who didn't seem to hold Paxton in such high esteem. Aisha shrugged.

'Elira says I should not talk so much. It is true.'

Helen leaned back on the divan, glad of the warmth inside the caravan, the temporary respite from men in balaclavas with weapons. Her shoulder throbbed. She moved her arm tentatively, wondered if she could get it more comfortable. She gasped at the pain, closed her eyes, and felt the sweat start again on her face.

'You are hurting?' asked Aisha.

Helen nodded. She felt sick. When she opened her eyes, Elira was crouching in front of her. With gentle hands, she felt around Helen's shoulder, shushing her like a child as she winced.

Elira spoke to Aisha again.

'She says…' Aisha frowned, trying to find the words. 'The bone is in the wrong place.'

'Dislocated. Yeah, I thought so. Is your sister a nurse?' The girl looked puzzled. 'Or a doctor?'

Aisha laughed. 'Not a doctor. But she helps people when they are sick. In the village, we did not have a doctor. We did not have anything.'

'So you came here?' asked Helen.

Aisha sighed. 'Elira wanted me to go to a good school. When our mother died last year, she said we would get out. She paid some money… I don't know. They say we have more money to pay and must work on the farm until it is all paid.'

Debt slavery. 'I saw lots of people in the barn when they brought me to the caravan. What are they doing?'

'Potatoes. They are packing them in crates. Elira was with them at first. Until they came for me. But now she refuses to leave me and Gary says they can't take me to the place. They want to take her instead.'

'Which place?'

Aisha shrugged and looked away. For the first time, she looked scared.

'I don't know. They said there is a place where they take the girls, for men to make sex with them.' When she looked back, her eyes were wet with tears. 'I don't want to go. I want to go back to Albania. Or to school. I really, really want to go to school.'

'I'm so sorry,' said Helen. 'Look, there must be a way out of this. We need to get you and Elira to safety.'

The older woman said something sharp to Aisha and the girl

wiped her eyes on her sweatshirt. Then the woman turned to Helen, gestured to her arm.

'I help,' she said.

Helen looked to Aisha. 'What does she want me to do?'

Aisha grinned. 'She will put your bone back in the right place. If you let her. It will hurt, but then it will get better.'

Helen looked at the woman, her rotten teeth and tired eyes. Did she trust her? What did she have to lose? She couldn't fight off Gary Paxton with one arm.

She gazed at Elira a moment longer, then nodded. 'OK,' she said. 'Let's do this.'

# Chapter 40

Paxton tried to shift position, stretch out his aching back. The smell of exhaust fumes was making him feel sick. He wanted to be ready when they finally let him out of this bloody car boot.

They were going to do him in. Despite all the promises. Do him in, dump his body somewhere it wouldn't be found. No-one would know what happened to him. He wondered if anyone would care. He couldn't think of anyone, off-hand. Not even his boy. Cooper, maybe.

A sheen of sweat chilled his face, his scalp. He flexed his fists, promised himself he'd put up a decent fight, do some damage for them to remember him by.

Paxton had spent the day being driven around from one place to another. When he called Guren at dawn, he'd picked him up from the lane, driven him to the farm. Another man had taken Paxton's van keys. He'd get rid of it, Guren said. Anything connected with Paxton was contaminated now.

Back at the farm, Guren had promised him they'd help, that they would find the Oddfellow woman. But the boss wants to talk to you, Guren said. You've got to go and meet him. There's a truck coming to pick you up.

They had made Paxton leave Cooper tied up in the yard and taken his knife. Then he'd been hooded and put in the back of a truck smelling of animal feed. A long journey in the dark, hours bumping along, sometimes at speed, sometimes inching through traffic. When he got out, he was in another barn somewhere. Men in balaclavas had pulled off the hood, given him a bottle of water and a plastic-wrapped pasty to eat.

A short break. Then he'd been hooded again. He heard a car drive in, the boot open. They'd lifted him up, chucked him in and forced the door down before he'd been able to put up a decent resistance. That was when he realised. Anything connected with you is contaminated now. Including you. They wanted rid of him.

They'd not tied him up, though. Was that an oversight, or did they just not think they needed to? Fists would be no defence against guns. Paxton pulled off the hood, stared into the darkness of the boot. Waited.

The car had been driving for about an hour, he guessed. The last half hour had been slow, stopping and starting. City traffic. They halted again. Then he felt a shift in angle. They were driving slowly downhill. A turn, and another. Then the car stopped and he heard the handbrake go on. A brief shudder from the engine, then silence.

He tensed himself. Footsteps. A bleep, then the boot swung open.

Paxton uncoiled, shifted to his knees to give himself some leverage, ready to take out the first bastard who came at him. No-one did. They'd all stepped well back, no doubt expecting an explosion of violence as soon as they opened the lid. Right, then.

He stood, one foot on the lip of the boot. They were in an

underground car park. The ramp they'd come down was at the end of a row of cars sheathed in protective covers. He might get out of here alive, after all.

He jumped and ran, launched himself at the smallest of the men, driving a fist into his stomach. The guy went down with a grunt. Paxton didn't wait to finish the job. He sprinted for the ramp.

Something hit hard, right behind his knees. He yelled and tried to stay upright. His legs buckled and he pitched forward on to the oil-stained concrete. Seconds later, a large boot planted itself on his lower back. He could see the baseball bat swinging loose next to his head. He reached out, tried to grab the weapon. The man swung it, caught him painfully across the knuckles.

'Stop. Or I'll swing for your head next.'

He tried to rise from the ground, but the foot was heavy. There were more boots now, more legs, all around him. He deflated. One punch. That's all he'd managed. Not much.

'Don't be an idiot.' The guy with the bat pulled him up. 'We're taking you upstairs. Don't try any more shit.'

Dazed, Paxton allowed himself to be led to a lift that sped silently upwards. They emerged into a tastefully furnished living room, all beige suede sofas and low glass coffee tables. A hotel, maybe? The curtains were closed. Paxton had no idea where he was, or what time of day it was outside.

The man with steel-rimmed glasses was sitting in an armchair, watching him with an amused air.

'Good journey, Mr Paxton? Take a seat and let's talk about the mess you have gotten yourself into.'

# Chapter 41

I t wasn't like Helen to be late. Nick was pissed off. He was stuck in the flat, baby-sitting a schoolgirl, while she swanned around the countryside with her posh boyfriend.

He'd seen the smarmy bastard draw up in his flashy Range Rover and watched from the window as he kissed Helen on the mouth, like someone who had the undisputed right to do so. First, she goes off with a bloody film star, now this. He remembered her expression that morning when he'd handed her a mug of tea. She'd spent Saturday night at a country house, she'd said. Tea on a silver tray in the morning. Posh bastard in a four-poster bed the night before, Nick thought.

Not that it was any of his business who Helen went out with. There had never been anything between them, not in that way. After losing Richard, she'd been so devastated that anything other than friendship had been out of the question. And he'd had plenty of other company. Nothing serious, nothing to distract him from work. The stuff they'd been through together had somehow made it harder to imagine making a move. He imagined her blue eyes widening with surprise, shock, maybe embarrassment or distaste. He couldn't risk it.

Didn't stop him from being fed up when she left him hanging around, though.

His mobile rang. He grabbed it, ready to give her an earful. But it wasn't Helen. He didn't recognise the number.

'Yeah?'

'It's Amy. From the hotel?' She sounded agitated, out of breath.

'Yo, Amy. How's things?'

'Where are you?'

'Rochester. Bookshop on the High Street. Why, what's happening? Are you all right?'

'I'm sorry, Nick.' Her voice was strained and high, as if she was trying not to cry. Or as if she was scared of something.

'Hey, now. What's up?'

He heard a man's voice, faint, laughing. Shit. Paxton, he thought. He's gone back to the hotel.

'Amy, is he there? Paxton? Just say yes if he is.'

There was an indistinct noise, then a new voice on the phone.

'We've got people right outside, boy,' said the sneering voice. Nick recognised it from the dozens of hate-filled, insinuating videos the man had posted online. Sebastian Johansson, the self-styled Captain Jonnie.

'I know who you are,' said Nick. 'Don't you touch Amy.'

'Amy's being a good girl. She won't get hurt if you behave yourself. Listen, boy. I know your game. I know what Paxton did to you. And I know you've been after him. Well, we want him too. Someone's been talking. I don't trust him. I don't trust you; I don't trust anyone.'

Nick frowned. What did this horrible piece of shit want?

'He's gone. He's not at the hostel, he's not answering his

phone. We had a meeting fixed up today; he didn't show. Where is he, Wilson, with your clever journalism skills? Where's he gone?'

Nick gazed out at the street. 'You want my help?' He saw a couple of lads loafing around on the street, kicking a can about. Short-cropped hair, pimples, khaki gear. Were they the 'troops' Johansson was boasting about?

'I think Amy would appreciate it if you could assist us with our enquiries.'

Nick gritted his teeth. Sod it, what harm could it do to turn one of his enemies on another? Let them take each other out.

'He was here,' he admitted. 'Rochester, last night. He tried to break into this shop. But he legged it afterwards and I've not found him yet.'

'Rochester? He's off up that farm,' said Johansson.

'Farm?' Nick frowned. Johansson had said that before, when he was talking to Paxton. That Paxton would take ages to earn money driving a van for those bastards out at the farm. 'Which farm?'

'You've been very helpful,' the man said. 'I'll be sure to put in a good word for you, next time my boys are looking to give someone a going over.'

'Put Amy back on,' said Nick, but the line had gone dead.

He blew out his cheeks. The boys in the street were still there. One of them looked up at the window and saw him. He grinned, waved. Nick let the curtain drop. Should he go to Dover, see if Amy was all right? But he'd promised Helen he'd wait here until she got back. He looked at his watch again. Quarter to three. She'd said lunchtime. This was ridiculous. He tried her mobile, but it went straight to voicemail.

He'd give it ten minutes, then call the hotel and see if Amy was OK. Ring the police if she didn't answer.

Something was nagging at him. The gang, the criminal lot that the man in the pub had told him about – were they the ones at the farm? Johansson had known about it, but he'd been trying to get Paxton away from them to work for him. So that would put Guren Hasani in the gang at the farm.

Nick opened his laptop, put Hasani's name in the search engine again and scrolled through the results until he found it. Guren Hasani, a former director of Agriland Development, based in Leicester. Home address, Stamford Road in Leicester. Resigned as director in 2019. He'd dismissed the result – but had that been too hasty?

He searched for the company name. A basic website described it as a land management company, specialising in agricultural land which could be repurposed for development. It listed dozens of small farms all over the country that the company owned, with or without planning permission for housing or commercial use. Loads in East Anglia, especially around Cambridge and Norwich. Some in the Midlands; a few in Essex. He couldn't see anything in Kent.

Maybe his hunch was wrong. Just to be sure, he opened the UK Land Registry website and found the UK companies' land ownership database. Agriland Development had a long list of holdings. He scrolled through, clicking past page after page of addresses.

Finally, he found it. Ratcliffe Farm, thirty acres of land east of Fort Lane, Rochester, Kent. He copied the postcode. An online map showed him the farm, just north of where he'd been driving yesterday morning, between the Medway and the Thames rivers. Fort Lane led up towards the Thames. That had to be it.

Nick zoomed in to look at a satellite image of the farm. He could make out two big barns, a house, a scattering of what looked like old caravans. Some of the surrounding fields were covered in plastic polytunnels. He swapped to street view to see what was visible from the road. There was no company sign on the metal gate across the entrance, nothing that showed that this was Ratcliffe Farm. Just a security camera on a pole and a padlock on the gate.

He double-checked with the Agriland Development website. Ratcliffe Farm wasn't listed. Why not?

Because they wanted it kept quiet, he supposed. For whatever nasty business they were doing up there.

He should get out there, take a look. Not too close, just have a stroll down that lane and see where it went. He would go just as soon as Helen was back.

The door downstairs creaked open. Finally. Then Sophie came up the stairs, looking pale and tired.

'You're back early,' he said.

'Not.' She went to the fridge, took out a can of soft drink. 'Want one?'

He checked his phone, saw with a shock it was after half past three. 'Yeah, thanks.' He looked at her narrow back. 'Heard anything from the police today?' She shook her head and closed the fridge.

'Where's Helen?' she asked.

Nick took the can, opened it. 'I don't know,' he said.

'She said she'd be back when I was home.' The girl's mouth turned down. 'In case there was news about Dad.'

'Yeah, I know.' He took a swig, then grabbed his phone again. 'To be fair, it's not like her to be this late. Not without phoning.'

He tried her number again, his anxiety mounting. Voicemail, again. Shit, shit, shit. Why had he let her go off with that bloke, with Gary Paxton on the loose? What if posh boy had dropped her off and she'd gone for a wander around Rochester on her own and run into Paxton? Why hadn't he thought about that before? He'd been too caught up in feeling annoyed about her boyfriend. It hadn't occurred to him she might be in trouble. And what about Amy? He cursed himself for getting distracted by his research.

He rang the hotel. She answered on the fourth ring. It sounded like she'd been crying.

'Amy. Have they gone? Are you OK?'

'Yeah. But they're nasty people, Nick. They trashed the place. Broke the windows, threw food around. Sprayed bad words on the walls. One of them did a poo on my bed. Nasty, nasty people.'

'Aw, shit. Amy, I'm so sorry. I'll come by when I can and help you clear up, yeah? And you should report it, really.'

She sighed. 'I know. Don't worry. My granddaddy and grandma got it worse than this. It's just… what makes them like that?'

'They're just evil bastards,' said Nick. 'No sense in looking for a reason.'

He'd go over and help her as soon as he could. Cleaning the place up was the least he could do. But first, he had to find Helen.

He looked again at the map, open on the laptop in front of him. If Paxton had been up at the farm – and if Helen had run into him somewhere and he'd taken her there…

'I think I'd better go and look for her. Are you all right on your own, Sophie?'

'It's Wiz, actually. Are you going on your motorbike?' He saw a gleam of excitement in her eyes.

'Yeah. Just a quick run up north of here. There's somewhere I want to check out. Won't be long.'

She stood in front of the door, looking mutinous. 'She's my friend, too. I want to go with you.'

He hesitated. He was only going for a quick look. And he had promised Helen not to leave the girl on her own. What if Paxton came back here while he was out? Or if Johansson sent his thugs over? Perhaps it would be safest for them to stick together.

'OK,' he said. 'Put on a pair of jeans and a jacket. I've got a spare helmet. Let's go.'

# Chapter 42

Nick rode along Fort Lane, past the turning to the farm. He didn't want to do anything to draw attention to them. Wiz, riding pillion, was so light he kept forgetting she was there. He pulled in by a farm gate a hundred yards on.

The girl hopped off the bike, her cheeks pink. 'That was cool.'

He smiled. 'Glad you enjoyed it.' He stashed their helmets away. Maybe it would be best to leave the bike out of sight from the road. He pulled it up on the verge, leaned it against a litter-laden hedge hung with shreds of plastic bags. Bottles filled with piss lay in the undergrowth, chucked out by drivers too busy or lazy to stop. God, this place was grim.

'Look.' He pulled up the map on his phone with the satellite overlay. 'We're here. That's the farm. I don't fancy going down the front drive, but I'd like to get closer. If we go over this gate and into the field, then keep beside this hedge, we get to the polytunnels. Then we should be able to see the back of the barn, where the caravans are.'

He looked from his well-worn motorbike boots to her thick-soled black stompers. 'We're going to get muddy. Hope you're

OK with that.'

Wiz looked at him as if he was mad. 'Do I look like I care?'

He scrambled over the gate and held out a hand, but she was over already, stomping through the ploughed field. He grinned. Bolshy, determined – no wonder Helen liked her. He was getting to like her himself.

They paused at the corner of the field. He'd been right. The polytunnels were ahead of them, row after row of plastic stretching across the field. He scanned the scene for people. There was a smudge of moving colour – blue, red – inside the tunnel furthest from the hedge. People moving around, tending to whatever they grew in there.

He crept towards the closest tunnel and ducked down to look. Inside, the ground was covered in straw all the way along. Three rows of bushy green-leaved plants grew vigorously along its length. Skunk? But there was no smell, and the weed needed more heat than this.

'Strawberries,' said Wiz, who had crept up beside him. 'Come on. If we crawl, they won't be able to see us from outside.'

She set off on her hands and knees. Nick followed, moisture from the wet straw soaking into the knees of his jeans. They were about half-way along when she dropped to her belly, almost covered in straw, pressed into the side of the plants. Nick followed suit, heart thudding. What had she seen?

'What about this lot in here?' asked a voice. English, local by the sound of it. 'Will they do us another year, or do they need replanting?'

Nick peered around the strawberries. He could see four legs at the end of the tunnel, blue jeans tucked into green wellies. One guy ducked down and looked into the tunnel.

Nick edged back behind the plants, heart thumping.

'This is only the second year,' he said, his accent eastern European. 'They should be good this summer. They look healthy. Leave them.' He stood, and Nick breathed again.

The men walked along the rows of strawberries, discussing planting plans. Nick was feeling ridiculous. Had he been wrong? Was this just a normal Kentish farm, growing soft fruit?

The men stopped right next to where Wiz was hiding.

'What's going on with the girls?' asked the local guy. 'Guren said one of them is refusing to go.'

'Yes, it is a bit of a problem. We got Gary to talk to her. Guren thought he'd sort her out. But he says she's too young, could be trouble. Wait a bit, maybe. She can work on the fields, or in the barn. There's a new lot coming next week, anyway. Romanian girls, all looking for romantic English boyfriends.'

They laughed, boisterous.

'What's up with Gary, then? That's not like him. Has he fallen in love?'

'I don't ask questions. Why don't you ask him later? He's coming back to deal with the woman,' said the eastern European guy.

Nick's head went up. Which woman?

The men turned and walked further down the row, bantering about the Romanian girls.

Nick felt sick. What the hell had they walked into? It sounded like some kind of people-trafficking operation. And Gary – that had to be Gary Paxton, didn't it? Which meant he wasn't there now, but he was on his way. To deal with the woman. Helen? Was she somewhere on the farm?

He should get them both out of here, back to Rochester. Then call the police. He wasn't close to DCI Sarah Greenley in the way Helen was, but she would at least listen to him.

He heard a rustle in the straw. Wiz was off again, crawling towards the front of the row.

'Come back,' he called, as softly as he could. She didn't answer. He crawled after her as fast as possible without making too much noise.

She crouched in the arch at the end of the polytunnel. One of the big barns was just beyond.

'You stay here,' she breathed. 'I'm smaller. I can get closer without being seen. Find out what's going on in the barn.'

'No. We need to get out of here,' said Nick.

Too late. She ran across the muddy ground, black jumper covered in straw like a moving scarecrow. Nick looked back down the row to where the two men were still talking. It didn't look like they'd heard anything. They were facing away from him, heading to the far tunnel, the one that had people working inside.

Wiz reached the barn and crouched by the side of it, edging along the galvanised steel wall. As she reached the corner, Nick heard a low growling sound. The next second, two German shepherd dogs slunk around the corner, teeth bared. Wiz turned towards them, fear on her face.

Shit, thought Nick. He bloody hated dogs. He looked around for a stick.

The dogs circled around Wiz, bellies to the earth, nosing towards her. She backed towards the wall. Nick found a discarded bamboo cane on the ground. They'd bite through it in seconds, but it was all he had.

The dogs barked. Nick emerged from the tunnel, readied

himself to run to defend Wiz. A kid in a hoodie ran around the corner of the barn and grabbed the dogs by their collars.

'Down!' he called to them. 'Come on, guys, it's just me. Calm down.' The animals quietened, tails wagging, pushing against his skinny legs as he rubbed their ears.

The boy stared at Wiz in astonishment. 'What the hell are you doing here?'

The two men had turned at the noise. One, the local bloke, ran towards the teenagers.

'Oi, what's going on? Who's that?'

'Nothing,' said the kid. 'She's just a customer. She's been helping me out, selling bits and pieces around town.'

Nick shrank back into the tunnel as the man strode past.

'I told you. Don't bring no-one here unless you've got my say-so. Yeah?'

'Yeah. Sorry, boss.'

The guy took Wiz by the arm, looked into her face. 'You don't tell no-one you've been here. Right?'

'Why would I? It's a shit-hole.' Sulky even under extreme danger, thought Nick, full of admiration.

The man let her go, turned back to the kid. 'You got the money?'

He dug into his pocket, pulled out a roll of cash. 'Yeah.'

The man counted it, handed a couple of notes back. 'Better. Go get stocked up. Tell Guren I said half a kilo this time. OK?'

The kid nodded.

Nick hit the floor as the man walked past him, over the field. The dogs, docile now, slunk back around the barn. Nick lay still for a moment, wiping the sweat from his forehead. Christ, that had been close. But who was the kid who'd come to Wiz's rescue?

He crawled out of the polytunnel. The teenagers clearly knew each other. They seemed to be having a massive argument. God, thought Nick. Now is not the time. How the hell were he and Wiz going to get out of here?

Wiz tugged the boy's arm and dragged him over to the polytunnel.

'Shit,' the boy said, seeing Nick for the first time. 'I've seen you on the telly. You're a reporter.'

'Yeah,' said Nick. The kid was lanky, unhealthy-looking. His hair fell long and greasy over his eyes. He looked petrified.

'You've got to get away from here,' he said, urgently. 'It's not a good place. Bad shit goes down.' He was scratching the back of his hand, a shiny pink patch of eczema surrounded by wrinkled dry skin. 'Some bloke got knifed a couple of weeks ago.'

'Come with us,' said Wiz. 'You can stay at the shop. I'll look after you.'

He looked at her, helpless. 'I can't. I work for them. You don't understand.'

She shook her head. 'Mad. Right, how do we get out of here?'

The boy looked over at the men standing in the fields. A group of people who had been working in the tunnels had joined them. The men were ordering them around, pointing across the field to different tunnels.

'You can't go back that way. They'll see you. I have to go to the house to get my gear. You'll have to come with me, go up the drive and out on to the lane.'

'But they'll see us,' said Wiz.

The boy shrugged.

Nick sighed. 'You two go first. That's what they'll expect to

244

see. Then, when Wiz is clear and at the end of the drive, I'll make a run for it. Can you keep the dogs in order, mate?'

It was a terrible plan, but they didn't have another.

# Chapter 43

The sleek black Mercedes purred to a halt at the end of Fort Lane. The man in the back seat leaned forward, passed a brick of cash to Paxton from his briefcase. He wore leather gloves, dark glasses.

'Go, now. But you understand, we need to know where that letter is. My boss will be very unhappy if Miss Oddfellow disappears before telling us everything she knows.'

'Yeah. Got it.'

'And then – only then – you need to wipe up your other mess, with the reporter who runs around town looking into things that are none of his business. Once that has been done, we will move you out of the jurisdiction of the United Kingdom. We have routes, connections, operations overseas. We will find a use for you. Do not fear, Mr Paxton. We look after our more talented operatives.'

Paxton pocketed the cash and reached for the door handle. It didn't open.

'Driver?' came the voice from the back seat. 'You can unlock Mr Paxton's door now.'

It clicked, and he climbed out of the car. He realised he was trembling. Fuck's sake. He gulped in the damp evening air. The man scared him. He wasn't a mug; he knew that the people he dealt with were thugs, that violence was the language they understood best. But he was fluent in violence, understood its shifts and nuances. In any group of people, he was usually the one prepared to go furthest, inflict the most damage.

The man didn't look like he'd ever laid a manicured finger on anyone. It was his air of complete assurance that was chilling. If he decided to take you out, you wouldn't see it coming. There would be no chance to fight, no struggle. It would just happen, as slowly or as quickly as he wanted, agonisingly painful or so fast you simply ceased to exist.

The window purred downwards. 'Go on, Mr Paxton.'

He started to walk. His legs felt shaky, his knees bruised from where he'd gone down on the concrete garage floor. He flexed his right hand, felt the ache in his knuckles. When he was past the metal gate, he turned and saw the car disappear down the lane.

Breathing more easily, he continued down the path. About halfway along, he saw two kids walking towards him, deep in argument.

He stiffened. Something was wrong. It was the girl, Chapman's daughter, with the county lines kid, Levi. What the hell was she doing here? She was covered in straw, like she'd been crawling around a barn. He waited, let them get closer.

They were within ten yards of him when the girl looked up. She stopped, clutched Lev's arm. He looked up too, guilt written on his face.

'All right?' he asked Paxton. 'I've just been picking up supplies. And introducing a new courier. She's going to help us break into new markets. Aren't you, Wiz?'

The girl glared at him. 'If you say so.'

Paxton doubted that. But the county lines business was Guren's affair. He had enough to worry about already. He looked from Levi to the girl. Had he told her about his involvement in the break-in? But if so, why would she still be hanging out with him? Wouldn't she have reported him to the police?

His head hurt from all the possibilities. 'Go on, then,' he said. 'Get out of here.'

The teenagers broke into a run. He turned and watched them go. Weird. Throwing occasional looks over his shoulder, he continued down the drive. He felt exposed, wanted his knife back in his pocket, Cooper by his side. He'd spent most of the day feeling vulnerable, unable to defend himself. It wasn't a feeling he enjoyed.

A second later, Nick Wilson pelted around the corner from the farmyard, running hell for leather down the drive. Cooper was close behind him, little legs pumping as he raced to catch up.

Paxton's lights went on. Finally, a situation he knew how to deal with. He stepped to the side of the path, head down, letting Wilson get closer. Wilson was so intent on running, he didn't see him at first. Then he clocked a figure, hesitated for an instant, kept running. A second later, the full realisation of who he was running towards bloomed in his face.

Give him credit, he kept running. He tried to swerve past Paxton, like a scrum half with the ball and the touchline in sight. But Paxton had the advantage in weight and height. He waited until Wilson was almost level, let him think he might just make it. Then he shoulder-barged him, the shock of high-speed contact knocking the reporter to the ground.

Before Wilson could get his breath back, Paxton was on him, pinning him to the ground, sitting astride his skinny chest. One hand around both wrists, grinding them into the gravel, the other free to inflict damage. The reporter yelped. Of course, remembered Paxton. He'd broken his wrist before. It would be fragile, vulnerable. Which one was it? He squeezed tighter.

He sat back, wanting Wilson to feel the fear before his fist smashed into his face, breaking teeth and cheekbones, wrecking eye socket and nose cartilage.

'Wait,' said Wilson. 'Do you really want to do this on camera? Say hello to the viewers.' He grinned and waved over Paxton's shoulder.

Shit. Was he being filmed? Paxton turned his head to look.

Something happened underneath him, so quickly he could barely remember afterwards what it had been. Wilson wriggled, twisted, got him off-balance. Then a savage blow to the nuts. He gasped, retched, and rolled over to protect himself.

The reporter was on his feet again, running down the empty driveway. Outside the gate, Paxton could see a motorbike with the dark-haired girl astride it.

'Go after him,' he shouted to Cooper, scrambling to his knees. 'Bring him down.' The dog looked at him quizzically, then nuzzled his head into his side and started to lick his hand.

# Chapter 44

The door to the caravan opened, letting in a blast of cold air. Helen opened her eyes.

'Gary,' said Aisha, sitting up on the bunk. 'What has happened to you?'

Paxton stood in the doorway, staring at Helen. She swallowed her fear, lifted her chin, and stared right back.

He wasn't in much better shape than she was. His jeans were covered in mud or oil, the knees ripped out of them. He was unshaven, eyes dark-ringed in his puffy, pale face. Six years in prison had not been kind to him. She felt a slight lessening of her fear. Perhaps she had a chance. Then she saw the knife in his hand, the dull silver of the blade catching the light.

His eyes flicked to Aisha and back.

'Get out, you two,' he said. 'Go to the packing shed.'

Elira took Helen's hand.

'We like Helen,' said Aisha. 'She's our friend.'

'Fuck's sake.' He walked to the bunk and pressed the tip of the knife against Elira's neck. Her eyes widened and her fingers gripped tighter, but she said nothing.

'Go,' said Helen. Unlike Aisha, she had no faith in Paxton's better nature. She didn't want the sisters in danger. 'Go on, Elira. Take Aisha. I'll be all right.' She disentangled her fingers.

Paxton drew the knife slowly across Elira's neck. 'One chance,' he said, bending down to look the woman in the eyes.

She sat very still. Then she blinked acquiescence.

They left in silence. Helen watched them go, grateful that they had at least tried to protect her. They would know. They could tell people who Helen was with. If anyone came.

She got to her feet. She was an inch or two taller than Paxton. It didn't make up for the knife, or her arm in the improvised sling, but it made her feel better.

'Sit down,' he said.

'People trafficking, is it? That's a bit low, even for you.' The hatred that she usually kept locked safely away in her guts rose up, corrosive and acid.

'I said, sit down.' He pressed the knife tip against her cheek. She batted his arm away, catching her breath as the sharp blade pierced her skin with a hot pain. She raised her hand to her face. A thin trickle of blood ran down her cheek, wetting her fingers. She backed to the end of the caravan, where the gas fire hissed.

'You know how this goes,' he said, his voice rough. 'You do what I say. You tell me what I want to know. Either now or later. Later will be painful. Messy.'

She did know. During long insomniac nights, Helen still relived the hours she had spent at Paxton's mercy. The pain, burrowing into her head until she could think of nothing else. The humiliation of defeat. There was no holding out against what he would do. What he was prepared to do, to get the information he wanted. But what did he want to know?

251

She watched him advance, the knife easy in his hand. She sat.

'Better.' He stopped, stood over her with his wide boxer's stance.

Helen pressed her back against the flimsy wall behind her. 'What do you want? Where's Gus? What have you done with him?'

He frowned. 'Who?'

'Oh, come on,' said Helen. 'Don't mess me around.'

'I ask the questions.' His chin jutted forward, reasserting his control. But he had looked genuinely confused when she asked about Gus. Maybe he didn't know everything. That was something she could work with. The longer Helen could keep Paxton talking, the more chance she had.

'Go on,' she said. 'Because I have absolutely no idea what you've brought me here for. Unless you're planning to sell me off to a brothel like that poor girl.'

A twitch of amusement at the corner of his mouth. 'Too old,' he said.

'Yeah, I noticed that. Aisha's under sixteen, isn't she? What are you – fifty? That's called child abuse in the real world.'

His brows lowered. He grabbed her chin, yelled into her face. She could feel the flat blade of the knife pressing against her neck.

'I am not a fucking nonce. I just drive the van, OK?'

He shoved her backwards and she fell against her bruised arm, flinching. Elira had done a good job; manoeuvred the shoulder back into position with remarkably little pain and rigged up a sling from a pillowcase. But it felt tender, vulnerable.

'Did you kill Thomas Chapman?' Helen asked. She should

stop with the questions, but she wanted to know. She thought of the pitiful bundle lying in the silt at low tide, of Wiz stoically waiting for news.

'Who?' he asked. This time she could see by his face he was lying. He smirked, not caring that she knew it. But he'd been angry when she talked about Aisha. He had some boundaries, even if they went far beyond those of most civilised society. She needed to work out what they were.

Paxton sat on the bunk opposite her. Helen kept her eye on the knife as he shifted his grip, tested the tip against his thumb. Eventually he looked up, and she saw he was ready to get down to business. She swallowed, wondering what was coming.

'Right. There's a letter from a woman called Nancy Love. You have it, or you know where it is. Tell me now and we're done.'

Nancy's letter. What on earth would Paxton – or any of the thugs at the farm – want with that? And how the hell did they know about it? Bewildered, she played for time.

'And what will happen after I tell you? You'll drive me back home in your van, drop me off and wish me a nice life?' Helen's throat was dry. She tried to hold Paxton's gaze, see if he would tell her the truth.

He looked over her head, a little smile twisting the corner of his mouth.

'What do you think?' He let out a high-pitched snicker. Helen felt cold. She remembered that sound, the cruelty of the bully enjoying his power.

She tried to keep her voice steady, to deny him the satisfaction of seeing her fear. 'I think you would kill me. Otherwise, you'll be back in prison before I've put down the phone to the police.'

He looked at her then. 'So you'd shop me, Helen? You're not going to pretend you wouldn't report me if I let you go?'

She shook her head. 'No point. You wouldn't believe me, would you?'

'No.'

They stared at each other for a long moment. This man wants to kill me, Helen told herself. He doesn't just see it as a regrettable necessity. He wants me dead. She tried to find a calmness, an acceptance of his intent. If she was going to survive this – and by God she was going to try – she had to overcome her fear, keep her head clear.

She glanced around the caravan walls, smelled the oppressive fug of the gas fire and the grubby bedding. She would die here in this caravan, unless she could talk her way out. She didn't know where the letter was. But Paxton didn't know that.

'Nancy Love has been dead for almost two hundred years,' she said, trying to make it sound like a normal conversation. 'I think she wrote a letter to her sister on the day she died, and gave it to a young boy to deliver. He was scared off, possibly by the man who murdered her. The boy kept the letter. Is that the one you want?'

He was frowning again, as if the story was new to him. 'Yeah. I suppose so.'

'OK. Good to be clear, isn't it? I don't have the letter. I've been working on finding it. I have some ideas, but I haven't had time to confirm them yet.'

'Don't give me that shit. You know.'

Helen sighed. 'Gary, why would I pretend? I don't want to be tortured before I die. No point, is there? I'm dead either way. I might as well tell you what I know and get it over with.'

He was watching with narrowed eyes. Would he buy it?

'I'll tell you what I've learned so far. But first, tell me this. Have you read much Charles Dickens?' she asked.

'Are you taking the piss?'

'Not at all. Nancy's messenger boy was Charles Dickens. It helps me explain if you know at least something about his work.'

He rolled his eyes. 'Fuck's sake. Yeah, I read some of his shit at school. *Great Expectations*. All right?'

Helen beamed. 'Excellent. He set it here. Did you know that? It starts close to where we are now, out on the marshes, the young boy helping the escaped convict from the prison ship. And it finishes out here too, on the river, with Pip trying to save Magwitch from being recaptured and sent back to prison. Remember?'

He nodded, his face sulky. 'I know. I grew up near here. Chatham.'

Helen had a sudden image of him as a schoolboy. The kid who always looked bored, couldn't see the point. The one who messed around in class, got into fights and nicked people's lunch money. When she'd been a schoolteacher, she'd worked hard to reach those kids; with little success. But sometimes they would tell you stuff in detention after school. Hair-raising stories of neglect or casual violence, chaotic homes.

'Did you really? So did Dickens. His father worked at the dockyard, so the family lived in Chatham before they moved to London. Then he moved back to Kent towards the end of his life, near Rochester. Gads Hill.' She sensed he was getting impatient with the biographical details.

'Anyway. He had this letter from Nancy Love. I know he

255

kept it for decades. You know the Mudie book? The one you forced Thomas Chapman to steal from my hotel room?'

He stared at her, impassive. But his lack of response told her she'd been right.

'Well, Dickens wrote a note in the back, in shorthand. I've been decoding it. It's about Nancy's letter. He says he hid it.'

Helen was rapidly cycling through all the possibilities. She needed to persuade him to let her out of the caravan. She thought again of *Great Expectations*, which seemed to resonate with him. At least he'd remembered it.

'When your friends picked me up, I'd been visiting St James's Church near Cooling. That's where *Great Expectations* starts, in the graveyard.'

'Where the kids' graves are,' said Paxton, unexpectedly.

'That's right. According to the shorthand note, he hid the letter somewhere linked to the novel. He said he had given it into Pip's safekeeping.' She held his gaze as she changed the details of the letter. 'I thought one possibility was that Dickens had hidden the letter at St James's. But there was nothing there.'

She paused, trawling through her memory. She'd been planning a Dickens tour of Kent to complement the London tour, and had spent hours poring over maps and potential locations. Where would work?

Paxton was leaning forward, eyes alight with interest. 'Go on, then.'

'So I'm thinking, what about the end of the book? The Thames, where Pip and Magwitch row a boat out to meet the steamer. They stayed near Gravesend, then rowed downstream – about here, I guess?'

'Here?'

256

'Well, north of here. Up by the river. Somewhere that hasn't been in regular use since Dickens's time, or the letter would have been found. Somewhere that Dickens might have had access to as a famous local author. And I thought, what about the forts? They were building them while Dickens lived at Gads Hill. He'd have been interested. Maybe they showed him around?'

'The forts? They're derelict,' said Paxton. 'We used to go up there and mess about when I was a kid.'

She smiled. 'Even better. You know them already.'

Forts guarded the mouth of the Thames and the Medway, dating back to the Napoleonic era. The Victorians had built more, running up the estuary from Tilbury in the north and Gravesend south of the river. Helen hadn't been out there yet, but had seen photographs of the brooding old structures close to the Saxon Shore Way. There would be walkers, maybe birdwatchers out on the marshes. A chance of escape.

'I've been all over Shornemead,' said Paxton. 'There's nothing there. It's just an old gun emplacement. And you can't get into Cliffe Fort, now. Private land. Owned by an aggregate company.'

Helen nodded. 'That's the one, then. Cliffe Fort. It'll be undisturbed. What do you reckon, Gary? Shall we have a look?'

She held her breath for a long moment. Would he go for it?

# Chapter 45

They trudged through the bleak landscape. The sun was disappearing over the marshes to their left, casting a bruised purple twilight that gave the scene an uncanny atmosphere. Great pools of water – former gravel pits – shimmered with flocks of grey geese. An elegant white bird with a kinked neck rose from the marshy grassland and flapped slowly over their heads towards the river.

Paxton had a tight hold of her elbow. She could hear his breathing, labouring as they hurried over the rough ground. His dog – a puppy, still quite small – ran ahead, then circled back to his heels. Narrow paths criss-crossed the land. It was a nature reserve, with an information board near the entrance about the different species of birds that overwintered there. Gus would love it, Helen thought, irrationally, as if they might come across him emerging from a hide.

Gus. What had happened to Gus? She'd been so intent on her own escape, she'd almost forgotten about him.

She'd also forgotten how early the sun set at this time of year. There were no bird-spotters out with their binoculars, no dog-walkers. Just Helen and Paxton, and the steady drone of machinery from the aggregate yard that bordered the site.

'Hang on,' she said. They'd walked to the reserve from the road that ran north from the farm and climbed on to a raised bank which gave a better view of the pools and hedgerows. She paused and pointed towards the dim shape of the fort in the distance. 'We need to be over that way, to the left. We're going to end up on the wrong side of the creek.'

'Nah,' said Paxton. 'Can't get through that way. That's the road where all the lorries go. They have security guards and stuff. If we follow this path, then you can get across the creek and come out the other side.'

'Right,' said Helen. 'I keep forgetting you know it.' This was weird. From a distance, they must look like a normal couple, taking their dog for an evening walk.

Her arm ached. She found it hard to walk with him hanging on to her. She cursed her bruised shoulder. If she'd not been injured, she could have run for it, fought him off. Maybe. She was hyper-aware of the vicious knife in his right hand. Her cheek stung from the cut he'd inflicted earlier.

They came to the end of the hedgerow, where Paxton had said they could cross the creek.

'Shit,' he said. They looked down at where the bridge had once been. The broken timbers had been cleared away. It was a steep scramble down into the creek, and the ground looked treacherous, boggy. A drainage pipe spanned the creek, narrow and slick with algae. Maybe, thought Helen. It wasn't too far to run back to the road.

'Why don't you try it, see if you can get across?' she asked.

'Don't take me for a mug.' He gripped her arm. 'You reckon you can get over on that? Go on then. I'm right behind you.'

Maybe she could run ahead to the fort while he crossed the pipe behind her. Maybe she could reach the lorry drivers, the people working at the aggregate plant. Any chance was better than none.

Three, maybe four paces. She pushed through the branches of the hedge and stood on the muddy bank. She held on to a slender wand of willow, trying to find her balance. One step out on to the pipe. She looked straight ahead at the indigo sky. Another. She felt the slight skid of her boot on the slippery surface; waited. Let go of the willow. Two more steps and she'd be on the bank.

One more and her foot skidded sideways. She lurched forward, flung herself towards the bank. She landed among brambles, tore her hands as she grabbed at them to stop her slide. Her feet scrambled against the slick mud and she plunged knee-deep into freezing water.

'Are you all right?' shouted Paxton. She looked up, saw him crawling commando-style across the pipe on his hands and knees. The dog was tucked into his jacket, nuzzling his neck.

'Yeah.' Helen braced one boot against a half-submerged tree branch and tried to climb out of the creek. Her left boot was stuck in the sucking mud. She tried to crawl out, but was held firm by the bog that clung around her ankle. She heaved at it, sweat starting out on her forehead.

'My foot's stuck.'

Paxton got to the far side and inched down the bank towards her. He extended his hand.

'Come on.'

She grabbed it with her good hand. The powerful grip enclosed her fingers, circled her wrist. She gasped as he heaved her up, her arm jolting so hard she was worried it would dislocate the other shoulder. But it worked. She knelt on the bank for a moment, getting her breath back.

'You have to be careful round here,' he said. He unzipped his jacket, set the pup back on the ground, scratched behind its ears. He didn't look evil; he looked normal. A normal, tired middle-aged bloke playing with a puppy.

For the past six years, Helen had been haunted by the thought of him. This monster who had killed without remorse, inflicted pain without flinching. He'd become an ogre in her mind, a terrifying presence in her nightmares, invincible.

He was still, she reminded herself, capable of those things. And his aim was to kill her once he'd found out what she knew. But he was a human being, not a monster. Which meant she had a chance.

'What happened to you?' she asked, on impulse.

He looked up, startled. 'What do you mean?'

'Something went wrong. You're not stupid. I don't believe people are born evil. Why are you like this?'

He got to his feet, climbed up the bank. 'There's nothing wrong with me. If you live in a fucked-up world, you have to fight. You'd be a mug not to.'

'But there are other ways...'

'Listen, Helen. Most people in this world don't have time for books, or the theatre, or worrying about whether people are nice enough to ethnic minorities or refugees or gays. Most people just want to feed their kids and live in a decent world where they get a decent chance, yeah?'

Helen followed him. 'Do you have kids, then?'

He didn't turn round. 'A boy.'

'See much of him?'

'No.'

She caught him up and they continued down the path

through the hedgerow.

'I'd like kids,' she said. 'One day.' I might already have had them, she thought, if Richard was still alive. She swallowed down her bitterness. They'd made a connection, of sorts. Paxton might find it harder to do what he planned to do to her once he realised there was nothing hidden in the fort.

He turned and looked at her, and she saw again the sneer, the bully's laughter.

'Bit fucking late for that,' he said.

Maybe, thought Helen. It was the first time she'd voiced the thought aloud. Perhaps it had been Lady Maria's goading that put it in her head. But it was true, she realised. She did want kids. She hoped she'd have the chance to try.

Helen looked past Paxton to where the fort sat on the horizon, its stone walls touched with silver. An almost-full moon had risen behind them, casting its pale light over the watery landscape.

'Almost there,' she said.

# Chapter 46

They skirted around an enormous heap of sand, diggers parked around the base, and joined a muddy path beside the Thames. Helen gazed out across the dark river, its oily surface marbled with moonlight. It smelled vegetal, of seaweed and rotten wood. There were strings of lights on the far side of the Thames, cranes swinging from vast container ships at the port on the Essex shore. Too far away to be of any help.

The path, closed in now with chain-link fencing, turned inland where a huge conveyor belt cut across the site. The rickety-looking structure ran from a dock in the river to the sand heap. Nothing was moving, but she could hear the rumble of machinery. There would be someone there, someone she could appeal to. She tried to ease away from Paxton, get ready to run.

The path ran under the conveyor belt. As they approached, a man in a hard hat and orange reflective jacket came through and held up a hand. Thank God, thought Helen. A chance.

'Wait there!' he shouted. 'I'm starting it up.'

Paxton stood still, holding her elbow tight. 'Quiet,' he murmured.

The man turned his back and threw a switch. The noise got louder, clattering and squealing as the metal gears and cogs started to turn and the belt moved, grinding along with its load of sand. Now or never.

'Please help me,' she called, yanking her arm away from Paxton and running towards the man. 'He has a knife.'

The man half-turned, surprise on his face. Before he could react, Paxton was on to him. In one swift movement, he grabbed his shoulder, spun him around, and buried the knife in his throat.

'No!' shouted Helen. She tried to pull Paxton's arm away, but it was like wrestling with an iron bar. The dog snapped at her, jumped up, got its needle teeth into her hand.

The man writhed for a few long seconds. A horrible gurgled scream as the blood poured out around the knife, pulsing over Paxton's hands and down the orange jacket until the white sand under their feet was sodden with it. Then the noise stopped and the man was still.

Paxton dropped the body on to the sand. The dog let go of Helen, licked at the pool of blood. She dropped to her knees beside the body, felt his wrist for a pulse, knowing it was useless. The machinery ground on, a deafening cacophony.

'You stupid cow. That was your fault, that was. You killed him.'

She stared up at Paxton, barely able to believe what had happened. Despite his angry words, he looked calm, quite calm. Despite the viscous blood coating his hands, spattered across his face and soaking his sleeves. His face was at rest, as if he had dealt with a minor inconvenience, not killed another human being.

He bent and wiped the knife clean on the man's jeans, then

folded the blade and slipped it back in his pocket. He put his hand to the dog's collar and pulled it away.

'Cooper, leave it. Come on.'

He pulled her up, his hand rough on her shoulder, then pushed her through the gap under the rumbling belt carrying sand and gravel above their heads. She tasted it in the air, gritty on her lips and tongue.

The fort walls were ahead of them. Two storeys of grey stone blocks, rectangular windows like a Victorian factory. The windows were barred with metal shutters. Between them and the walls were a barbed wire fence and a dry moat, overgrown with brambles.

'Round this way.' She followed along the dusty path towards a small hut, the light on. The door stood open. She glimpsed a chair with a desk and a computer. A half-drunk mug of tea, a calendar on the wall, a child's drawing. Helen's legs stopped working. She pressed her hands against her mouth, swayed on her feet. Acid rose in her throat.

'Move.' Paxton shoved her in the back.

They climbed up the aggregate heap to the back of the fort, where the piles of sand and gravel met the walls. A window, unbarred.

'Go on. Get in.'

Helen stepped through. This could be the last place on earth I see, she thought. She did not much care. The shock had numbed her capacity to feel fear, to feel anything.

The moon reflected silver off a big pool of water. Much of the interior was flooded. She scrambled down from the window on to rubble, where the fort had crumbled.

It was quieter inside, the roar of the machinery muffled by the great stone walls. She could make out shadowy concrete shapes, the remains of gun emplacements and iron tracks. A control tower to one side. She walked to the water's edge and saw her own shadow stretch across it, biting into the moon-mirrored surface.

The man had died right in front of her. She'd brought that death to him, as certainly as if she'd been holding the knife herself. She had stood next to him and heard his dying scream. Yet she knew nothing of him, not even his name. The fact of the death was so enormous it crowded out all other functional thoughts. A family somewhere had been smashed, because she had called to a stranger for help.

Paxton's shadow appeared next to her. 'Right,' he said. 'Where are you going to look for this letter?'

She walked into the water, feeling the cold seep through her boots. It closed around her ankles. The ground was uneven and she stumbled into holes, over blocks of stone.

'Hey! What are you doing?'

Helen kept walking. The water reached her knees. Dimly, she remembered her plan. Get out of the caravan, keep talking to him, go somewhere there would be other people, get help. She'd talked about Charles Dickens, *Great Expectations*, the convict's attempted escape on the river. Fooled herself she could break through to him, reason with him.

There would be no help. She had no words. She kept walking into the water. The still surface shimmered in ripples around her, the cold clasping her waist. She let her hands trail in the water, fingers numb.

'Helen, wait.' He sounded oddly frightened. 'It's dangerous. You don't know how deep it is.'

Something tore across her thigh, ripping into her skin. She gasped. She was caught on something. Cautiously, she sought

266

the source. Wire, barbed wire, wrapped around her right leg. She tried to uncoil it; her fingers clumsy with cold.

Paxton splashed through the water towards her. 'What's happening? Helen, talk to me. We need to find this letter. Remember? Nancy Love, the letter that Dickens hid.'

She turned her head then and looked at him. It was as if he'd forgotten it already, as if the man had not been real to him. An obstacle, a thing in the way. Like Richard had been. Like she would be, once he knew she'd been lying about the letter and the fort.

'Don't be stupid. Come on, you've got to help me. Like Pip, yeah? Like he helped Magwitch on the marshes?'

Helen stared at him. Was it possible that this man was comparing himself to Dickens' mysterious and tragic character? That he saw himself as some kind of hero? She shook her head, turned her attention back to the wire. It was attached to something on the ground beneath her feet. She felt around in the black water, trying to find a loose end.

She thought of Nancy Love, the actress, playing politics in a game with stakes too high for her to win. The real Nancy, murdered by Tom Buller. Buller was once a soldier, like Paxton. Dickens had taken Nancy's murderer and transformed him into one of the most vicious, callous thugs he ever wrote.

Paxton isn't Magwitch, she thought. He's Bill Sikes. She thought of the end of *Oliver Twist*, the desperate Sikes holed up on Jacob's Island in the Thames at Bermondsey. His attempt to escape the mob, swinging above the stinking creek of Folly Ditch.

'What are you doing?' The little dog was in Paxton's jacket again, licking his face. 'What is it? You've changed. You're not

267

trying anymore.' He sounded put out, disappointed. 'Do I have to remind you what happens when you don't co-operate?'

He waded out further. The dog wriggled out of his arms, dived into the water.

'Cooper, you stupid animal.' He splashed after it. The little dog emerged, its wet head slick as it swam through the water. It was heading for the undergrowth by the wall on the river side of the fort, where small animals rustled. Rats, Helen supposed. Something squealed, then disappeared into the water with a splash and ripple.

She shuddered. Could rats swim? She had a sudden horror of the rats swarming to where she was stuck, attracted by the blood in the water. Gnawing away at the edge of the wound.

'I'm stuck,' she shouted. 'Stuck on some bloody wire.'

He turned, a smile on his face. 'I told you to be careful. I suppose you want my help, now.'

She took a breath. 'Yes.'

'Yes what?'

'Yes, I want your help. Please.'

He walked towards her, deeper into the cold water. The water came almost to his chest by the time he reached her. He stood in front of her, the knife open in his right hand, testing the blade against his thumb.

She watched the knife. He would know soon, if he did not already, that the letter was not here. And she was trapped by the wire and the water, in a place where nobody ever came.

'Where's the letter, Helen?'

She could not see his face. His head was a silhouette against the moonlit sky. He would see her, though. Would he know if she lied?

'I don't think it's here,' she said.

'What?' He grabbed a fistful of her hair, forced her head back.

'I thought it might be,' she said. 'But this place is ruined. There's nowhere to hide it. I need to think again. We both do, if we're to find that letter for your boss.'

He pushed his face close to hers. She could smell his breath, sour with hatred and fear.

'You've been stringing me along. I should leave you here. Let the rats get you.'

'But then you'll never find it. What are they going to do to you, Gary, if you go back without it?'

She waited. He let go of her hair, spat into the dark water. She saw it floating, a clump of white bubbles on the tar-black surface.

'Cut the wire,' she told him. 'I'll help you. But you have to get me out of here first.'

'Show me where it is.'

Her hands were so cold, they hurt; her fingers numb. But she tried to make them gentle as she took his knife hand in both of hers.

'Under the water. Round my leg.' She guided the knife down, under the surface. His eyes, so close, locked on to hers. His breath, shallow and soft.

'Like this,' she whispered.

She turned the knife, drove it up with all her strength. Kept pushing, twisting, lifting. He howled.

Across the water, the small dog froze, lifted its head, and howled back.

# Chapter 47

Nick rode out to the farm behind the convoy. First went four unmarked police vans, stuffed with tooled-up officers itching to get their hands on Guren Hasani and his criminal gang. The team had been assembled and briefed at breakneck speed after he and Wiz had explained the situation to DCI Sarah Greenley.

They'd been trying to get something on Hasani for months, she said, but had met only silence and fear. The chance to break up a people-trafficking organisation, a modern slavery gang and a county lines drug-dealing operation in one swoop meant resources were no issue for once.

Sarah was in a car following the vans, alongside the officers from Rochester overseeing the operation. To Nick's surprise, the policewoman had been grateful enough for the information to allow him and his team along to film the raid. Good PR, Sarah had said, after the debacle at Dover. Behind the police car, at a decent distance, came Angus and Simon. Simon was driving while Angus steadied the camera, although there was little of the bleak landscape to be seen through the dark windows.

Nick followed on his bike, Wiz riding pillion. He knew

he shouldn't have brought her, but she'd been desperate to come. It couldn't be that dangerous, with all the police around. She'd promised to keep behind him and Angus until the arrests had been made. Needless to say, he hadn't told Sarah he was bringing a sixteen-year-old girl as part of his team.

It was dark by the time they arrived at the turning. The convoy paused out of sight of the security camera, while one officer got out and took a pair of bolt cutters to the padlock on the gate. Then they were in, driving at top speed along the driveway where Nick had tussled with Paxton. He was going to enjoy seeing that meathead brought to justice again.

The police vans pulled into the dark farmyard just as a black SUV roared out of a barn, heading straight for them. The vans fanned out to block the driveway and the SUV braked, then reversed rapidly. Nick pulled off his helmet, trying to see what was happening. Angus was leaning out of the car, camera on his shoulder.

One of the police vans roared after the SUV, down a muddy track. Nick heard brakes squeal, voices shouting. Police officers piled out of the other vans, running with batons raised into the farmhouse, the barn, yelling for anyone inside to get down. Nick parked the bike and jumped off.

'Get into the back of our car and stay there till I say,' he told Wiz.

He ran to the car and yanked open the door. She slipped in, eyes wide beneath her helmet. Nick gave a breathless running commentary to camera as police emerged from the farmhouse building, marching out a couple of men and a woman and depositing them in the van.

Nick and the team ran over to the barn. Big tables covered with plastic packing crates ran down the centre of the vast,

chilly space. Along the walls were lines of mattresses. People
– dozens of them – sat on the mattresses, shivering in the
chilly night. Some scrambled to their feet, started to run. The
place was cacophonous. Three guard dogs were chained by
the door, barking their heads off. The police were shouting,
men gesticulating and yelling.

Nick noted a line of buckets on the far wall. The smell made
it clear these were the bathroom facilities. He pointed, got
Angus to film them. A female police officer escorted out two
trembling women wrapped in blankets, and Nick followed
with his team.

'Get out of the way,' the police officer yelled at him.

He raised his hands. 'Sorry. Have you found Helen yet? Or
Gary Paxton?'

One woman whipped her head around. She was young, still
a kid.

'You know Helen?' she asked. 'Are you her friend?'

'Yes! You've seen her? Is she here somewhere?' he asked.

The girl nodded vigorously. 'She was in the caravan with
us. Then Gary came and sent us to the barn. I'm scared for
her. I think something bad is going to happen.'

The police officer paused. 'Which caravan? Show me.'

Three police officers ran along the row of caravans, the girl
leading the way. Nick and Angus ran with them. Panicked
faces were pressed against the windows, women with tears
streaked down their cheeks.

'Christ,' said the woman police officer. 'There are dozens of
them.'

The girl stopped outside one ramshackle caravan. 'Here.'

There was no light showing. Nick's mouth was dry, his
heart hammering. How long had Paxton been alone with

Helen? What had he done to her? He prayed to the God he only called on in extreme circumstances. Deliver us from evil. And don't let us be too late.

'Get back,' said an officer. He booted the flimsy door down and flashed a torch around the interior.

It was empty.

'This is the right one?' the police officer asked.

'Yes. Look, that's my hair scrunchy on the bed,' said the girl. She grabbed it and pulled her long blonde hair back into a ponytail. 'He must have taken her somewhere.'

'Where would they go?' Nick jumped at Wiz's voice.

'I told you to stay in the car,' he said.

The female police officer rolled her eyes. 'For God's sake, get out of the bloody way. We're going to clear these caravans.' She talked into her radio. 'We need more transport here, and somewhere to take all these people. There's bloody loads of them.'

She moved off. Wiz and the girl were staring at each other.

'Are you all right?' Wiz asked.

'I'm scared. What's going to happen to us?'

Wiz shrugged. 'The police will look after you, I suppose. I don't know.'

'Will they send us back to Albania?'

'I don't know.'

'Listen,' Nick broke in. 'Why don't you both sit in the car? It's not safe until the police have found all the bad guys. And we need to find Helen.'

He shepherded them back down the lane to the farmyard. Sarah Greenley came running across the muddy ground, bulky in her stab vest and jacket.

'What's going on? Who are these girls? Have you found

Helen?'

'Not yet. She was here, though. One of the girls saw her with Paxton, in a caravan. No-one there now. I thought they should get in the car, out of the way.' He didn't want to tell DCI Greenley that he'd brought Wiz here himself on the back of his bike.

The policewoman nodded. 'OK.' She held open the door of the police car. 'This one.'

Wiz threw Nick a dark look as she sat in the back. Like him, she wasn't keen on the police. Nick bent down to talk to them.

'Don't worry. She's nice, really. She'll look after you.'

'Thank you,' said DCI Greenley, raising an eyebrow. 'You stay here with them. I've got a job to do.'

She walked off towards the farmhouse, where lights were now blazing. Angus and Simon filmed as the police escorted out a procession of hefty-looking men, handcuffed behind their backs, and loaded them into a van. How did they know who was a suspect and who was a victim? Nick wondered. Maybe they didn't; maybe they'd have to sort it out down at the police station. He hoped they'd find one with enough cells.

'Nick, Aisha knows something.' Wiz was tugging at his arm. He crouched down to listen.

The girl's face was pinched and anxious. 'I wanted to help. When Gary pushed us out of the caravan, I stayed outside by the window. I listened to what they were saying, but I didn't understand everything.'

'What did you hear?'

'First, she talked about me, said I was too young for him. That made him angry. Then she asked him if he killed someone. Thomas someone?'

Wiz gasped. 'Thomas Chapman. My dad.'

Aisha clasped her hand. 'I'm sorry. I didn't know. But he didn't say. He asked, "Who?" like he didn't know who that was.'

'OK. What else?' asked Nick.

'Then there was some stuff I didn't understand, someone who had been dead for two hundred years. And Helen said she thought he would kill her if she told him about a letter.'

Nick swallowed. Bloody Helen, never shying away from the truth. The woman was absolutely fearless.

'Nancy Love,' said Wiz. 'Helen was looking for a letter from Nancy Love, a woman who Charles Dickens knew when he was a kid. She died two hundred years ago.'

'That's right! There was a lot of talk about Gary reading books at school by – what was the name you said? Charles Dickens? I have heard about him, I think. An old English writer.'

'Go on.' Nick's neck prickled. Whatever secret Helen had been chasing, they seemed to be getting close to it now.

'She was talking about where this Charles Dickens had hidden the letter. And she said she had looked in a church, but it was not there. And then about the river – about people in boats on the river near here. But then a man came to look for me and I had to go to the barn.'

The river. Nick pulled up a map on his phone. They weren't far from the river; you could see the gantries and lights from the docks over the fields.

'Wiz, help me out here. What's up by the river?'

She looked at the phone with him. 'Nothing. Just a load of gravel pits full of water. You get bird-spotters up there. There's a rifle range further up the river, over towards

Gravesend.'

Gravel pits. Graves. Guns. None of this was sounding good, thought Nick. He switched to the satellite view on the map.

'What's all that white stuff by the ponds?' he asked.

'Sand, gravel, stuff like that. There's a company that owns all the land round there, digs it up and puts it on lorries. And that's an old fort.' She pointed to a curved wall, a row of buildings. 'Me and Lev used to go there sometimes. It's cool out there. Lots of sunken wooden boats on the shore, rotting away.'

Wooden boats. Nick was grasping at straws here, but if Helen and Paxton had been talking about boats on the river, maybe it was worth a try.

# Chapter 48

Paxton staggered backwards, the blade in his guts. He fell, floundered in the water. It closed over his head, flooded into his open mouth. The cold shot through him like electricity. He kicked furiously, broke the surface, struggled for a foothold.

The need to clear water from his lungs was more urgent than the tearing pain in his stomach. He coughed, felt his muscles rip against steel. Somehow, he steadied his stance. The water held him, supported him. He coughed again, retched. He found the handle of the knife.

Hold it there, he told himself. Don't try to take it out. He remembered the training, the early days in Iraq. The shaven-headed special forces veteran, showing them the fine art of hand-to-hand combat. If a knife goes into you, keep it in place. It plugs the wound, stops you from bleeding out.

He raised his head. She was three paces away, watching him, her eyes wide with shock. All that training, and he'd let a woman turn his knife back on himself. The shame of it was almost worse than the pain.

A knife to the guts. It was deep, felt serious. He had half an hour, maybe an hour, if he wasn't bleeding too hard. Before the stomach acid ate through something vital. A painful, protracted death. If he could get help quickly, he might live. But how?

He thought of the hut, the office by the aggregate yard. There'd be a phone. His mind flicked to the body he'd left on the sand. No matter.

He waded for shore. He'd like to finish her off, but there was no time. Anyway, she was stuck. Eventually, the cold or the exhaustion would get her. She'd sway, stagger, slip under the icy water. No-one would know what had happened to her. Maybe one day, they'd drain the pit and find her skeleton, gnawed clean by vermin.

The water was below the knife, now. He looked down, saw the leather handle protruding above the waistline of his jeans. The pain was worse out of the numbing embrace of the water. Things were slipping out of place, dragging. With an effort, he locked the pain away.

His legs were heavy and unresponsive. He saw a block of concrete at the edge of the water. Don't sit down, he told himself. Keep going. You have to keep going.

He sat on the edge for a second to get his strength together. Water streamed to the ground. Not just water. He glanced down at the knife, the steady pulse of blood around it. Not good. His heart rhythm was fast, skipping, trying to keep up.

He looked across the moonlit pool. She still watched. Her face was wet, tears coursing down it.

'What… what you crying about?' His voice was barely there, the effort to fill his lungs was too difficult. He shivered. It was so cold.

'I had to do it,' she said. Her voice rang clearly across the water. 'You were going to kill me.'

He grunted assent. 'Not dead yet,' he said.

She received that in silence. Then: 'You will be.'

'I tried to help you, didn't I?' His voice sounded whiny, even to his own ears. The boiling pit of his guts clamoured for his attention, sent him urgent signals. In a minute, he thought. I'll get up and go in a minute.

'You killed that man. Just because I asked him for help. He had a family. They don't even know he's dead yet.'

Was that what had upset her so much? Paxton tried to remember the first time he'd seen someone killed. Not at a distance, through night goggles or down a scope, when you might as well be playing a video game. Close by. He had a flash of memory: one guy he'd trained with, blown to pieces by an IED as they'd checked the perimeter of the base, patrolling together. Paxton had been five paces behind; had stopped to light a cigarette.

He remembered his panicky call over the radio, his attempts to find a large enough piece of the body that might still be alive. Finding the head. The look of surprise on the man's face. He couldn't even remember his name now.

'You killed Thomas Chapman. Wiz's dad.'

'That was business,' he said. Cooper came trotting up to him, put his muzzle on his knee. Paxton laid his hand on the little fellow's head. Smooth, warm.

'It was murder,' said Helen, her low voice vehement. Paxton was weary. He had no energy left to reply. His head felt heavy.

'You murdered Richard,' she said. Her voice had dropped to a whisper. Paxton tried to remember.

Richard? Which one was he?

# Chapter 49

'I know it's a long shot,' said Nick. 'But they've not found her anywhere on the farm. We know Paxton was with her, and they were talking about the river. What do you think?'

Sarah Greenley tapped her fingers together, brain whirring almost audibly. 'We caught the SUV. Paxton wasn't in it, and we've not found him. We've got roadblocks in place; he won't get far now. But if they left before we arrived...'

She waved over an officer. 'Come with me in the car. We've got a potential lead for Paxton. He's dangerous. Nick, you can lead the way – but don't do anything. Wait for us to check the area first. All right?'

Nick grabbed his bike helmet and pulled it on. 'Thank you.'

He tore out of the farmyard, up the track and on to the road north, towards the promontory he'd seen on the map. It was less than a mile. He followed the signposts to the RSPB nature reserve; turned left off the road on to a single-lane track, Salt Lane. For once, the headlights of the police car behind him were reassuring.

He stopped by a gate covered in warning signs. Private property, Thames Aggregate. No unauthorised entry. Lorries need constant access. Guard dogs patrolling, CCTV in operation. The police car pulled up beside him and the window rolled down.

'The main entrance to the nature reserve is round the corner, but then you have to walk for a mile or two to the river. It'll be quicker down here,' said the police officer at the wheel. He jumped out to open the gates. Nick kicked the accelerator and roared through, down the narrow road, throwing up white dust that clogged his nostrils. The road broadened. There was a wide lake to his left, glittering in the moonlight as the wind ruffled its surface. A railway track ran parallel with the road, leading dead straight down towards the river.

He could see the fort now, solid stone walls looming against the white heaps of sand. He drew up in a skid of gravel by a small hut. Once he'd killed the bike engine, he could hear the machinery, a relentless grinding.

He dismounted, ran towards the hut where a light shone. The door was open, no-one inside. A phone was ringing on the desk. He picked it up.

'What's going on?' asked a voice.

'I dunno. Just got here,' said Nick.

'Switch the bloody thing off, then. It's been running for hours. And tell Rob to call me back, yeah? Where is he, anyway? I can't get through to his mobile.'

'I don't know.' Nick replaced the receiver.

He walked out of the hut, feeling uneasy. A pile of rubble behind him led up to a window in the fort wall. The police car parked just beyond his bike, headlights slicing through the dark.

Two officers got out. The man pointed to something Nick couldn't see around the corner of the fort, and they ran

281

towards it. Sarah Greenley turned to him and held up her palm. Wait there.

Yeah, right. Nick climbed the pile of sand to the gap in the wall and looked through. The moon shone on a pool of water, the smooth surface barely moving. Rubble and debris cluttered the base of the stone walls, overgrown with weeds. He stepped through into the empty fort, swearing as a stinging nettle caught him, and scanned the dark enclosure. He could see no-one. The place was quiet, still, protected by the stone walls from the wind and noise outside.

Maybe there was something out the front where the police officers had gone. Where the wrecked boats were, down by the river. He turned to go.

Then a dog barked, a flurry of yaps coming from the water's edge. Nick scrambled down the rubble, climbing over concrete blocks and iron rails. The ugly little dog jumped up, snarling. A puppy, some kind of bull terrier. Paxton's dog.

He rounded a concrete block by the side of the pool. A figure lay slumped on the ground. A dark stain spread from it, draining down to the water. One hand was clasped around the handle of a knife, buried in its belly.

Nick pushed aside the yapping pup, crouched beside the man, and took a long look into his face. The eyes were open, glazed. Gary Paxton. Dead.

Nick straightened, scanning the fort.

'Helen! Helen, are you here? It's Nick. Come out. It's safe now.'

Nothing. The dog continued to yap. Nick stood at the edge of the pool, a sudden feeling of icy fear. He remembered Wiz's dad, drowned in the Medway river.

His eyes raked across the water. How deep was it?

Bubbles. There were bubbles where the water rippled in the centre of the pool. Nick ran into the water, gasping at the cold. Ankle deep, then knee high. Harder to push through. When it reached his hips, he plunged in and swam. He could see nothing through the dark water. Where the hell was she?

His hand touched something solid. Christ, no. He surfaced, took a breath and dived down again. Something floated ahead of him. An arm. He grasped it, pulled it towards him. She was drifting, face down. He got his shoulder under her torso, heaved her above the surface, heavy and unresponsive as a sack of cement.

He tried to pull her away, swim her to the dry land. But she was caught on something. He found it, a strand of barbed wire around her leg. Shit. He pulled her body upright, clasped her belly from behind and pulled in sharply, the best imitation of a Heimlich manoeuvre he could manage in the circumstances.

Foul-smelling water trickled from her mouth.

'Come on.' He pulled again, driving his fist into her diaphragm.

A deluge of water, then – thank God – a gasp.

'That's it! Good girl. Come back. God, Helen…' He was babbling, tears of relief running down his face.

She retched, coughed, staggered, almost fell back into the water. He held her tight.

'Lean on me. On my shoulder. That's right. I've got you.'

She was so cold. How long had she been there, caught on that wire? She was sobbing and coughing, convulsive gasps against his ear.

'It's OK. Sarah Greenley's here. She'll find us in a minute,' he said. He bloody well hoped she would; he wasn't sure how long he could hold them both upright in this freezing pool.

She was trying to say something.

'Paxton,' he heard.

'Don't worry about that bastard,' said Nick. 'Dead. You'll never have to worry about him again.'

She muttered something he didn't catch.

'It's all right.' He adjusted his hold, his arms straining with her weight.

'I killed him.' She lifted her head, gazed at him with anguished eyes.

'Yeah,' said Nick. He'd been trying not to think about how that knife had ended up in Gary Paxton's guts. But there was only one possibility, really.

'Murderer.' Tears ran down her wet face.

'No.' He raised his voice. 'You killed him in self-defence. He was going to kill you, yeah? He had the knife. He attacked you.'

She shook her head.

'Helen, listen to me. I can see a cut on your face. Was that him?'

She blinked assent.

'Right. So that's what you tell the police. That's what happened. He attacked you with the knife. There was a struggle. You managed to turn the knife back on him. Then he crawled out and left you here to drown.'

A flashlight and a shout at the window behind him.

'Nick! Is that you?' Sarah Greenley. Thank God.

'Yeah,' he yelled. 'I've got her. She's caught on some wire. We need cutters to get her free.'

The woman came running down to the water. 'Thank goodness. Helen, are you all right?'

Paxton's dog jumped up and DCI Greenley subdued him

with a quick smack on the nose.

'Down!' The dog slunk back.

'She was under the water when I got here,' said Nick. 'She's freezing. Can't talk. Probably needs hospital treatment. Christ knows what's in here.'

'Right. I'll call an ambulance,' said DCI Greenley. She shone her torch on them. 'And for you too, if you've been swimming around in that.'

She spoke crisply into her radio.

Nick whispered in Helen's ear. 'All right? Self-defence. Don't let that bastard take you down with him.'

'I stabbed him,' she whispered.

'You stabbed him in self-defence. And probably saved loads of people's lives in the future. Including mine.'

She said nothing.

DCI Greenley scanned the fort. 'Do we know what happened to Paxton?' she asked.

'He's right behind you.' Nick tried not to smile as the policewoman jumped out of her skin and whirled around. 'He's dead.'

She crouched by the body on the ground, put a hand to Paxton's neck. 'Yes, I can see that. Any idea how that happened?'

'He was like that when I got here. He was going to kill Helen, though. I guess it must have happened in a struggle,' said Nick.

DCI Greenley straightened up, looked at him for a long minute.

'Perhaps,' she said.

# Chapter 50

Sarah Greenley was sitting beside her bed when Helen opened her eyes. She closed them again, feeling the ache in every part of her body. She didn't want to talk to anyone, least of all the police.

'Helen. How are you?'

She sighed. 'OK.'

'Good. Can you tell me what happened?'

She cast her tired mind back. The water, the knife. Paxton. The caravan. The farm...

Her eyes snapped open. 'Gus. Have you found Gus?'

'Who's Gus?'

Helen struggled to a seated position. Her arm felt heavy and sore; various scratches and cuts stung.

'Gus Cumberland. He was with me in the church in Cooling. They kidnapped him – drove him away in his Range Rover. Then, when I tried to get help, they picked me up and took me to the farm.'

'Sir Augustus Cumberland, from that big estate near Canterbury?' The policewoman stared at her, her face pale with shock. 'He's a friend of the chief constable. Right, I'd better call it in. Don't go anywhere.'

Fifteen minutes later she was back, looking confused.

'Helen... you're sure about the kidnap?'

'Yes! They almost drove into me after bundling him into the back. They knocked down a wall. It dislocated my shoulder.'

Sarah sat down again. 'That's... very odd. I've just spoken to a local beat officer. I got someone straight round to Vylands to talk to the family. Sir Augustus was there, and rather surprised to see us. He says there must have been some mistake.'

Helen sank back against her pillows. 'I don't understand.'

'No. Me neither.'

They were interrupted by a young doctor who peered at the various monitors Helen was attached to, detached them, checked her dressings were in place and pronounced her ready to go home.

'Do you have a friend you can call to collect you?' he asked. 'You shouldn't drive if you can help it. You'll need to rest for a while.'

'I'll take it from here,' said Sarah, before Helen could answer. The man withdrew. She pointed to a plastic bag on the chair. 'Your clothes were all soaked. I borrowed these from one of my taller colleagues. Get dressed. But we need to talk about Gary Paxton before I can take you anywhere.'

Sarah left the room and Helen pulled on a pair of men's jogging bottoms and a sweatshirt with a football logo. The clothes felt weird, but at least they were clean and dry. She glimpsed her face in the little mirror beside the bed, put a finger against the adhesive tape that held the cut closed on her cheek. It might leave a slight scar, the doctor had warned, but shouldn't be too noticeable. Helen wondered if she would ever look in the mirror again without thinking of Gary Paxton.

'I stabbed him,' she said, when Sarah came back in. 'He

killed the security guard when I called to him for help. I was
– I think I was in shock. He killed him right in front of me.'

Helen paused, realised she was shaking. She sat on the bed.

'Then I walked into the water. I don't know why. I wanted
to get away from him. But he followed. He was going to kill
me. He'd told me that already.'

She took a deep breath. Nick was right. She would not let
Paxton take her down with him.

'He had the knife in his hand. I was caught on the wire; I
couldn't run away. I turned the knife back on him.' She looked
up at Sarah, defiant. 'Am I under arrest?'

The policewoman's face was stern, but her tired eyes were
full of compassion.

'No. You're a witness and a victim. We'll come and take
a full statement later today. Not me, a couple of colleagues.
Now, where do you want to go?'

Helen hesitated. She didn't have her phone, she realised. Or
her keys. Everything had been in her overnight bag, in Gus's
car. Should she go to Vylands?

'Where's Nick?' she asked. 'I'd like to see Nick Wilson.'

Sarah called him up as they walked to the car park. 'He's in
Rochester,' she reported. 'At a bookshop. Does that make any
sense to you?'

Helen nodded. 'Yes. That's fine.'

They approached Sarah's small silver hatchback. Helen
stopped. An angry-looking puppy was flinging itself against
the window in the boot.

'Is that…?'

'Paxton's dog. Yes. Sorry, are you bothered by dogs? The
poor thing was frantic when the pathologist was examining
the body. I've got plenty of space, and a couple of pups at

288

home. My partner likes animals. I thought I'd take him in.'

Helen tried not to flinch as the creature barked its head off. She didn't share Sarah's love of dogs, but she supposed it wasn't the animal's fault that it had belonged to Gary Paxton.

'He's called Cooper,' Helen said, settling into the passenger seat. She looked again at the ugly little puppy. 'I think he was the only thing that Paxton actually cared about.'

# Chapter 51

'I've never eaten food like this before,' said Aisha, holding up a forkful of egg fried rice. She took another mouthful and nodded. 'It's good. I like it.'

'Best Chinese takeaway in town,' said Wiz, her face brightening. 'Dad always went there.' The light died again and she lapsed into silence.

'He was right,' said Aisha. She smiled and reached for Wiz's hand, squeezed it.

When Helen had arrived, she'd found the flat above the Rochester bookshop full to bursting. Wiz had refused to be parted from her new friend. Aisha's older sister, Elira, was asleep in the master bedroom, exhausted by her ordeal. Lev had curled up in an armchair, deep in a manga comic, not talking to anyone. Nick was camped out on the sofa, working on his laptop.

Then a family liaison officer had arrived with the news they had been dreading. The body retrieved from the river on Sunday was that of Thomas Chapman.

Wiz had received the news in silence. She'd pushed away Aisha and Lev, both of whom tried to comfort her. Helen watched in anguish as the girl crumpled to the floor and curled herself into a ball. There was nothing anyone could do to salve that pain.

At lunchtime, the policewoman had suggested they get some food. They had kept her busy washing up and making tea for everyone. Helen felt she was in the way, waiting for the officers to come and take her statement. Nick had told her to think through what she was going to tell them, to make sure it was clear she'd acted in self-defence. But there was no room to think about anything.

Nick himself was busy editing the package his team had filmed of the raid on the farm. He shovelled in food with one hand, the other holding his phone as he liaised with commissioning editors and lawyers. Helen usually felt comfortable with Nick, with his easy-going banter and passion for his work. But she didn't like the way he kept glancing at her, his gaze wary. He knew what she'd done to Paxton. She worried about what he'd think about that, no matter what he said.

She couldn't face the Chinese food. The flat felt too full of people, smells, noise, and trauma. Helen wanted to get out and walk, but her body was leaden. Everything hurt. And Sarah had told her to stay where she was until the police had taken her statement.

'I'm so tired. I think I'll lie down on the sofa in the shop,' she said. She picked up her copy of *Oliver Twist*, discarded on the coffee table.

It was quiet and dim downstairs. The blinds were down, keeping out the light from the street. Helen stretched out on the sagging leather. The shelves of books were companionable, their musty smell comforting, but she was too wired for sleep. Whenever she closed her eyes, the horrors of the night pressed in.

Distraction. She turned the pages of her paperback, drawn inevitably to the scene at Folly Ditch where Bill Sikes met his dreadful death at the end of a rope. His dog, she noticed, had died too, leaping to a broken neck. Oliver's Nancy had been thoroughly revenged, unlike the real-life Nancy Love.

What had Dickens done with Nancy's last letter? *I will give it into the safekeeping of Mr Pickwick*, he'd written in his shorthand note. But Pickwick was a fictional character. Did that mean Dickens had used the letter in his fiction – had taken Nancy's letter, and her memory, and subsumed them into his first great novel? The character of Nancy did not seem much of a tribute to the actress who'd befriended him.

Helen flipped back through the book. Nancy had been praised by Fagin's gang as a consummate actress, she noticed. She'd stood up for Oliver when Sikes threatened to beat him, defied Fagin, and dreamed of a better life. Perhaps Dickens had felt he'd done her justice. But Helen was not satisfied. She'd found Nancy Love; she'd visited the street where she lived and the graveyard where she was buried. But she was missing something. The secret that Nancy had hinted at in the previous unfinished letter to her sister.

The safekeeping of Mr Pickwick. What would Richard have made of that? she wondered. She thought of the portrait of his great-grandfather, the same amused eyes and high forehead. It was the closest thing Helen had to a photograph of Richard. She wondered if she'd ever be able to get together enough money to buy it. Maybe no-one else would want it. Would a collector buy a Victorian portrait of a little-known stranger?

Wait.

She sat bolt upright. Then she took the stairs to the flat as fast as her aching body would allow.

'Wiz, where's that box? The one from Cobham Hall, with the Dickens illustrations in it. The ones you said the collectors would like.'

The girl looked up, surprised. 'It's under Dad's bed. I thought I should put it somewhere safe.'

Helen knocked softly on the bedroom door. She could hear gentle snoring. She slipped into the darkness, but Elira didn't stir.

Helen pulled the box out into the living room. 'Help me take it downstairs.'

'What are you doing?' asked Aisha, as Nick carried it down to the desk.

'Looking for Mr Pickwick.' Helen handed the portrait of Albert Brooke to Nick. 'Take that a second.'

She lifted out the cardboard-mounted prints. A litany of villains: Magwitch, Uriah Heep, Quilp, Fagin. Back in time, to the start of Dickens's career. Mr Jingles. Sam Weller. Mr Pickwick, in his breeches and waistcoat, standing on a chair to address the Pickwick club. The very first illustration of *The Pickwick Papers* by the first illustrator, Robert Seymour. Property of the Cobham Hall estate, perhaps bought at the sale of Dickens' goods after his death. Possibly once owned by Dickens himself.

Helen turned it over. The cardboard frame had a pasted paper back. She hesitated.

Nick handed her a penknife. 'Go on.'

She took it, hands trembling just a little. She inserted the point, cut cleanly through the paper, peeled it away.

A sheet of writing paper, dirty and creased from being much-folded and carried about in a twelve-year-old boy's pockets. The handwriting was black ink with extravagant loops and many underlinings, like the unfinished letter Helen had found in the Canterbury prompt book.

She began to read.

'My dear Sister,

'I hope this letter finds you well and my Niece and Nephew fully recovered from their illness. What a fright they gave us all! Please convey a kiss from their Aunt Nan. I am mindful that you have had your share of troubles of late, Frances. I pray this letter will not add to them.'

Helen looked up at Wiz and Nick. 'This is it. This is the letter I've been looking for.' She wished there was someone to share it with who would understand her excitement. Hester, perhaps. Emmanuel. Gus? She still didn't understand about Gus.

She turned back to the page.

'I hope you will not object if I revert to the habits of our youth and share with you my burden. I am in what we once called A Grate Dele of Trubble.

'My time on the stage, I fear, is coming to an end. As you may have guessed, I have half a year to settle my situation. I have hopes, even expectations, that the Duke (dear A! How you would like him) will make me a settlement, as he has done for other ladies. But much remains to be decided. The King is mightily opposed, and there are those who would see me dead before set up in the way I wish to be.

'I had hoped that the intelligence I have would protect me, but it may, instead, be a dangerous knowledge.

'Sister, I am afraid. The Duke, dear man, forbids me to speak of what I have learned about his late brother's child. And yet, I believe secrecy is now the most dangerous policy. If only A. would make it known, it would be a great thing for the country and would improve his own position regarding the succession. Yet he tells me that is the last thing he wishes for.

'So, let me tell you, dear Frances. Shortly after you have this letter, I will proclaim this dreadful secret from the London stage, and it will become common gossip. By this letter, you will understand that I have done this not to create Trubble for others, but to secure my safety and future.

'The Princess, in whom all now place their hopes, is not the true daughter of Kent. A. has told me the truth – that his brother was unable to sire a child, or indeed to attempt such a thing, and had been in such a case for five years or more before his death. The girl V. is the child of his man, ordered to take his place in the royal bed chamber, to the great confusion of his poor wife. Trust me, however, if she has not sought to turn the situation to her advantage, as which of us would not?

'The child and her mother are the puppets of this Ponsonby. And the child will be Queen, when her uncle dies, unless the truth is known – and we shall all be ruled by this despicable man, her true father. Is that not the most dreadful thing you have ever heard?

'He is, they say, a dangerous enemy. Well, we shall see. This week I am to perform a comic monologue, after the main drama. Tomorrow night, the topic will change – and all will hear, including my dear Duke. What happens after that, I cannot tell. But we shall have No More Trubble from Mr Ponsonby, I hope.

'I am once again sending this by my little friend Charley. Pray you give him a bun, a kiss, or a penny, whichever comes soonest to hand. Keep the letter, dear Frances. It may be of importance if… but no, let me not think on that.

'Your ever-loving sister, Nancy Love.'

# Chapter 52

'What does it mean?' asked Nick.

Helen was on her feet, pacing around the shop. 'That Queen Victoria shouldn't have been Queen. That she was illegitimate, not really the daughter of the Duke of Kent. That another of George III's sons should have succeeded to the throne instead.'

'Blimey. So that would mean – our Queen shouldn't be Queen either?' asked Nick. 'That's… pretty major.'

Helen nodded. 'Yeah.'

And it would mean that Gus's family should have been on the throne. That Gus's mad father should be cousin to the King of England, as Lady Maria had put it. And Gus himself. What would it mean to Gus? He'd told her he was not interested in the past, in the royal claims. Did he mean it? He'd admitted how much it would mean to his mother and sister.

Wiz was reading the letter again. 'She says she has half a year to settle her affairs. What does she mean? Is she sick? Is she going to die?'

Helen stopped her pacing, sat on the arm of the sofa next to the girl. 'I think it means she was pregnant,' she said. 'Six months until the baby is born.'

Which, of course, would have been scandal enough on its own in 1824. Nancy must have known how the royal family would have reacted to her and her child. A mixed-race actress, giving birth to the child of a Duke in direct line to the throne. And not, by the sound of her, a woman prepared to go quietly, to be fobbed off with a pocketful of cash in return for silence and obscurity.

Helen appreciated for the first time Nancy's absolute peril. And she'd reacted not by running away, promising silence, but by threatening to proclaim the royal family's darkest secret from the London stage. She'd decided that attack – full frontal attack – was the best form of defence.

Who was the Ponsonby she'd been so afraid of? The Duke of Kent's man, Nancy had written.

'Nick, can I use your phone?' She looked him up. Sir John Ponsonby Conroy, baronet. Equerry to Prince Edward, Duke of Kent; later controller of the Duchess of Kent's household during the childhood of Victoria. There was a portrait, an upright man in military uniform with mutton chop sideburns and a self-satisfied sneer on his thin face.

He'd been commissioned into the Royal Artillery and served in the Napoleonic Wars, before coming to the attention of the Duke and being appointed his equerry, shortly before the Duke's marriage. The Duchess, Victoria's mother, had relied heavily on him after her husband's death.

Helen thought back to Tom Buller, the man suspected of Nancy's murder. He'd been a soldier, also in the Royal Artillery. Had they served together? When Ponsonby saw his own position – and that of his patron and daughter – threatened by Nancy Love, had he turned to his former comrade-in-arms? A quick shove down the steps at London Bridge, a blow to the back of the head extinguishing the threat.

She heard the words in Paxton's voice: 'That was business.' But it had been murder.

The doorbell rang.

'That'll be the police for my statement,' said Helen. She tried to keep her voice steady. 'It might take a while. I'll talk to them down here, stay out of your way. Do you mind going back up? Keep that letter safe, Wiz.'

She walked slowly through the shop, heart beating hard. Self-defence. Nick was right: Paxton had intended to kill her. Not right at that moment, perhaps, not at the point she'd seized the knife. But if she'd waited until he was ready, it would have been her blood coagulating in the sand at Cliffe Fort, her body cold in a mortuary.

The light from outside dazzled as she opened the front door. The man outside was a silhouette, the sunlight creating a halo around his blond head.

'Thank God, Helen. I've been so worried about you. Then I wondered if you'd come back here. Where have you been?' He held out his arms.

It was Gus. Looking like a prosperous young farmer, his hair neatly combed, in a Barbour jacket and clean jeans. Blue eyes bright, as if he'd never lost a night's sleep in his life.

'What happened to you?' She stepped outside and closed the shop door.

His smile slipped; a little boy expecting praise and being disappointed. 'Aren't you pleased to see me?'

'Of course.' She tried to dredge up a smile, backed up against the closed door as he leaned in for a kiss. 'But you were kidnapped. I saw it. What happened?'

298

He shook his head, laughed. 'That's a bit over-dramatic. Just a couple of local kids, idiots trying to steal the Range Rover. They drove off in a panic, then dumped me by the side of the road when they calmed down a bit. I walked into the village and called our estate manager. Then we went back to the church, drove around for ages trying to find you. Where did you go?'

Helen watched his face. The story was almost plausible, she supposed, if it didn't sound so practised. And there was something disturbing about his guileless blue gaze. Somehow, she didn't believe a word.

'I… it's a long story. But we're both safe. That's the main thing,' she said.

'Yeah. We even found the car, eventually. They'd dumped it on the motorway. The garage has given it a going-over. It's fine.'

He reached out to her face, touched her cheek. She winced. 'Who did that?'

Why did he assume it was deliberately inflicted? She shook her head.

'I got caught by some wire.'

'OK.' She could tell he didn't believe her. 'Looks sore.'

'Do you know a place called Ratcliffe Farm?' she asked.

His eyes shifted sideways, then back to meet her gaze. 'I know of it. It's up on the marshes, isn't it? Out by Cliffe somewhere. Must be bloody hard to farm, I should think. Terrible drainage.'

'Do you know a man called Guren Hasani?'

He shrugged. 'I don't think so. Why?'

'That's where I went for help, after you were driven away. I met him there.'

'Jolly good. I'll have to thank him for looking after you,' said Gus. His smile slipped again and his face flushed dark red. 'He didn't hurt you, did he? Helen, my God, if some low-life foreigner has been taking advantage of you…' He clenched his fists.

'He didn't hurt me.' What do you think he might have done to me? she wondered.

'Thank goodness. Well, that's all right, then. Listen, I'm on my way back to London. I'll give you a lift. I think it's time we got back to our poor Nancy, don't you? That shorthand note you were working on. The hidden letter.'

He smiled, his face confident again. Helen was certain she had not told Gus there was a hidden letter. She'd never told him she'd deciphered the shorthand note. My poor Nancy… Dickens' own words. He must have seen the transcript in her notebook, she realised.

She remembered how she'd hunted for the notebook, the night after her stay at Vylands. He must have found it, read it while she was in the shower, put it back in the wrong place. And then… he'd asked her about it, so casually. And she'd pretended she hadn't started work on it yet.

She'd been puzzling over how Gary Paxton knew about the letter from Nancy Love. The letter that proved Gus's family's claim to the throne, which Wiz had just carried upstairs.

Helen saw the green Range Rover parked on the far side of the street, gleaming. What would happen, she wondered, if she got into that car with Gus and he drove away? She didn't think she wanted to find out.

'Sorry. I have things to do this afternoon. The police will be here any moment. But can I have my bag back? And my coat?'

He looked confused. 'The police?'

'Never mind about that. My things. They were in your car. When I was in the church. Before the – before the kids tried to steal the car.'

'Of course. Sorry, I forgot. I don't have them with me. But come and see me in the London Bridge flat when you get back. We can have dinner and admire my view. Maybe pick up where we left off?'

Helen nodded. Gus kissed her un-scarred cheek.

'Take care, sweetheart. See you very soon.'

She suppressed the shudder until he had driven away.

# Chapter 53

Helen stood at the tall window, looking down into the square. The crocuses were up, a glitter of shimmering gold and purple in the pale March sun. She took a sip of mint tea, replaced the cup in the saucer.

'I thought I should warn you. There's bound to be press interest in the inquests,' she said. She turned to face Emmanuel.

His expression was almost comically startled. 'That's very… thank you, Helen. I'm just relieved you're safe.' Of all the problems he'd expected to encounter in his role as head of the English Department at Russell University, she doubted he'd considered how to handle a member of staff who'd stabbed a man to death.

'And Sir Augustus?' he asked, cautiously.

'I've not seen him since I got back from Rochester,' she said. 'I couldn't get through to his mobile. When I rang Vylands, I was told he was out of the country for several months, seeing to business overseas.'

He nodded. 'Yes. I've been trying to contact him too. His office says he's in Monaco.' He waved Helen to the armchair beside his desk. 'The thing is…' he tailed off, looking uncomfortable. She sat down, smiled at him encouragingly.

'It may be for the best,' he said. 'Helen, you've been honest with me. This is in complete confidence, all right?'

She nodded. 'Of course.'

He took a deep breath. 'I spoke to some former co-workers at Harvard. Sir Augustus had spoken to them a year ago about the possibility of sponsoring a Dickens fellowship there. They'd done due diligence; discovered a few things about the family that made them uncomfortable enough to turn it down.'

Helen raised her eyebrows. 'What sort of things?'

'Well… politics, mainly. His father – you know about him?'

'I know he's in a secure mental health unit.'

'Yes. Before that, in the late nineteen sixties, Sir Ernest Cumberland was involved in the British Nationalist Movement, along with Oswald Mosley and his cronies. He put up the money to fund rallies and marches through Jewish areas of London.'

Helen put down her cup and saucer. 'Gus's father was a fascist?'

'He gave the Nationalist Movement thousands of dollars. He wrote letters to the newspapers, saying that Britain had been on the wrong side during the Second World War.' He gave a wry smile. 'You see why Harvard was concerned about accepting the family money.'

'I see.' Helen thought of the glamorous Lady Maria and her awkward daughter, their troubling politics and obsession with their royal heritage. 'And they think Gus is involved too?'

'No.' Emmanuel steepled his fingers. 'Not necessarily. But my friends in the US said there were concerns about the source of the family fortune. His father set the company up. Sir Augustus has been running it for the last twenty years, making serious money. But before that, the family was on the brink of bankruptcy.

'Vermillion holds an enormous amount of land, both directly and through trusts in Luxemburg and Monaco. Land is illiquid and the family's finances are hard to understand. It's unclear how the company produces enough income to sustain their outgoings.'

Helen thought of Gus's plans for eco-tourism, green subsidies, and rare breed meat production. She'd wondered at the time how he would make it pay.

'Is there any sign that the – what was it? British Nationalist Movement? – is still getting money from the family?' she asked.

'The movement wound up in the nineteen seventies. But Ernest has been linked with a few other groups since,' said Emmanuel. 'He funded the British Nationalist Party in the nineties, before the episode at Buckingham Palace.

'Sir Augustus doesn't seem to be involved in politics. But there was enough unease about the Cumberland family and the Vermillion money for him to be politely shown the door.'

Helen was silent. Someone, Nick had said, was funding the British Patriot Party. Pouring money into it, funding rallies and coaches and social media campaigns, ensuring demagogues like Captain Jonnie had plenty of cash to splash around.

Nick had been looking into the funding. He said he'd found a link between the BPP and the organised crime group at Ratcliffe Farm via a land ownership company. Agriland, the company that owned the farm, had also donated to the BPP via a subsidiary, he said. And Hasani had once been a director. But the land ownership company itself was owned by an offshore trust based in Monaco, and he'd had trouble finding out anything more about it.

Nick had never mentioned Vermillion, and Helen had not told him about her suspicions of Gus. Perhaps she should. But that would complicate an already complicated situation.

'I'm worried that I may have put you in a difficult position regarding Sir Augustus,' said Emmanuel, his voice awkward and formal. 'I hope that's not the case. It sounds as if you have quite enough going on in your life.'

Helen saw concern and embarrassment in his kind face. 'Don't worry. I'm not planning to see him again,' she said. She'd called Vylands to ask for her stuff back. It had arrived by courier the next day. No note.

Emmanuel looked relieved. 'Let's talk about something else, then,' he said. 'How's your research into Charles Dickens coming along? *Oliver Twist*, wasn't it? You said you had something to show me.'

Helen smiled, reached into her bag. 'Indeed. I think Hester and I can identify Dickens' inspiration for Nancy with a fair degree of confidence.' She opened the folder on his desk and sifted through the pile of photocopies.

'Here's the record of Nancy Love's baptism, from St Saviour's church in the Borough. And that's the record of her burial in St George the Martyr. This is the coroner's report, and this is the newspaper report of her murder that I found in the book which may have belonged to Dickens.

'This newspaper report describes her funeral and theatrical career. I even found a playbill from the University of Kent's theatrical collection, which features her as an actress at the Surrey Theatre, playing a role that seems to have influenced Dickens' portrayal of Nancy.

'This is a photograph of the shorthand note in the back of the Robert Mudie book. It's in Dickens' hand. He talks about "poor Nancy" and mentions a letter she'd given him.'

Emmanuel leafed through the papers, his face creasing into a smile. 'This is magnificent, Helen. What a coup! I can get you admin support, and of course I'd be delighted to co-author with you and Hester, if that's really what you would like. We'll have to think about where to submit it. And the university press office will help us with a publicity strategy.'

Helen grinned. 'Thanks. I thought you'd be pleased.'

'We should have lunch, celebrate your new position. Maybe Hester could join us? Let me get Jessica to book somewhere decent.' He reached for the phone. Helen raised her hand.

'Sorry, I'm meeting a friend. But I'd love to do that another day.'

Emmanuel nodded and read Helen's transcript of the shorthand note again. He looked up over his spectacles.

'I don't suppose you have any idea what he meant about this letter from Nancy Love? Wouldn't it be amazing to find it?'

Helen smiled. 'Wouldn't it? I don't suppose it's survived all that time. But we can always try.'

She descended the stairs, eager to get out into the sunshine. Jeremy Fraser materialised from the shadows of the stairwell. He reached out an arm to bar her path before she could dodge around him.

'Congratulations,' he spat, not attempting to hide the bitterness in his thin face. 'I suppose you encouraged him to force me out. Out with the old, in with the new?'

Helen sighed. 'I had nothing to do with it. Emmanuel said you'd accepted a generous offer of early retirement. He needed someone to fill the position.'

His venomous eyes glanced from side to side. He leaned in and lowered his voice.

'You may think you and Professor Brown have won. But I have friends too. Questions will be raised in Parliament about the running of this university. The woke brigade in charge, banning white male authors from the curriculum. Some of us value tradition. Some of us think there's nothing wrong with patriotism.'

'Some of us are writing a new paper on Charles Dickens, white male author,' Helen shot back. 'Do look out for it.'

She pushed aside his arm and escaped down the stairs.

'Enjoy your retirement, Jeremy.'

# Chapter 54

Nick was in the Russell Square cafe already, guarding a table by the window. He waved and she squeezed through the press of people to join him.

'How did it go?'

Helen laughed. 'Poor Emmanuel. I think he was rather shocked. But he'll get over it. He'd already confirmed they were offering me the renaissance literature chair, so he couldn't take it back. He was pleased about the Dickens stuff, anyway. A big coup for the department.'

Nick raised his hand to attract the waiter. 'I bet. Congratulations, Professor Oddfellow.'

She grinned. 'That's going to take a while to get used to.'

'You didn't tell him about the letter, did you?'

She shook her head. 'No point. A long-dead woman repeating hearsay about a discredited scandal. I've looked it up. There were plenty of rumours about Ponsonby and Queen Victoria's mother at the time. But no proof. And the letter isn't proof, just more gossip.'

His warm brown eyes narrowed. 'Whatever. You're holding back. I can tell, you know. Why don't you want that letter published?'

She smiled, looked down at the menu. 'I think I'll have the tuna salad. And some fizzy water.'

'Don't try to distract me. I saved your life, remember?'

She reached across the table and squeezed his hand. 'I do remember. And that makes us equal, doesn't it?'

He sighed. 'At least tell me what you've done with it. I was looking forward to making the documentary that brings down the British royal family in the Queen's platinum jubilee year.'

She laughed. 'Sorry to disappoint. I have given it into the safekeeping of someone I trust.'

She thought fondly of the portrait of Albert Brooke in his Indian gear, hanging on the wall of her one-bedroom flat, the letter safely hidden behind it. Wiz had given her the portrait, insisting that she didn't want paying for it. Helen planned to get it valued and find a way of giving the girl the money. She was going to need it, although the sale of the Dickens illustrations to the museum should tide her over for a while. They'd discussed what should happen to Nancy Love's letter. Nobly, Wiz had left it to Helen to decide.

'Don't you trust me?' Nick was still holding her hand across the table. He began to stroke her fingers with his thumb. Helen's heart speeded up. His palm was warm and smooth, his dark eyes soft. There was something immensely comforting about Nick.

He understood her – at least, he came as close as anyone to understanding. He knew what she'd done to Paxton, and why. He would never judge her or try to hold her back in life. He was fun, clever, utterly trustworthy. And yet she was keeping secrets from him.

'How's your undercover guy?' she asked, gently pulling her

hand away.

Nick grimaced. 'Coming home from hospital tomorrow. He's going to move back to Manchester. I've hooked him up with a production company there. But he says he's not doing any more of that stuff. Even though we're up for a Bafta for the immigration documentary.'

'You can't blame yourself. He knew the risks.' Helen knew Nick would blame himself, all the same. His reporter had been cornered by two of the thugs he'd been hanging out with and badly beaten.

'Sure he did.' Nick poured the water. 'Are you not having a glass of wine? I thought you'd got things to celebrate.'

'Yeah. I have.'

He looked up, alerted by the change in her tone. Helen took a sip of water. She'd need to start telling people soon. Nick deserved to hear first.

'I'm pregnant,' she said. 'Almost two months. So not public knowledge yet.'

'Shit!' His face showed only dismay. 'Who…' He tailed off. 'That bloke in Rochester. The posh one. I didn't think you were seeing him anymore.'

Helen held his gaze. 'Yeah. Him. And I'm not. He's… I haven't told him. To be honest, I don't know where he is. Haven't seen him since Rochester. I'm not sure I want him involved. I'm going to do this on my own.'

Nick pushed back his chair. 'Blimey, Helen. Are you sure? I mean, it's a big deal, being a single parent. And they're expensive things, babies.'

She smiled. 'True enough. Don't worry, Uncle Nick, I'll be sure to call on you for babysitting duties. The new salary will help. Also…' She reached into her bag, pulled out a letter on stiff paper. 'It's from Crispin's solicitors. I got it last week. He left me his estate, the old darling. There's inheritance tax to deal with, but it should mean I can sell both our flats and buy somewhere bigger.'

Somewhere without four flights of stairs to climb each time she got home. She was already feeling incredibly tired at the end of the day.

Helen had thought long and hard about whether to keep the baby. She'd been horrified when she first realised she was pregnant, furious with herself for being so careless. How could she possibly have Gus's baby?

She didn't know if he'd set up the operation that took her to Ratcliffe Farm, or what his involvement with Hasani's business was. She didn't know if he was behind the funding of the British Patriot Party, or the attack on the immigration centre. Sarah Greenley had told her the police had visited Gus at his London flat, the day after Helen had given her statement. He'd been evasive, refused to answer questions without a solicitor, and left the country the next day. She'd added, with obvious discomfort, that her chief constable had let it be known that further investigations into the Cumberland family would be unwelcome. For once, Sarah had sounded cowed.

But Helen wanted children. She remembered telling Paxton that, as they walked across the nature reserve. Faced with the prospect of imminent death, she'd instinctively wanted more life. Too late, he'd told her. It wasn't, but she knew it might be soon.

'I'm good with children,' said Nick, cheerfully. He seemed to have recovered from his shock. 'My brother's kids love me.' He leaned across the table, kissed her cheek. 'Congratulations, girl. So long as it's what you want. I'll help, however I can. And it's so cool that Crispin's helping too. From beyond the grave.'

Helen burst out laughing. 'He'd love it, wouldn't he? Do you think I should call the baby after him?'

She raised her glass of sparkling water.

'To Crispin, and help from beyond the grave.'

# Enjoyed Folly Ditch?

If you enjoyed *Folly Ditch*, please consider leaving a review online. Reviews really help readers like you to discover my books.

Helen Oddfellow will be back! To follow her continuing adventures, why not sign up to my free readers' newsletter? You'll be the first to know about talks, events, special offers and giveaways. You can also get a free e-book of the Helen Oddfellow novel The Crimson Thread. Sign up at annasayburnlane.com.

# Notes and acknowledgements

Many of the places featured in Folly Ditch are real and can be visited. Particularly worth a trip are the Dickens Museum in London, the cathedral and castle in Rochester, St James' Church in Cooling and the Cliffe Pools RSPB nature reserve, from where you can see Cliffe Fort (although it is not possible to go inside). Other places are fictional.

Some of the history – such as Charles Dickens's stint as a child labourer while his father was imprisoned in the Marshalsea Prison - is true. However, the plot, people and action of the novel are entirely fictional. Nancy Love and the Cumberland family, past and present, are figments of my imagination.

Thanks to Claire Wood and Hugo Bowles from The Dickens Code project, who talked me through Dickens's shorthand; Jo Baines at the University of Kent's Special Collections & Archives service; Leon Litvack of the Dickens Letters Project for talking to me about how to spot a fake Dickens letter. Inaccuracies and liberties taken with the facts are mine alone.

Books consulted: Michael Slater: *Charles Dickens*; Claire Tomalin: *Charles Dickens: A Life*; Lee Jackson: *Walking Dickens' London*.

# About the Author

Anna Sayburn Lane is a novelist and journalist. She lives on the Kent coast. Anna has published award-winning short stories and was picked as a Crime in the Spotlight new author at the 2019 Bloody Scotland International Crime Writing Festival. Her 2018 debut novel Unlawful Things was shortlisted for the Virago New Crime Writer award.

**You can connect with me on:**
- https://annasayburnlane.com
- https://twitter.com/BloomsburyBlue
- https://www.facebook.com/annasayburnlane

**Subscribe to my newsletter:**
- https://annasayburnlane.com

# Also by Anna Sayburn Lane

Helen Oddfellow never intended to become a sleuth. But she can't resist a mystery.

As an academic researcher and London tour guide, Helen is equally at home reading in a dusty archive or walking the streets of the capital. Her drive to uncover the truth takes her into some unexpectedly dangerous places. Uncovering secrets can come at a high cost.

**Unlawful Things**
**A hidden masterpiece. A deadly secret buried for 500 years. And one woman determined to uncover the truth.**

When London tour guide Helen Oddfellow meets a historian on the trail of a lost manuscript, she's intrigued by the mystery – and the man. But the pair are not the only ones desperate to find the missing final play by sixteenth century English playwright Christopher Marlowe. What starts as a literary puzzle quickly becomes a quest with deadly consequences.

Unlawful Things was shortlisted for the Virago/The Pool New Crime Writer Award. It is the first Helen Oddfellow mystery.

"A fully action-packed thriller with fantastic characters and a great story line – very highly recommended!" Donna's Book Blog

**The Peacock Room**
**A literary obsession. An angry young man with a gun. And one woman trying to foil his deadly plan.**

When Helen Oddfellow starts work as a lecturer in English literature, she's hoping for a quiet life. But trouble knows where to find her.

There's something wrong with her new students. Their unhappiness seems to be linked to their flamboyant former tutor, Professor Petrarch Greenwood. When Helen is asked to take over his course on the Romantic poet William Blake, life and art start to show uncomfortable parallels. Disturbing poison pen letters lead down dark paths, until Helen is the only person standing between a lone gunman and a massacre.

"This is a clever, slow burn of a thriller that builds the tension gradually up to a nail biting end." Orlando Books.

**The Crimson Thread**
**A theatrical curse. A shocking discovery in the cathedral.
Only one woman can unravel the mystery and prevent
more bloodshed.**

When Helen Oddfellow goes to Canterbury for the opening of
an Elizabethan play unseen for 400 years, she is expecting an
exciting night. But the performance is disrupted by protests,
then a gruesome discovery in the cathedral crypt draws her
into a desperate hunt for a murderer.

  Is the play cursed? The actors think so, but Helen doesn't
believe in curses. As friends go missing and Helen herself is
threatened, she pursues the clues through the ornate tombs of
the cathedral and the alleyways of the ancient city. Mysteries
from the distant and not-so-distant past are exposed. Can
Helen find the killer – before he kills again?

"Another beautifully written page turner. I am now well and
truly hooked by these thrillers underpinned by real historical
events." Amazon reader review.

You can download a FREE copy of The Crimson Thread when
you sign up to my monthly readers newsletter at my website,
annasayburnlane.com.

Printed in Great Britain
by Amazon